Dinah started to remind Captain Moberly of her vow not to marry a seafarer, but somehow the words would not form.

He gazed about the room. "You have your choice between Mr. Richland Senior or Junior."

Dinah bit her lips to keep from giggling. "Captain, I order you to cease matchmaking for me." A playful thought nudged Dinah's mind. "That is, unless I am permitted to serve the same office for you."

He gave her a slight bow. "Fair enough. Make your selection and present me to the lady."

She stared around the room, seeking a likely candidate. "Hmm. Well. How about…no, not her. And then there's…but no, she would not suit." She released a dramatic sigh. "I fear not a single match can be found for you in our city, sir."

Kindness would not permit her to tease about pairing him with any of her acquaintances. Kindness? Or perhaps something far more selfish?

D1173432

Books by Louise M. Gouge

Love Inspired Historical

Love Thine Enemy
The Captain's Lady
At the Captain's Command

LOUISE M. GOUGE

has been married to her husband, David, for forty-six years. They have four children and six grandchildren. Louise always had an active imagination, thinking up stories for her friends, classmates and family, but seldom writing them down. At a friend's insistence, in 1984 she finally began to type up her latest idea. Before trying to find a publisher, Louise returned to college, earning a B.A. in English/creative writing and a master's degree in liberal studies. She reworked the novel based on what she had learned and sold it to a major Christian publisher. Louise then worked in television marketing for a short time before becoming a college English/humanities instructor. She has had ten novels published, five of which have earned multiple awards, including the 2006 Inspirational Readers' Choice Award. Please visit her website at www.louisemgouge.com.

LOUISE M. GOUGE

At the
CAPTAIN'S COMMAND

Love Inspired

Recycling programs for this product may not exist in your area.

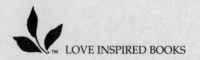 ™ LOVE INSPIRED BOOKS

ISBN-13: 978-0-373-82865-4

AT THE CAPTAIN'S COMMAND

Copyright © 2011 by Louise M. Gouge

www.LoveInspiredBooks.com

Printed in U.S.A.

I will receive you and will be a Father unto you,
and ye shall be my sons and daughters,
saith the Lord Almighty.
—*II Corinthians* 6:17b–18

This book is dedicated
to my beloved husband, David,
who has stood by my side through my entire
writing career, encouraging me, helping me with
research, reading my raw manuscripts and giving me
the gentlest of corrections. Oh, and best of all,
he gives me the male perspective and insights a
woman sometimes can't quite grasp. He also gives
me the benefit of his military experience in the
U.S. Army, during which he served in the
101st Airborne in Vietnam. Every March 11,
I thank God for bringing David safely home to me.

Acknowledgments:

In addition, I want to thank
my amazing critique partners for their
wonderful suggestions and research tips:
DiAnn Mills, Ramona Cecil, MaryLu Tyndall
and Laurie Alice Eakes, all gifted authors
in their own rights.

Finally, I'd like to thank my insightful editor,
Melissa Endlich, who sets the bar high for
writing excellence. I'm proud to be writing for you.

Chapter One

May 1780
St. Augustine, East Florida Colony

The instant Dinah saw the three naval officers, she ducked into the mercantile and hid among the stacks of goods. To her relief, the men, grandly uniformed in indigo wool, gold braid and black bicorne hats, continued up St. George Street. Yet she could not help but notice the well-formed profile of the captain among them. A strong jaw. High cheekbones. Jet-black hair tied back in a queue. She wondered what color his eyes were.

What was she thinking? She quickly turned her attention to a display of awls and knives laid out on a shelf.

"How may I help you, Miss Templeton?" The rotund, middle-aged proprietor approached her, admiration gleaming in his dark eyes. "Some silk for a new gown, perhaps? My latest shipment of lace has arrived and—"

"No, thank you." Dinah lifted her basket of lavender flowers from her arm and held it like a shield as the widower moved closer. Coming in here had been a mistake.

"I do not require anything." Tension tightening in her chest, she hurried toward the door.

He reached it first, and his eyebrows arched. "I have tea from China and…"

Dinah drew herself up to her full height and lifted her chin. "Please allow me to pass, Mr. Waterston."

He mirrored her posture, although his shorter height did not reach hers, and he sniffed. "I must say, Miss Templeton, for a girl with no family, you certainly do put on airs. Would you not prefer to be mistress of your own home instead of living with Mr. and Mrs. Hussey?" His shoulders slumped, his gaze softened and his lips curved into a gentle smile. "You could do worse than marrying a responsible merchant such as myself."

A twinge of pity softened her annoyance. "As I have told you before, sir, we truly would not suit."

Even if she found the merchant's offer appealing, which she did not, his reminder of her orphaned state did nothing to recommend him, nor did his reference to her living situation. She did indeed have relatives, but they were all far away. And yes, she would like to be mistress of her own home. But in truth, not one of the many unattached men in St. Augustine suited her, in spite of her friends' attempts at matchmaking. After four years in this small city, she had no doubt God had consigned her to a state of spinsterhood.

"I wish you a good day, sir." She slid past Mr. Waterston and walked out into the street, lifting a silent prayer of thanks that the encounter had ended without unpleasantness. She encountered quite enough unpleasantness every day at home.

Coming to this city had not been her preference, but she'd had no other choice. Even before the beginning of the war that now raged in the northern colonies, she had felt twice displaced. Her parents died when she was very small, and her relatives had been unable to take her in. Then, when the dear spinster ladies who reared her died of a fever, the elders of the Nantucket Friends Meeting placed her with the Husseys, for Mrs. Hussey had also been reared by the Gardiner sisters. Once the war began to escalate, Artemis Hussey insisted upon removing to this safe haven, where no rebels could threaten to tar and feather him for his Loyalist views. Over these past four years, he had grown more and more disagreeable and usually aimed his dissatisfaction at Dinah rather than at his wife, Anne.

But as Dinah continued on her way, thoughts of Artemis vanished amid the chatter and clatter along the dusty street. When she reached the Parade, the grassy common in front of the governor's house, she approached several well-dressed ladies who were whispering behind opened fans, their admiring stares aimed across the green lawn.

Elizabeth Markham, a friend near her age, beckoned to Dinah. "Did you see those handsome naval officers who just passed this way?" Her fair cheeks bore a rosy hue, as they always did when the subject under discussion included fine-looking gentlemen.

Dinah stared in wonder at the phenomenon upon her friend's countenance, for she herself never blushed. "I did see them, yes."

"Indeed, they are proper-looking gentlemen." Elizabeth's mother sent her daughter an indulgent smile, then touched Dinah's arm. "Dear Miss Templeton, you must join us for tea at the Rose Room." She waved her hand to take in the others in her little gathering. All the ladies added their approval of the invitation.

"I thank you, Mrs. Markham." Dinah nodded toward

her basket of lavender. "Perhaps after I complete my errand. Tea would be just the thing." She hurried past the group.

The ladies' jasmine and rose perfumes mingled with earthy street smells, all swept along by a warm ocean breeze. Throughout the Parade, vendors hawked their wares, everything from cast-iron kettles to candles to live chickens to freshly cut meat, while the squeals of children at play echoed across the lawn. Two gentlemen Dinah knew from St. Peter's Church doffed their hats, bowed and greeted her with the customary pleasantries. She returned a curtsey but excused herself from further conversation. Instead, she continued up St. George Street toward her destination, maintaining her distance from the British uniforms. They no doubt were on their way to Fort St. Marks, and her objective was a little farther away.

To her right lay Matanzas Bay, and a new ship—a British frigate, if she was not mistaken—bobbed in the mild current, sails furled to its three tall masts. Last evening, she had heard the bells ringing from the Anastasia Island watchtower, signaling a ship's arrival over the bar. No doubt those officers came from the vessel.

After a walk of perhaps a hundred yards beyond the city proper, she saw to her dismay that the officers had continued past the fort and turned in at the military infirmary, her own objective. She released a long sigh. Perhaps she could slip into the building without notice. If she had not promised to bring the lavender for Dr. Wellsey's patients, she would delay her errand and return to have tea with Mrs. Markham and the other ladies until the officers went elsewhere.

The familiar odors of sickness and lye soap met Dinah's nose even before she opened the hospital's front door, for all the windows of the building were open. She dismissed her own discomfort. Dr. Wellsey's patients suffered enough with wounds and diseases. Perhaps the fragrance of her flowers would help diminish the unpleasant smells.

Hurrying into the wide entry room, she brushed her straw hat off and let it hang by its ribbons down her back. As she made her way toward the surgeon's office, she caught a glimpse of the officers in the next chamber. With haste, she slipped into the small office and then out the side door to the herb garden to make certain the plants had sufficient water. Through the hazy glass of the back window, she saw the captain bent over a man on a cot, one hand resting on the sailor's shoulder. Every nuance of the officer's relaxed posture bespoke sympathy and concern, not the hauteur one might expect. He had removed his hat, revealing a broad, smooth forehead. Now he lifted his gaze toward the garden window, and she ducked back into Dr. Wellsey's office, her heart pounding. She hoped the captain had not noticed her presence, or if so, had assumed she was a servant.

Setting her basket on the floor beside the desk, she capped the inkwell and sharpened the feather quill. If not for her and Joanna, the good doctor's wife, his infirmary and home would be in complete disarray. She found a cloth and dusted his bookshelves and journals, taking care not to disturb the many carefully labeled bottles. Once while dusting, she had lifted a small urn of medicine and hours later was still able to smell the pungent odor of bear grease on her fingers.

The deep rumble of male voices echoed from the inner chambers of the infirmary. This would be the best time to make her escape unnoticed. Pulse racing, she made certain everything was in order, then placed the basket of lavender in the center of the desk. Dr. Wellsey or his assistant could disperse it throughout the rooms as they saw fit.

She hurried into the entry just as the doctor and his guests emerged from the back chamber.

"So you see, Captain Moberly, we make every effort—why, Miss Templeton, what a surprise."

Dinah gasped. "Captain Thomas Moberly?"

"Miss Dinah Templeton?"

They spoke at the same time, and the entire company laughed. Relief flooded Dinah. This changed everything regarding these men. Or at least regarding the captain.

He strode across the wide room and lifted her hand to kiss it.

"My dear kinswoman, how delightful to meet you at last." His thick black eyebrows arched and his blue eyes sparkled. *Bright blue, like the sky.* The fragrance of woodsy shaving balm tickled her nose. Doubtless the officers had visited the bathhouse before coming into the city.

"And I am pleased to meet you, Captain." Dinah curtseyed, then glanced at Dr. Wellsey, who wore an agreeable smile and showed not the slightest surprise. "Why, doctor, did you plan this?"

Dr. Wellsey chuckled. "I fear I cannot claim the credit, though to be sure, it is fortuitous."

"Indeed it is." Thomas released her hand and summoned his officers with an authoritative wave. "Miss Moberly, may I present Mr. Brandon and Mr. Wayland. Gentlemen, this is my sister twice over. My younger brother is married to her cousin, and my sister is married to her brother."

As the two officers stepped forward, Dinah saw in

their eyes the usual look of sailors new in port—as if they might devour her on the spot. She tried not to recoil. This was the very thing she'd hoped to avoid by evading these men. At least when the first officer kissed her hand, he had the grace to temper his expression with respect. "I am honored, Miss Templeton."

"Miss Templeton." The other man, a lieutenant who was younger by far than his companions, gripped her hand a bit too firmly. "Who would have thought to find such beauty in this backward colony?" His breathless speech was etched with an aristocratic British accent.

Seeing a storm brewing on the captain's brow, Dinah gently twisted her hand from the lieutenant's grasp. "How kind of you, sir." She honored them with another curtsey before focusing on her kinsman, whose expression now seemed as protective as her own brother's. How strange that the idea brought on a twinge of disappointment. Strange and foolish. The captain was a seafaring man and as such could never become the object of her romantic interest. Why, she would as soon marry the little merchant as a man who always deserted his wife for the sea. No, this man could be her friend, as he was to her brother Jamie, but no more.

"What brings you to St. Augustine?" Dinah gazed again into the captain's warm blue eyes. "Have you brought news that the war is over? That the rebels at last have been defeated?"

The other men responded with condescending chuckles, but Thomas's expression turned grave. "Would that it were so, dear lady. Unfortunately, each time we think we have crushed them, they return like the phoenix." Sorrow flitted across his eyes, but he seemed to blink it away. "To answer your question, my crew and I have been assigned to join the other two frigates now patrolling these waters and to defend St. Augustine and the St. Johns River from invasion by the Spanish fleet and pirates."

"Effectively taking us out of the war." The lieutenant's tone echoed with annoyance.

"Yes." Thomas shot him a frown. "And giving us a respite from death."

"Not to mention—" Mr. Brandon's brown eyes twinkled. "Giving us an opportunity to enjoy a decent roast beef at one of the fine taverns in this fair city. A man wearies of salt pork and weevil-ridden biscuits." He shuddered comically, and the other men voiced good-natured agreement.

His remark sparked a scheme in Dinah's mind. "If you gentlemen will excuse me, I must take my leave. I hope you will enjoy St. Augustine. It truly is a lovely city, and we appreciate the regiment at Fort Saint Marks and the naval ships in our harbor." She turned to Dr. Wellsey. "Doctor, the lavender is on your desk. Will you see to it?"

He glanced over his shoulder toward his office. "Ah, yes. Thank you, Miss Templeton."

After the appropriate *au revoirs,* Dinah added, "Until we meet again, Captain Moberly."

She restored her hat to her head and paused to re-tie the ribbons and renew her plan. As soon as they left, she would come back and ask Dr. Wellsey where the officers were lodging, then send Thomas an invitation to supper so they could share family news. Perhaps he had information about Jamie, whose merchant ship was always in danger from pirates. And no doubt the captain would like to hear about his sister and brother, who dwelt on a plantation deep in the East Florida wilderness.

Before she could think of how to word the missive,

the captain emerged from the building and stopped her with a light touch on her arm. Looking up from beneath her hat brim to see a smile as gentle as his gaze, she stifled the foolish giddiness threatening her composure. Gracious, he was handsome. But how featherbrained of her to think such things. After all, she had heard from his sister that this gentleman was one and thirty, an entire decade older than her own one and twenty years. Another reason not to make him an object of her interest. And with all those marriages between their families, he was practically her brother. Wasn't he?

"Yes, Captain Moberly?" Could he hear the squeak in her voice?

"Perhaps we can arrange to see each other soon to exchange family news." Thomas clamped down on the strange wave of feeling that surged through him in response to her glorious smile. This was the lady his good friend Jamie called his "delightful little sister." But instead of the child Thomas had expected to meet one day, here stood a tall, beautiful young woman in a pretty lavender frock that enhanced her dark-brown eyes. Eyes that exuded kindness and generosity. Eyes a man could get lost in. He mentally shook himself. What foolishness. He'd been too long at sea, too long out of society and the company of lovely ladies.

"Why, yes, I would like that very much, Captain." Her voice had a pleasing, mellow tone. "Will you come to supper this evening? I cannot promise roast beef, but perhaps something just as tasty."

The innocence of her invitation gave him pause. No matter how much they regarded one other as a family member, other people might not see the matter in that light.

"You know, of course," she said, "that I live with my foster sister and her husband. They will be more than pleased to meet a true British naval hero."

Thomas grinned, feeling foolish. Had she discerned his hesitation? "And I would be honored to meet them. Where and what time shall I come?"

She gave directions and named the time, but while he committed them to memory, he fought the urge to shift his manner of viewing her. Not since his wife's death had he seen a woman of such innocence and genteel grace. But whereas dear little Ariel had flitted through life without a serious thought in her brain, Dinah's steady gaze invited confidence in her intelligence.

Guilt stung him for making such a comparison. After four years, he still missed Ariel, still missed the hopes he'd held for the infant son she could not safely deliver. In time, he had come to think it best for a naval officer not to marry, for service to his father, his king and his God—in that order—took precedence over one's personal interests. But even if he found his heart engaged by some winsome lady, Thomas had no intention of emulating his sister and brother, both of whom had married common Americans. While a man could have good friends of a lower rank, such as Dinah's brother, Jamie, these ill-advised unions no doubt had caused some grief. But he would not think of that until he stood face-to-face with his sister, Marianne, and brother Freddy.

"Until eight o'clock, then?" She bestowed another of her pretty smiles upon him, striking a chink in the four-year-old wall around his heart.

Belay that, you dolt. He must regard her as a sister and no more.

"May the hours hasten by until then." He bowed with an extra flourish, hoping to lash down his wayward emotions through humor. His reward was an equally overdone curtsey. What a delightful creature.

She turned and walked away, leaving behind a hint of lavender in the air.

Thomas withheld a sigh. At least now he understood the temptations into which his sister and brother had fallen.

Chapter Two

Her heart merry over the unexpected encounter with Thomas, Dinah hurried back down St. George Street toward the Parade. Whether or not she saw much of him, his mere presence in St. Augustine would help to mitigate her usual sense of being cut off from her family. With Jamie at sea most of the time and her cousin living at Bennington Plantation, Dinah often felt lonely.

Of course she realized the handsome, charming captain would become the object of matchmaking for every mother of an eligible daughter in the colony. She tried to think of someone who might suit him, but for some reason, the idea nettled her. Moreover, what colonial miss would be worthy of such a distinguished gentleman, a renowned captain in His Majesty's navy *and* the son of a British earl? No, Dinah would leave the matchmaking to the ambitious mothers. She would turn her efforts toward giving the captain a pleasant supper as a reward for his heroic naval service.

The thought of seeing him again so soon warmed her heart, and she became aware of May's humid heat rolling over her face. On days like this, she longed for the cooler summers of her childhood home. But in Nantucket, winters could be deadly, while in East Florida winter generally offered a pleasant respite from both heat and cold. Still, when she pulled a linen handkerchief from her pocket and dabbed at the perspiration on her forehead, she recalled the need to complete her errands before the late-morning sun began to scorch the city and intensify its less pleasant odors.

In the Parade at the poultry vendor's cart, she purchased two plump hens and asked the man to deliver them to her house. Artemis would fuss at the expense, but she was spending her own money. And no doubt he would be more than pleased when he learned they would have such an illustrious guest. If her foster sister's husband had the slightest sense of humor, she would keep the captain's identity a secret until he arrived at their home. But Artemis did not do well with surprises. As it was, she could just imagine how he would fawn over the captain. She'd best prepare him.

Hastening toward home, she shoved away her uncharitable thoughts. If Anne could be content in her marriage, Dinah would try not to dislike the man. But in the five years she had lived with them by mutual necessity, he had changed much—and none of it for the better.

Pausing in front of the bakery, she inhaled the inviting fragrance of fresh-baked bread. Cook would be hurt if Dinah brought home someone else's baking, but perhaps it would be wise to make a purchase anyway. Cook would have enough to do preparing fish, chicken and pies for Thomas without having to start bread in the middle of the day. And what about vegetables? Dinah had not checked the garden since picking squash three days ago. Would there be enough green beans—?

She laughed at her own frantic thoughts, for she had no need to impress the captain. Not only had their family connections provided instant and reciprocal friendship, but she was sure he would appreciate whatever meal she served. Long months at sea guaranteed a hearty appetite for fresh fare.

Continuing toward home without the bread, Dinah felt her emotions settle further. She truly must not permit her feelings for Thomas to go beyond friendship. Their relatives had already teased her about another marriage between their families, but for her it was not even a remote possibility. Her father had died at sea eighteen years ago when she was barely three, leaving her without any memory of him. Her brother was the captain of his own merchant vessel and spent his life away from dear Marianne and their precious son. Would Jamie return from England in time for the birth of their second child in a few weeks? Dinah had no wish to live that way. As disagreeable as Artemis was, at least he lived at home, and Anne need never suffer loneliness. No, Dinah would never marry a seaman of any kind.

After passing through the gate of her fenced yard, she plucked several long stalks from the rosemary bush along the path to the house. She sniffed the pleasant, woody herb, and her mouth watered. She would give it to Cook to roast with the chickens. Yes, tonight at supper, Thomas would be amply rewarded for his service to His Majesty and the people of St. Augustine.

When Artemis came home from the government offices for his midday meal, he sat at the head of the table with his brown eyes narrowed and focused on Anne. "Mrs. Hussey, I saw chicken feathers strewn about the yard in front of the kitchen house. If we are to have such an expense in the middle of the week—"

"If you please, Artemis." Dinah would not permit him to bully dear Anne.

"If *you* please, *Miss* Templeton." His harsh glare settled on her. "I am speaking to my wife. If you must sit at table with us, I will not have you interrupt." His gaunt face lined with tension, he turned back to Anne. "As I was saying, if you must have meat in the middle of the week, could Cook not at least gather and clean the feathers for bed pillows or chair cushions or some useful purpose?"

Dinah exhaled a quiet sigh, refusing to permit his rudeness to injure her feelings.

Always placid, Anne gave him a serene smile. "I shall see to it immediately after dinner, my dear." She pursed her lips and sent Dinah a meaningful look. "Sister, dear, what shall we do with those feathers?"

"Of all the—" Artemis thumped his fist on the table. "What has she to do with their use?"

Dinah pressed her lips together. Oh, how she wished she'd not told Anne that Thomas was coming to dinner. How she wished she could give this intolerable man his due.

"Why, my dear," Anne said calmly, "Dinah bought the chickens."

Artemis's hawk-like glare darted back to Dinah. What he was thinking, she could not guess. His sinewy jaw muscles clenched with anger, but confusion filled his eyes, as if she'd never before contributed to their food stores. Indeed, she paid half of all the household bills while using only one third of the resources.

"There. You see." He waggled a bony finger at her as if she were a naughty child. "This is exactly why you should entrust your paltry fortune to me, Miss Templeton. You will be destitute before you reach three and twenty years if you continue such spending." He scooped up a spoonful of bean soup and ate, but his glower forbade any response. "In these four years, I have laid before you the names of seven worthy gentlemen willing to marry you and take you off my hands, and you have rejected each and all. If you must be a spinster, give me charge of your money, and I shall make certain it carries you into your dotage."

Prickles of anxiety closed Dinah's throat, and she set down her spoon and stared at her cooling soup. Messrs. Panton and Leslie, managers of a store on Treasury Street, kept her inheritance in safekeeping, as they did the funds of several other citizens. Yet every time Artemis brought up the subject, the same fears assaulted her. Without a husband's oversight, would the gentlemen truly look out for her interests? Whom could she trust? Certainly not one of Artemis's political cronies to whom he had tried to manacle her. And Jamie was not in East Florida often enough to provide protection for her. Only by living with Anne and Artemis could Dinah feel safe. And despite Artemis's insinuations otherwise, he needed her financial contributions to maintain a suitable house for a man of his position.

Anne coughed softly. "Sister, dear." The warmth of her gaze and the unwarranted family endearment soothed Dinah's nerves. Always, in the midst of these unpleasant discussions, she felt certain Anne addressed her as "sister" to gently remind Artemis of the heart bond the two women shared. "Thee must tell Artemis why thee bought the chickens."

Forcing herself to recover, Dinah sniffed. "La, I cannot think he would be interested, but if you insist." She gave Artemis the sweetest smile she could muster… and waited until he'd placed a spoonful of beans in his mouth. "I fear your table will be overcrowded again this evening, for I have invited Captain Thomas Moberly to dine with us."

As she'd hoped, he gasped and then fell into a fit of coughing. Anne jumped up and dashed to his end of the table, pounding him on the back while sending Dinah a chiding glance. Dinah bit her lip to keep from laughing, but the hurt in Anne's eyes soon dispelled her merriment and replaced it with shame.

"Forgive me, Artemis." She stood and fanned him with her napkin, taking in a heavy dose of his apple-scented hair dressing. "I did not mean to shock you—" Would God forgive this lie? Would Anne?

"No, no, not at all, dear sister." Artemis sputtered. "Captain Moberly, is it? Well, now, I'd heard this morning that a third British frigate had arrived last evening to protect our city, but I had no idea of who the captain was. To think, Lord Bennington's heroic son quartered here and coming to my humble home." He waved his hand to dismiss Anne. "Thank you, my dear. I am well. Please be seated."

With order restored, Anne signaled Cook to bring dessert. As Artemis dug into his cornmeal pudding, his dark eyes almost twinkled. Dinah imagined he was thinking of ways to turn this night to his political advantage, for that was his practice with every situation. She must brace herself for whatever he might do.

"Hmm." Artemis stared at Anne with a stern expression. "Mrs. Hussey, are you certain chicken is the best we can serve? Is there no beef or lamb to roast? Have you spoken to the butcher about a bargain on a good cut of meat? And what of dessert?" He tapped his chin thoughtfully. "And do have Cook clean up those chicken feathers. What will Moberly think if my yard is strewn with trash?" He turned his stare toward Dinah. "Miss

Templeton, this afternoon you must run across the back-yard to the Ethertons' house and hire their eldest daughter to help Cook serve supper tonight." He stood and tugged at his lapels. "I'll not have the earl's son think we cannot afford to serve him properly." He stepped away from the table and stopped by the door, his lean form casting a thin shadow on the tabby floor. "And make certain the girl wears a clean apron."

"Yes, Artemis." From his authoritative tone, Dinah understood that Thomas was no longer her guest, but Artemis's. Whatever hopes she'd had for becoming better acquainted with her kinsman and exchanging news about their shared family must now be abandoned in favor of this disagreeable man. Dinah felt her annoyance dispel. Surely there would be ample opportunity to befriend Thomas. She must not become reliant on him, she knew, but for the moment it comforted her to have a kinsman nearby. Oh, she was looking forward to supper!

Chapter Three

"A very fine meal, Mrs. Hussey. I have never tasted anything quite so delicious. Rosemary is the perfect herb to enhance the flavor of roasted chicken." Thomas pressed his napkin to his lips and sent Anne a pleasant nod. "Your hospitality warms this seafarer's heart, just as your table delights my palate."

Dinah's roasted corn turned dry in her mouth while an ache settled in her stomach. Of course the captain's compliments to Anne were appropriate. As the married woman of the house, she deserved his honor and gratitude. But still it stung Dinah's feelings not to receive a little credit for arranging this evening *and* the menu. Never before had she felt like such a spinster, an old maid, a redundant woman in the house she paid to live in.

"Thou are most welcome, Captain Moberly." Anne smiled with all the humble graciousness of their Quaker upbringing. "But thy compliments should go to Dinah." She signaled to the serving girl to remove their plates and bring dessert. "We are so pleased that she chanced to meet thee and invited thee to supper. Are we not, Mr. Hussey?"

Dinah hid a smile. She should have known Anne would not accept praise without sharing it. Her friend always turned attention away from herself and gave credit to others.

"Indeed, we are, Mrs. Hussey." Seated at the head of the table, Artemis was a different man this evening, all affability and manners. He turned to Thomas, who sat on his left. "And so pleased for her kinship to you and to us."

The captain nodded his appreciation of the cream-covered peach pie the maid set before him. "Ah, Miss Templeton, I did not know of your kinship to Mr. and Mrs. Hussey." He gazed across the table at her, and a pleasant feeling warmed Dinah's heart. Thomas was more than easy to look at and, for a naval captain, not the least bit intimidating. "You must tell me more about your family."

"Well," Artemis said, "it's not as if we're blood relations—"

The captain slid his attention to Artemis briefly. "But I should like to hear Miss Templeton recount the connection."

Artemis coughed into his napkin. "Yes, of course. Miss Templeton, do proceed."

With great difficulty, Dinah withheld a laugh over the captain's gentle rebuke to Artemis. After all, this was not exactly a jolly tale she'd been asked to relate.

"Both Anne and I were orphaned, she first, and then I. Two dear spinster sisters, daughters of a whaling captain, took us in and reared us. And thus we consider ourselves foster sisters." She sent a fond look to Anne. "I know her far better than I know my own brother, who was absent nearly all of my childhood."

Memories flooded her with sadness. "Aunt Matilda

and Aunt Eunice, as we called them, died when a fever struck Nantucket, and by that time Anne and Artemis had married." She drew in a deep breath to still the sorrow that tried to close her throat. "I was left alone." Indeed, she had felt alone all her life, abandoned by all, even God, despite the tender care of the Gardiner sisters. They had never known quite what to do with her excessive energy, while Anne had been all quiet compliance to their Quaker ways.

The captain leaned forward. "I grieve that my question has distressed you, dear lady." The light from the candle centerpiece reflected in his blue eyes and deepened his compassionate frown. "You need not go on."

"Not at all." She forced a smile and dug into her pie, determined to enjoy its sweet flavor. After a moment, she continued. "It's not as if we were the only people to suffer in this life." Jamie once told her Thomas's wife and son had died a few years ago. To fully regain her composure, she swallowed another bite of pie before going on. The gentleness in the captain's countenance invited her confidence and stirred within her a deeper, fonder sentiment toward this good man.

"When that dreadful rebellion began in Boston, most Nantucketers took a neutral position on the growing war due to their Quaker convictions. But a few foolish young men who...well...they—"

"They tarred and feathered several Loyalists." Artemis sniffed with indignation. "Had we not left, I cannot imagine what they might have done to me."

The captain kept his attention on Dinah, and the intensity of his gaze sent a wave of encouragement through her. He truly wanted to hear this story from *her.* "If Anne and Artemis had not permitted me to come to St. Augustine with them, I've no idea what I would have done." She would not mention her cousins in Boston who supported the rebels' cause. Her break with them had been the worst of all cuts to her heart. At least her brother had forsaken his interest in the rebellion and now dedicated himself to his import business, avoiding the war altogether.

"It would seem to me," the captain said, "that Nova Scotia or Newfoundland would have been a wiser choice, being closer to Nantucket. Why did you three not remove to one of those loyal English colonies?"

As much as Dinah enjoyed his kind attention, she felt compelled to look to Artemis for an answer. He had made the decision for them all, while her choices had been few: stay on the island of her birth and be shunned or even starved, take refuge with her rebel cousins in Boston or come to East Florida. "Artemis, perhaps you might enlighten Captain Moberly."

Artemis's eyes brightened, and he took a sip from his water goblet. "Well, you see, Captain, East Florida holds many more opportunities for advancement than those northernmost colonies, which already had established societies." Tugging at his ruffled cravat, he grew more animated as he warmed to his topic. "When the Crown obtained East Florida from the Spanish in '63, it provided great opportunities for a man with any degree of ambition."

"So you had no plans to return to Nantucket?" Thomas lifted his chin. "Did you not think we would quickly defeat the insurgents and have order restored?"

Dinah thought she detected a hint of humor in his voice, although she could not imagine why. After five years, the war continued on, and the rebels seemed to grow stronger and more determined with each passing season.

As if mirroring the captain's posture, Artemis lifted his chin, and his eyes narrowed. "*When* order is restored by the efforts of our brave military—" he lowered his chin and gave the captain a fawning smile "—courageous men such as yourself—nevertheless, I shall never be able to forgive or forget the cutting words of my childhood friends as we departed." Anger flashed in his eyes, but he seemed to remember himself. "No, Captain, I shall not return to Nantucket. St. Augustine is my home now."

"And these four years," Anne said, "have been more than pleasant, have they not? Here amongst other Loyalists and the British citizens who have settled here, those of us who have been displaced have come to appreciate our English heritage more than ever."

She glanced between Dinah and the captain, and Dinah quizzed her with a look. At the lift of Anne's eyebrows, Dinah gave her head a little shake. She must cut short her friend's matchmaking. As engaging as Thomas was, with all his travels at sea, he would make a poor choice for a husband. At least for Dinah.

"And how we do appreciate Governor Tonyn." Calmer now, Artemis puffed out his chest like a rooster. "I'd not been here two months before he employed me as a clerk, and he has personally seen to my subsequent promotions."

Dinah could detect no hint of boredom in Thomas's expression as they related their stories, but surely it was time to inquire about his interests. "Now it's your turn. Please tell us about your move to our city."

He lifted one shoulder in a shrug Dinah found charming for one of such august rank. "There is little to tell. My ship is the HMS *Dauntless,* a forty-six-gun frigate, which you may have seen in the harbor. After three years in Admiral Rodney's fleet, I've been given the duty to join His Majesty's other two frigates in protecting St. Augustine and the St. Johns River from the French and Spanish fleets. And of course any colonial vessels foolish enough to wander this way." He took another bite of his pie. "Delicious. My compliments to the cook."

Artemis shifted in his chair, and from the narrowing of his eyes, Dinah guessed what he would say. "And while you protect our shores, by chance will you be responsible for ridding us of pirates?"

"I suppose you are referring to the one they call Nighthawk." The captain appeared more interested in his pie than the question. He ate another bite and seemed to savor it.

A wave of satisfaction swept through Dinah at the thought of pleasing the captain's palate. If she had not dried those peaches last fall—

"I do indeed refer to Nighthawk, and I will be nothing short of disappointed if you do not apprehend this brigand and sink him." Artemis's lips curled into a sneer as he spoke. "I have dabbled a bit in commerce, and he has stolen my wares. *Mine,* Captain Moberly." He clenched his jaw and shoved away his pie. "Our mutual friend Captain Templeton was delivering molasses to Jamaica when this pirate accosted him. Of all the cargo on the ship, he seized only my barrels. It was a dreadful loss."

Dinah took a turn at clenching her jaw. "At least Jamie and his crew were not harmed."

"Thank the good Lord." Thomas gave his head a little shake. "I hear strange reports about that fellow Nighthawk. He seems to avoid bloodshed. Perhaps that reputation encourages merchant captains to give him what he asks for. Most pirates are murderers as well as thieves."

"Do you mean to say—" Artemis's eyes bulged "—that these merchant captains permit this pirate to rob them? That you think Templeton just handed over my molasses?"

Dinah huffed out a breath to express her indignation. "I am certain Jamie did all he could to protect your precious cargo…short of being shot or losing any of his crew."

Thomas's wide-eyed gaze darted between her and Artemis, and she wished she'd tempered her cross tone. "I agree, Miss Templeton. In fact, I know how fiercely he would defend the wares entrusted to his care. To reassure you, let me say that I had the privilege of advising him in regard to refitting the *Fair Winds* to provide support for increasing his firepower. She now sports twenty-four guns and a crew trained to use them. That is a defense equal to many smaller British frigates. Should a pirate show an inclination for carnage, Jamie will have the wit, will and resources to engage him in battle."

Artemis continued to grumble, but Dinah's heart overflowed with happiness for all this good captain had done for her brother. "You must know how grateful Jamie is for your help. He has told us of your father's involvement in preventing impressments of the *Fair Winds*' crew. The earl's patronage has no doubt been the single most important element in Jamie's success as a merchant captain." Dinah also did not doubt for a moment that the earl's patronage had ensured Jamie's loyalty to England and the Crown, despite his former support for the rebellion. "When you next write to Lord Bennington, please convey to him a sister's gratitude."

Pain ripped across his eyes but disappeared so quickly Dinah wondered if she'd been mistaken.

"Yes, dear lady. I shall be pleased to convey your thanks to Lord Bennington."

"Ah, such a grand thing to be the son of an earl," Artemis said. "I've had the privilege of becoming acquainted with your brother Frederick, and I am deeply impressed by his management of Bennington Plantation. Your father must be proud of his four sons."

Again, Dinah saw a shadow flit across Thomas's face. Instead of responding, he lifted his coffee cup and sipped, focusing on his plate.

"Just think—" Artemis prattled on "—to have one's future all arranged and not to have to work one's way to success." He expelled a lengthy sigh. "Tell me, Captain Moberly, what is it like never to have doubts about one's future?"

The man's face was a mask as he turned a dead stare upon Artemis. "I serve at the king's pleasure, sir, but only the Almighty holds the future."

Artemis's animated countenance went blank. "Yes. Of course."

Thomas had long ago perfected the art of ending a discussion he did not wish to continue. Hussey was clearly ambitious, and his puffed-up demeanor did not invite confidences. A man had to be careful what he said to this sort, lest he take the bit and run with it. Thomas would not discuss family matters when there seemed to be some tension between Hussey and Dinah. Did the man treat her with honor, with respect? If not, Thomas would see things set to right.

Still, these St. Augustine Loyalists had decent manners, and Mrs. Hussey appeared to be the soul of

Christian gentility. But for the husband, Thomas might request the ladies' prayers regarding the tasks before him, for he *would* catch this Nighthawk chap, whom he must call a pirate merely because he was the enemy. But in truth, Thomas regarded him much like British privateers who gained wealth by raiding the cargoes of their foes. Still, the challenge to catch him was enticing, and success in the endeavor would ensure another feather in Thomas's cap.

As it was, he must find some way to speak with Miss Templeton alone without offending Mr. and Mrs. Hussey. A gentleman simply did not request a private conversation with a young lady unless he meant to court her. But the grief weighing down his soul clamored to be relieved, and his kinswoman's warm gaze invited his confidence...as well as some strange yet pleasant sentiments he could only attribute to their familial connections. That very morning, Dr. Wellsey had spoken of her good deeds among the sick and wounded soldiers from Fort St. Marks, citing her sympathetic disposition and natural kindness. Thomas had also noted her good humor, strangely subdued in Hussey's presence.

"Anne." Dinah's cheerfulness had returned, and her lively brown eyes shone. "Since the sun has not set, do you suppose it would be acceptable for me to show Captain Moberly our garden?"

Thomas wondered if she'd read his thoughts.

"Ah, yes." Hussey tossed his napkin on the table and stood. "A trip to the garden is just the thing after such a filling meal."

"Artemis, dear," Mrs. Hussey said, "I have need of thy help, if thee will, please." She rose from the table. "Dinah, do show Captain Moberly the garden. Perhaps he would like to take some of our abundance of squash to his ship's cook."

While Hussey blustered a bit before acquiescing to his wife's request, a riot of thoughts swept into Thomas's mind. Like most married women, Mrs. Hussey no doubt felt a duty to serve as a matchmaker for her unmarried friends. Still, if it worked to his advantage in this case, he would not complain. Dinah seemed to be a sensible girl, not likely to fawn over him or use artifice to gain his interest. But her cheerful countenance caused him to reconsider confiding in her for fear of ruining her merry mood.

As they stepped out the side door, a rich, sweet fragrance swept over Thomas. He quickly identified the source: a broad, lush, six-foot-tall bush filled with white, roselike blossoms. He breathed in the heady smell. "Gardenia, if I am not mistaken."

"Yes." Dinah moved close to the bush to sniff a bloom. "My favorite." She waved a hand toward a low wooden fence. "This way to the garden."

Just when they reached the gate, a gray-and-white cat pounced from behind a shrub and grabbed at the ribbons trailing from the waist of the young lady's flowered gown. The creature's claws snagged the back hem of the skirt, stopping her.

"Oh, Macy, hold still." She tried to twist around and grab the cat, but it tugged away from her.

"Hold still," Thomas echoed. He bent down and detached the claws, then lifted the cat into his arms. Its loud purr made him chuckle. "Yours?" It nestled into his neck, sending a familiar comfort through him. How long had it been since Wiggins died? Thomas's cabin on the *Dauntless* had been lonely since his little mouser had met its end.

"Yes, he's mine, the little nuisance." She reached for her pet.

Thomas tightened his grip. "Do let me hold him. My men would laugh to see me thus, and my steward will protest this hair on my coat. But I confess a weakness for cats." He stared into Macy's green eyes, and the cat lightly nipped his nose. He patted his muzzle with a gentle rebuke, then looked down to see the bemused expression on Dinah's face. They both laughed.

"A man so fond of cats is a rarity." She resumed walking into the garden, and Thomas fell into step beside her.

"I suppose." He shrugged and was rewarded by Macy's discovery of his epaulet tassels. The cat batted the moving woven strands and caught a claw on one. Thomas grimaced to see some gold threads pulled loose. "Uh-oh."

"Oh, now, *that* is the end." Dinah reached up to remove her pet, taking care with his entangled claws. "You must let me mend those braids. How will you explain to your steward that you were in a brawl with a fellow no bigger than your forearm?" She set the cat on the ground and tried to shoo him away, but Macy followed them down a row of squash plants until he spied a lizard and gave chase. Dinah's laughter resonated pleasantly around the garden. Not too high. Not too low. Not in the least giddy. Thomas would happily listen to that merry sound often.

"Do not trouble yourself. I shall tell Hinton I was attacked by a panther." Thomas inhaled the fresh fragrance of the varied plants. Beyond the vegetable garden grew a small field of lavender, casting a pleasant atmosphere about the place. A fig tree, several citrus trees and a grapevine-covered arbor graced sections of the landscape. An ancient oak tree stood sentinel in one corner of the green yard, its long branches reaching wide to cast shadows over a cast-iron bench that seemed to beckon them.

Orange and violet tinted the western sky, and a feeling of peace swept through Thomas. He gestured toward the bench. "Shall we?"

"Of course."

Seated beside him, Dinah gazed up, her eyes soft with concern. "What did you wish to tell me, Captain Moberly?"

He chuckled without mirth. "That obvious, eh?" He bit his lower lip while framing his words. With this intelligent, warm-hearted young woman, he sensed he could, for the most part, be candid. "Eight years have passed since my brother Frederick left England." Thomas would not mention the bitter rivalry that had plagued their childhood. "Marianne left to marry Jamie four years ago." Unexpected emotion rolled through his chest at the memory of the heartache her departure had caused. "I feel as if we are strangers." He stared off at the darkening eastern sky while he gained control. "Therefore, I must ask your advice on how best to tell my brother and sister about the death of our father. You see, Frederick now serves at the pleasure of our eldest brother."

Chapter Four

"Ooh." Dinah breathed out the word on a long, broken sigh, and her eyes burned with sudden tears. "Dear Captain, I am so sorry for your grief." She gripped his hand. In spite of the dim light, she thought she saw his eyes redden, and her heart swelled with compassion. Experiences with the sick and broken men at the infirmary had taught her that in moments like these, silence was the best comforter.

He covered her hands with his free one for a moment before gently pulling away. "I would not have your kind condolences misunderstood by Mr. Hussey."

He glanced toward the house, and she followed his gaze. There stood Artemis staring out through the dining room window. Dinah doubted he could see into their shadowed sanctuary, but she had no wish to feed his imaginings.

"Yes, of course." She rose and walked toward a sunlit patch of lawn. The captain followed. "To answer your question, I must ask one." She stopped and faced him. "Will your duties permit you a leave of absence to deliver your sad news in person?"

He stood with hands clasped behind him and stared

toward the line of trees at the edge of the property. "Your instincts seem to be in accord with mine. A letter would be too cruel, especially for my dear sister."

Dinah nodded. "Yes, and especially considering her delicate condition."

"Ah." Thomas's eyes widened. "Little James is nearing three years, is he not? Time to welcome a little brother or sister." A flash of pain crossed his eyes. "We must do nothing to cause her difficulty."

Dinah guessed he referred to his own wife's death in childbirth, but she would not seek a confirmation. "Do not be overly concerned, Captain. Marianne is strong and healthy. And in three weeks, Dr. and Mrs. Wellsey will be going to St. Johns Towne for her lying-in. You will be pleased to know that Mrs. Wellsey is a skilled midwife. I plan to accompany them. Perhaps you could travel with us." She would greatly enjoy his company on the arduous overland trip.

"Hmm." His black eyebrows bent into a frown. "I had hoped to put the matter behind me without delay, but perhaps this is the Almighty's way of managing the affair." He grunted. "In fact, I find myself grateful for the reprieve."

Dinah offered a gentle smile. "I understand." How good to hear of his trust in God, an attribute worthy of a superior leader, just like her brother.

Gazing down at her, he nodded. "I thank you." As if wanting to break their solemn mood, he inhaled a quick, sharp breath and glanced around the garden. "This is a charming place, both this property and this little town. Tell me, Miss Templeton, what keeps you busy here beside your good works at the infirmary?"

Dinah could see he wished to move on to a lighter topic, and she was pleased to comply. "You may be surprised to learn, sir," she said with a playful toss of her head, "that we have a very active social life here."

He chuckled. "Do tell me about it."

"Why, we have teas and parties and balls and picnics and no end of merry times. And of course the men go hunting." She gave him a sidelong look. "You will be in great demand, Captain. Every mother of a marriageable young lady will seek your company." Her teasing words threatened to stick in her throat. As before, she could not think of a single young lady worthy of this man, not even dear, wealthy Elizabeth Markham, for the girl rarely had a serious thought. Still, Dinah found herself nattering onward. "In fact, if you attend services at St. Peter's Church this Sunday, I shall make certain you are introduced to the cream of our society."

Again her words gave her pause. Growing up the son of an English earl, the captain no doubt had met truly exalted personages, perhaps even the king. Ignoring her uncertainties, she eyed him. "What do you say to that?"

Again he laughed. "I say that it would be imprudent of me to ignore your invitation if I expect to escape boredom in your fair town. In fact, I try never to miss attending worship services when I am ashore. And if I can be introduced into St. Augustine society at church, all the better." He raised one eyebrow the way Jamie did when he was about to tease. "Speaking of social matters, I must tell you that my lieutenant, Mr. Wayland, was quite taken with you. 'Twas all I could do to keep him from following me here this evening. If he asks me as your kinsman for permission to call on you, what shall I tell him?"

"Oh, my." She could still feel the young officer's too-firm clasp of her hand and see the overeagerness in his eyes. "You must tell him he would do better to pursue another." She kept her tone cheerful. "You see, I have vowed never to marry a seafaring man, for I will not live as a widow while I am wed." The slight dimming of his smile caused her a pang of regret, for she did not intend to disparage Thomas's profession. Nonetheless, she would not have sailors, even officers, coming to call. Of course, she would not count Thomas among the unwelcome ones, but then, he was her brother-in-law.

"Then I will do all in my power to protect you from such suits." He looked toward the house and offered Dinah his arm. "Miss Templeton, pray let us put Mr. Hussey at ease."

She thought she detected a tiny smirk on the captain's lips, but she dared not surrender to the giggle bubbling up inside her. "And let us escape these mosquitoes as well. This is the time of evening they come out to bother us." She waved away the insects trying to land on her bare hand. Inside they would be protected by the fine mosquito netting over the windows, an expense even Artemis had been eager to indulge in.

Halfway on their trip to the side door, the captain stopped, serious once again. "Are you well protected in this house, Miss Templeton?"

She blinked in surprise. "Wh-why, yes, Captain." Her heart warmed at his concern. Every word, every gesture endeared this man to her. Were he not a seafarer, she might even set her cap for him. But that was nonsense. He *was* a seafarer. And he was practically her brother. And he had made it clear at their first meeting he regarded her a sister. She need not even consider the difference in their ages…or their social ranks.

No, she would put away all such featherbrained thoughts of romance this very instant.

* * *

Thomas could not guess what had come over him. Somehow this delightful young woman's warmth and kindness had brought forth his tenderest emotions, not to mention his protective instincts. Perhaps his familial sentiments, so long submerged beneath his military responsibilities, were resurfacing in light of his imminent meeting with his brother and sister. Whatever the cause, he felt…*at home* with Dinah Templeton.

And now nothing would do but for him to discover the cause of the tension between the lady and Mr. Hussey. Overdone manners aside, the fellow had not hidden his annoyance with her. But why did she displease him? At first, Thomas had considered that the man might have designs on her. But Mrs. Hussey appeared to be as virtuous as she was attractive, as insightful as she was kindhearted. If the husband desired Dinah, the wife would surely not comport herself with such serenity.

Thomas searched his memory for scraps of conversations he'd had with Jamie Templeton regarding his sister. He could recall only that she had a modest inheritance to sustain her. Ah, perhaps that was the issue. Money. Thomas would not be hasty in his judgments but would watch for confirmation of his suspicions. His first impressions generally proved true. And when he met Hussey, a single line from Shakespeare's *Julius Caesar* had come to mind: "Yon Cassius has a lean and hungry look." If Hussey revealed himself to possess the same depth of wily ambition as the scheming Roman Cassius, all the more reason to investigate his treatment of Dinah.

As for the young lady's assertion that she would not wed a seafarer, Thomas acknowledged her decision was a wise one. As her friend, he wished only for her happiness. Still, the military man within him felt a bit of challenge, a surge of pride, even, that he could conquer that resolve, should he so desire.

Which, of course, he did not. But he was pleased to have a confidant who seemed to understand his situation. He should like to see Dinah well cared for. Even if he couldn't personally guarantee her happiness, he could not allow her to stay in an unsuitable situation. He would wait and learn what he could and if need be, he would act.

Chapter Five

Seated in St. Peter's Church, Dinah sensed someone's gaze on the back of her head, so she opened her prayer book, trying not to look over her shoulder. Her attempt failed. A glance across the aisle and to the rear revealed Mr. Wayland's bold stare and impudent grin, both of which ceased the instant a frowning captain nudged the young lieutenant with his fist.

Her heart lightened by the captain's protective gesture, Dinah turned back to face the altar, taking care not to knock loose her wide-brimmed straw hat by bumping into Anne's smaller chapeau. Anne gave her a smile, then returned her attention to her open Bible.

Dinah tried to refocus on her own prayer book, but the playful invitation in the lieutenant's expression lingered in her thoughts. Did he have no respect for this place of worship? While other unattached young ladies might find church the perfect place to engage the interests of young gentlemen, Dinah thought the practice bordered on heresy. It was all well and good to introduce Thomas to her friends after the service ended. However, one attended church services to consider God's mercies and worship Him. Indeed, this was the only place where Dinah ever felt the presence of God.

Pray though she might every day, believe in Him as she did with all her heart, she could never quite attain the serenity Anne had exhibited since they were children. Anne seemed to know God intimately, which surely gave her the grace to endure her marriage and even to love Artemis. For Dinah, God seemed distant, inaccessible, unheeding of her cries, uncaring about the loneliness she had felt all her life. Other than Anne, whom had Dinah ever loved who had not abandoned her?

She shook off her self-pity. Even if God chose not to speak to her, she would still choose to believe in His goodness and serve Him as best she could, just as Anne did. Anne, who sat here without complaint because there was no Friends meeting in St. Augustine. Here in St. Peter's, the lovely liturgy and insightful sermons bore little resemblance to Nantucket's quiet, but equally spiritual Quaker meetings, in which no one spoke unless guided by the Inner Light. Yet Anne often said how important it was to meet with other Christians to worship God, whatever form that worship took.

Although Dinah had never felt the Inner Light, she did find joy and comfort in repeating the prayers and singing the songs with the other congregants. Moreover, Reverend Kennedy's sermons always inspired her. No doubt Thomas would agree with her, for he had expressed sincere eagerness to attend today's service. Furthermore, when he mentioned the Almighty, he spoke with reverence. Surely he was a pious man. Dinah wondered if he had ever felt an inner light from God…and wondered if it would be poor manners to ask him.

* * *

As the service began, Thomas found himself distracted, not to mention infuriated by Wayland's insolent gaping at Dinah. No matter how lovely she was, he would not permit his officers or crew or anyone else to gawk at her as if they would breach her modesty. In the absence of her brother, and despite the useless presence of that Hussey fellow, Thomas would make certain every man knew she had a kinsman to whom they would answer.

With no small amount of effort, he managed to settle his anger and focus on the collective reading from his prayer book just as Dinah was doing. He wished he could see her face rather than the back of her charming beribboned hat. Her piety set an example for the other young ladies, several of whom had ogled him and his officers from the moment they had entered St. Peter's.

But alas, as he read the familiar words, his thoughts once again took their own direction. He may as well admit that Dinah drew his interest more than a little. Surely her familial connection and her compassion for his grief caused this longing to spend more time with her. And perhaps he could offer advice or solace for the sorrow he had seen in her eyes several times the other evening. Was that not the purpose of families?

Had he not been in church, he would have snorted in derision at his own thoughts. If his family were taken as an example, then blood bonds were often the cause of more pain than healing. Yet he longed to heal his relatives' griefs, longed to see to their needs just as he did for his crew. Indeed, after tending to several issues yesterday—letters to his crew's families gathered for the next ship to London, injuries and illnesses, wages paid to all, admonishments given to the men of weaker character to avoid drunkenness—Thomas could rest assured he had done his duty by those who served under him.

Duty. It was what he lived for, his purpose for being. And in addition to his crew, he performed his duty to his king and, long before that, to his father, who had impressed upon him the obligations of the nobility and their offspring. But what was his duty to Dinah?

Just as Reverend Kennedy stood to begin his sermon, Thomas lifted a silent prayer that he would know how to serve the young lady. Such a delightful, capable creature should be married, should be mistress of her own home. He had heard that few marriageable ladies lived in St. Augustine compared to the many unmarried men, and so surely she had received offers. But perhaps there was a dearth of eligible *Christian* men in the city. Clearly her heart was not engaged, yet she seemed to have no objections to marriage, except to a seafarer. Perhaps the Almighty would have Thomas interview potential suitors. Somehow the idea settled like lead in his mind. More to his liking would be to warn off any man who cast a glance in her direction.

As the minister and deacons made their way up the aisle at the close of the service, Dinah gripped the back of the bench in front of her to keep from turning around to look for Thomas. She would not, simply *must* not seek his company, for such behavior would be inappropriate.

But even before the front pews emptied, Artemis shoved his way into the crowd. "Come along, Mrs. Hussey." He glanced at Dinah and gave a quick jerk of his head. "Come along." Almost dragging poor Anne, he made his way toward the captain, who had already been surrounded by people clamoring for his attention.

Even Governor Tonyn approached the group of naval officers, and when people noticed, the way parted before him. Artemis almost jumped out of the governor's path, and Dinah bit her lip to keep from laughing. Thomas must have noticed as well, for he caught Dinah's gaze, his eyes twinkled, and he lifted one eyebrow. She gave him a tiny nod, then moved along the edge of the mob toward the door.

Standing inside the open front doors, Reverend Kennedy smiled warmly. "Good morning, Miss Templeton."

"Good morning, Reverend. Thank you for your lovely sermon. I was deeply moved." She curtseyed, then moved on to make way for others. Indeed, the sermon had been quite inspirational, and she longed to discuss the minister's words with someone who understood how it had touched her emotions.

Outside on St. George Street, she blinked in the bright sunlight and tugged at her hat brim to shield her eyes. Surprised to see that few parishioners had emerged, she attributed the phenomenon to the appeal of the captain and his officers. She glanced up at the clock on the spire of St. Peter's. Almost noon. Her stomach responded to that information with a tiny growl.

Soldiers from the fort eyed her and made remarks among themselves, so she stared down the street toward the Parade, hoping they would not approach. It was one thing to minister to these men when they were sick, but another thing altogether when they were hale and hardy and attempted to gain her interest. Soon her concerns about the matter ended when people began to pour from St. Peter's and go their separate ways.

"Dinah." Elizabeth Markham approached and touched her arm. "Why did you not join the rest of us in meeting Captain Moberly…and his very handsome lieutenant, Mr. Wayland?"

The wistful look in Elizabeth's eyes gave Dinah a laugh. Perhaps those two would be a good match. That is, if Mr. Wayland's bold stares had simply meant he had been at sea too long, not that he lacked Christian character.

"I have already met the gentlemen, Elizabeth." She looped her arm around her friend's. "The other day when we saw them walking down St. George Street, I had no idea the captain is none other than my brother-in-law."

Elizabeth gasped and then laughed. "Why, of course. Captain *Moberly*. I should have realized when I heard his name." She gave Dinah a sly smile. "Are there not several marriages between your two families?"

Dinah released Elizabeth's arm. "Yes, and those marriages are quite sufficient to join us as family."

Elizabeth smirked. "Of course. Well then, if Mr. Wayland proves uninteresting, perhaps I shall set my cap for the captain."

An odd annoyance cut through Dinah. How could anyone find that impertinent lieutenant superior to Thomas? But if she voiced the thought to Elizabeth, she would never hear the end of it. "Do enjoy yourself, my dear."

"Hmph. Just because you do not wish to marry a man of the sea." Elizabeth's pout was short-lived. "Oh, but won't it be grand to dance with these fine officers at the governor's ball?"

Dinah's heart skipped. "A ball? Oh, my. When? And what on earth inspired Governor Tonyn to this frivolity? Why, he despises such merrymaking." She could hardly contain her astonishment…and her excitement. "Tell me everything you know."

Elizabeth giggled. "There, you see. You are not as indifferent to the gentlemen as you pretend." She punctuated her words with a smirk. "As to the governor, well, I am of the opinion that he is impressed by the fact that Captain Moberly is the son of Lord Bennington. In his political world, such an august person surely must be entertained." She glanced toward the people emerging from the church, then leaned toward Dinah in a confiding manner. "The ball is to be held this Friday evening to officially honor the arrival of HMS *Dauntless*. Only specially invited guests may attend, and my parents and I are among them. *Mamá* told me about it the day before yesterday, and I have been begging for a new gown since then. But she says my old one will do because none of the *Dauntless* crew has seen it." She paused, and puzzlement crinkled her smooth forehead. "Did you not receive an invitation?"

"Ah, there you are, Miss Templeton." Thomas approached, looking a bit harried with his eyes wide and his lips in a thin smile. "I feared you had already left." People clustered behind him as if seeking his attention, but he focused on Dinah.

Her feelings in riot and confusion, Dinah dipped an unsteady curtsey and forced a smile. "Good morning, Captain." Surely if he was concerned about the possibility of not seeing her this morning, this oversight about an invitation could not be his doing. "I believe you have met my good friend, Miss Markham."

"Indeed we have just met inside." He swept off his bicorne hat and greeted Elizabeth with an elegant bow. "Miss Markham."

"Captain—" Elizabeth lifted her chin "—I should not

wish to scold you, but the omission of your kinswoman from the list of those invited to the ball in your honor is beyond—"

"What?" Thomas stared at Dinah, his eyebrows rising sharply. "Of course you were invited. I gave your name to Governor Tonyn's secretary." Now those strong black eyebrows bent into a stormy frown. "I shall investigate the matter and see it set to right. In fact, I shall escort you to the event myself." He blinked, as if surprised by his own words.

The crowd buzzed and hummed around them, but Dinah could not discern their words. A wave of heat began to surge up her neck and she quickly inhaled to stop it. She had never blushed in her life and would not begin to do so now.

"I thank you, my good kinsman." She raised her voice slightly for the benefit of their audience. "Now, if you will excuse me…" A quick glance down the lane revealed Anne and Artemis well on their way home.

Thomas followed her gaze, and his frown deepened. "My dear sister-in-law, may I escort you home? I should like to speak to Mr. Hussey on a matter of some importance."

He offered his arm, and Dinah set her gloved hand on his forearm, grateful for his gesture and for his familial address. That should prevent gossip. Or so she hoped.

They took their leave of Elizabeth, and the crowd dispersed, as if understanding they had been dismissed.

And now Dinah had only to contend with her giddy heart, which seemed to have a mind of its own regarding Thomas Moberly.

Chapter Six

As Thomas escorted Dinah away from the throng, his emotions warred within him. That Hussey fellow deserved a good thrashing for leaving a young lady to see herself home. Yet Thomas could not deny he welcomed the opportunity to serve in that capacity himself...not to mention he was relieved to escape the crowd of churchgoers who behaved as if they had never before seen an officer in His Majesty's navy. An oddity, to be sure, since he understood that the two other frigate captains and their officers also frequented St. Peter's. Today, their ships were on patrol, as his would be in another week.

Thomas wondered whether the gaggle of matchmaking mothers had pushed forth their daughters for introductions to the other captains. Whether gentlemen clamored for their attention and promised all sorts of diversions from hunting to billiards. What madness! It was all he could do not to laugh out loud at these colonials. While he might be admired in London Society, at least the ladies there exhibited a bit more decorum.

He glanced down at his companion and saw her pursed lips just below her hat brim. It was too much.

Suddenly lighthearted, he chuckled at the absurdity. Dinah tilted her head prettily, peered up at him and released her own musical laughter.

"Am I to assume," he said, "this is not the usual Sunday morning in St. Augustine?"

Her merriment increased until her brown eyes watered. "Oh, no. Well, perhaps our citizenry grows a bit more...*lively* whenever a new regimental officer arrives." She wiped away a tear and shook her head. "So you can imagine how they respond to the rare arrival of new *naval* officers."

"Unlike yourself." He meant to tease her, but his tone sounded wrong in his ears, more an accusation. More the way he would speak to an insubordinate sailor.

Suddenly sober, she gazed up at him, and he steeled himself to hear an affirmation of his ill-spoken words. But she did not speak for several moments as they continued down the narrow street.

"Tell me, Captain," she said at last, "do you enjoy discussions regarding religion?"

Surprised, but glad for the change of subject, he considered the question. "When I was a lad, my family did not speak of our faith, but we attended services without fail. One is expected to set an example whether as the son of a nobleman or as an officer in the military." He paused, hoping his reference to being wellborn did not sound arrogant. "Until I met your good brother, I do not recall ever having a deep conversation about religion with anyone."

Her lovely smile returned, and her eyes shone with pride. "Jamie is rather bold about such matters, is he not?"

"He is, much to his credit. My brother Robert and I have both benefitted by his concern for our souls." And their eldest brother, Lord Bennington, as well, although the newly-elevated earl might not acknowledge it.

"And of course Frederick and Marianne." Her eyebrows rose.

"Marianne has always been a woman of faith."

"Yes, she is much like Anne." She was silent for a moment, but her thoughtful expression kept him from speaking. "You do not mention Frederick."

"Mmm." He would not burden her with his fraternal discord. If their planned trip to Bennington Plantation became a reality, she would soon enough see how things stood between his younger brother and him, a thought that did not sit well on his mind.

"Mmm," she echoed, but her voice and expression held no censure, which Thomas found refreshing, reassuring.

They walked in companionable silence for several moments. At least Thomas hoped she felt as relaxed as he did. The day was fair, if hot, but a few shady oaks and breezes from the ocean gave them intermittent respite from the sun's rays.

She leaned into his arm in a sociable way but seemed unaware of her own movement. "My purpose in opening the subject of religion is that Reverend Kennedy's sermon caused me to think. We all require grace extended to us. And as we wish to receive it when we err, so should we extend it to those who have offended us."

He regarded her with interest. "Wise words, Miss Templeton." The young lady was not only beautiful, but astute as well. As he had assumed during the service, her mind had been on spiritual matters, not the matchmaking schemes that seemed to emanate from some of the other girls.

They neared the whitewashed coquina walls that surrounded her house, and his anger reignited at the thought of seeing Hussey again. "Of course there is a difference between personal affronts and breaking the law. One cannot extend grace to miscreants or any man not doing his duty."

She questioned him with a frown. "No, of course not. Do you speak of someone in particular?"

Thomas stared over the five-and-a-half-foot barrier that protected the courtyard to see Hussey stride from the house like a preening peacock.

"Ah, there you are, Miss Templeton. Why, Captain Moberly, how good to see you—" Hussey released the iron latch and swung the door inward.

Thomas did not pass through and saw to his satisfaction that his companion hesitated, too. "I cannot return the compliment, sirrah. What do you mean by leaving Miss Templeton at the church to find her way home unescorted?" He heard her soft gasp beside him, but he would not permit her to protect this toad, who now stared at him with mouth agape.

"B-but, sir, this is St. Augustine. We are a walled city, protected from interlopers and wild beasts by armed outposts on the walls, not to mention our well-armed garrison. Who would dare to—" he waved his bony hands about in a nervous manner "—*annoy* any of the ladies within our fair town?" The pitch of his voice rose to a squeak, and he tugged at his frilled cravat. "On a Sunday morning? In broad daylight?"

Thomas glanced down at Dinah, whose bemused expression gave him pause. Had he erred in his assessment of the situation? Too late, he recalled that Dinah saw to her errands unescorted during the week.

"In any event," the man said, "Mrs. Hussey and I

assumed she would spend hours gossiping with her friends, as is her custom. Is it not, Miss Templeton?"

"I would not say hours—"

"And of course, Mrs. Hussey and I are not given to gossip, especially after a worship service, therefore we returned home. But never mind." Suddenly all affability, Hussey gestured toward the house. "Do come in, Captain. We would be delighted to have you join us for our midday meal. A modest fare, but wholesome nonetheless."

A war of thoughts ignited in Thomas's mind. Hussey's suggestion that Dinah was a gossip while he was blameless of that shortcoming bordered on being not only a direct insult but also a lie. Grasping for self-control, Thomas quashed the desire to challenge the charge, but now he felt no need to apologize to this boor for his own error. As for spending time in this oaf's presence or obligating himself by accepting another meal, nothing could be more distasteful. Yet he still must address the missing invitation to the ball. Before he could respond, Dinah's lavender perfume wafted up to his nostrils, soothing his turmoil, and she gave him a sweet smile. All rancor disappeared. That is, all but his annoyance over the missing invitation.

"You are most hospitable, sir." Thomas took Dinah's elbow and guided her through the gate opening.

Hussey watched their movements with narrowed eyes, reminding Thomas of a viper. But the expression melted into an oily smile. Thomas would have to watch his words and actions around this man. And he would endeavor to deliver his next accusation with less force.

Waiting in the parlor for Cook to announce dinner, Dinah shifted uncomfortably on her straight-back chair.

She and Anne traded glances. All their efforts at pleasant conversation had failed, and Artemis seemed to have run out of things to boast about. Thomas sat, silent as a stone statue, balancing his teacup and saucer on his knees. From the glint in his eyes, Dinah could see he had more to say to Artemis, perhaps about the missing ball invitation. But for some reason, he had become taciturn the moment they had entered the house, no doubt in deference to Anne. Should Dinah introduce that topic?

"Captain," Anne said, "is there any way in which the people of St. Augustine might show their appreciation to thee and thy crew for thy protection of our coast? Perhaps the ladies might mend or sew for thee, as we have for the other ships' crews? Perhaps bake pastries or even prepare a picnic?"

His gaze softened considerably at her words. "How generous, Mrs. Hussey. I thank you for those offers and will not refuse them." He gave Artemis a sly look.

Dinah almost laughed. Anne had no idea of the opening she had just given the captain.

"We have never been received quite so well as by the people of this fair city." He took a sip of tea. "In fact, my officers and I anticipate a grand time at the governor's ball this Friday." He blinked with seeming innocence, and again Dinah could barely contain her laughter. "You have received your invitation, have you not, Mrs. Hussey?"

Now Anne blinked. "Why, no. But perhaps we were not meant to be included." She gave him a serene smile. "Despite the friendliness amongst our citizens, we cannot be counted as members of the city's elite society."

"Nonsense, my dear," Artemis blustered. "We are most certainly among the elite."

"But I put your name on the list myself." Thomas stared at Artemis. "In this charming yet small *walled* city, how could an invitation go astray? An invitation that came from the very office in which you are employed?"

"Well, if you must know—" Artemis's face grew red. "I do have the invitation in my desk." He stood and straightened his coat, then marched across the tabby floor and into the next room, his bedchamber. In a matter of seconds, he returned, waving the missive in the air. "A man cannot even surprise his wife."

Dinah pursed her lips and stared down at her tea to keep from looking at anyone else. Artemis would say anything to keep out of trouble with Thomas, as evidenced by his ignoring the captain's earlier scolding. Thoughts of that morning's sermon came to mind, and shame pinched her conscience. She truly must stop laughing at Artemis's expense, no matter how much he irritated her. Remembering Reverend Kennedy's sermon, she decided she must extend grace to him as the Lord extended grace to her.

"Oh, my dear Artemis," Anne said, "how kind of thee." Despite her words, her eyes and voice conveyed a muted rebuke. "I know what I shall wear, but Dinah must have a new gown. Now we may not have enough time to make it."

Dinah's heart skipped. She would love something new to wear to such a grand event, but unlike her cousin Rachel, she had never been a swift seamstress.

"Why does she require a new gown?" Artemis still looked flushed. "Such an unnecessary expense—"

"Now, Hussey," Thomas said, "surely you know ladies always must have a new gown for these occasions."

"I know no such thing." Artemis dropped back into

his wingback chair. "But now that my surprise has been ruined, I will tell the rest of it. Miss Templeton, I have arranged for Mr. Richland to accompany you."

Dinah saw Thomas's gaze cut quickly to her, but she felt too stunned to reply. Mr. Richland owned a plantation. Not only was the man a slaveholder, but he was many years her senior and even had a son near her age. Would Artemis never cease his efforts to marry her to unsuitable men? And what of the captain's statement, spoken in front of her friends, that he would escort her to the ball? She could not keep from looking at him and knew her expression conveyed the dismay she felt.

He sent her a reassuring smile. "But this will not do." His smooth, controlled words held a world of authority. "I have promised to take my sister-in-law to the ball myself."

"But—" Artemis's face contorted into a variety of expressions, from anger to confusion to helplessness.

Once again Dinah subdued her desire to laugh. Never before had anyone intervened for her as the captain had done today—*twice*. Her heart warmed even as she cautioned herself against putting too much into the matter. His words proved clearly that he regarded her as his kinswoman, and his actions were simply in keeping with that relationship. She dismissed the disappointment that tried to creep into her with that thought.

In any case, pleasant and a very good friend though the captain might be, he *was* in the navy.

Thomas wended his way through the streets back to the transformed Franciscan monastery that now served as military barracks. Billeted there, he and his officers found comfortable accommodations and respite from sea duty. Today, he would be pleased to find respite from his own nagging conscience. Not since his foolish adolescence and those first few years in naval service had he struggled so fiercely with his temper. In fact, his steady disposition was an attribute that had often earned him promotions over his fellow officers—that, and his father's influence, of course.

A stray thought interrupted his line of thinking. He had often wondered if his eldest brother would maintain Father's influence for him or if Thomas's advancements would cease. The uncertainty alone was unsettling, but not enough to cause him to abandon self-control. A captain's temperament must be dependable, not erratic. Therefore he must ascertain the cause of this odd rage within him.

Perhaps the fine church service had stirred his soul, for he found himself lifting a rare prayer that he might know the cause of this weakness. The hawk-like face of Artemis Hussey came to mind, but Thomas rejected such a simple answer. Yes, of course, the man was irritating. But even if he did not display sufficient generosity toward Dinah, he did permit her to live in his home during these difficult times for all Loyalists on these shores. And what choice did she have but to live with the Husseys?

The answer came in the form of another more confounding question that halted Thomas in his path. Why did the young lady live here in this city with such a disagreeable fellow when she could be safely and amiably housed at Bennington Plantation? Renewed anger surged through Thomas's chest, and he strode toward his barracks while more questions sprang to mind, all directed toward another man who had never been anything but disagreeable to him. A man who should have seen to Dinah's care just as he had to his sister's.

Frederick Moberly, his spoiled younger half-brother.

By the time Thomas reached his apartments and his steward had relieved him of his ceremonial sword and jacket and placed a cooling beverage in his hand, he had a fair understanding of what motivated his rage. He had no wish ever to see little Freddy again, much less to convey news of their father's death. Had he not promised to escort Dinah and Dr. and Mrs. Wellsey through the wilderness to the plantation, and were he not eager to see dear Marianne and her young son, he would dash off a note to Freddy to accompany their eldest brother's letter.

A wicked thought crossed his mind and he made no attempt to stop it. Perhaps the trip would not be so bad after all if he could witness Freddy's distress upon learning their father no longer lived and therefore could not ensure his employment.

Guilt smote him. What had Dinah reminded him of from this morning's sermon? Every person stood in need of grace from time to time and therefore should be willing to extend it to those who offended him. But then, Dinah did not have a brother like Freddy.

Chapter Seven

Few ladies in St. Augustine matched Dinah in stature, so borrowing a gown for the ball had been out of the question. Dear Elizabeth had saved the situation by donating her second-best overdress, a rose-pink linen, to which Dinah added a ruffled border made of Elizabeth's leftover fabric. Of course the new material had a brighter sheen, but nothing could be done about that. Underneath, Dinah wore her own plain white linen skirt. Anne praised her ingenuity, and even Artemis gave a nod of approval…accompanied by a frown rather than a smile. Dinah attributed his crossness to Thomas's insistence on escorting her to the ball in his honor.

In truth, she could barely grasp the idea herself. While everyone in St. Augustine knew who she was and she knew of them, she had never put herself forward for attention. Being at the captain's side would surely bring much notice, almost like a coming-out ball that launched young ladies into London's Society. Marianne, the captain's sister, once told her about these events, but Dinah had thought little more about them. Now she was not certain she wished for such recognition, for it might bring more unwanted suitors. Having looked over the crop of available local men and rejecting each and all, she could hardly find joy in that prospect.

Further, she had expended much energy subduing the elation that arose each time she envisioned walking into the governor's palace arm-in-arm with the captain. What nonsense that giddy feeling was. Thomas belonged at the top of her inventory of unsuitable gentlemen for all the reasons she repeatedly listed to herself. Why, even Artemis's latest candidate, Mr. Richland, lived in East Florida and never traveled farther than Jamaica. That made him a more suitable husband than the captain, but she would never consider the man.

Still, when Thomas arrived in a fine black landau complete with four matched grays and a liveried driver, she made no attempt to conceal her delight.

"Really, Captain Moberly," Artemis said as he, Anne and Dinah emerged from the house. "'Tis a short walk across the city. Why go to the expense of a carriage?"

Dinah noticed he did not seem too put out about the matter. She also noticed he had applied an exceptional amount of his apple-scented hair dressing. Her appetite for apples had diminished considerably since living in the Hussey household.

"But if we walk," Thomas said, "the ladies' slippers will be ruined. Many puddles from this afternoon's rain have failed to evaporate, despite the heat." He waved a white-gloved hand toward the bright evening sky, which would not become dark for another hour or so, then reached out to Anne. "Mrs. Hussey, you are a vision of loveliness."

"I thank thee, Captain." Anne accepted his hand to help her step up into the conveyance. Indeed, in her black damask gown, she presented a picture of modest matronly grace as she settled into her seat.

"Miss Templeton." Thomas turned to Dinah, and his blue eyes twinkled. "I am overwhelmed by your beauty." The humor in his voice at once dismayed her and made her laugh. What did he really think of her appearance?

"And of course, you, Captain, are the epitome of perfection." Her words, conveyed on a chuckle, nevertheless spoke the truth.

His shiny black hat sat on his shiny black hair, which was pulled back into a queue by an equally shiny black ribbon, and not a single hair was out of place. His dark-blue uniform jacket bore not a speck of lint. His white breeches were spotless. The golden threads of his epaulets gleamed. And his sword, polished to a brilliant shine, caught the remaining sunlight with a gold and silver sparkle. But it was his sapphire-blue eyes, leveled squarely on her, that sent her heart into a dizzy spin. She had never seen a more handsome man, not even his brother Frederick, whom he closely resembled. Not even her own brother, Jamie. And the elegant gracefulness with which the captain climbed into the carriage generated admiration…and fear within her. Of course she must dance with him at least once this night, and then he would discover her clumsiness, for in Quaker Nantucket she had never learned that skill. At least in the dim candlelight of the ballroom, he would not notice her patched-together gown, which until this moment had seemed acceptable for a St. Augustine fête.

But never mind. She had no need to capture his interest. As with all things, they would find reasons to laugh together, as good friends did at each other's shortcomings. Yet he seemed to have no deficiencies, and she would certainly not seek to find one.

Artemis clambered into the carriage behind the

captain and dropped his slender form next to Anne. His long fingers caressed the black leather seat and his wide-eyed stare scanned the gray carpeted flooring. "A fine coach, Captain. I believe this is the finest available to let here in St. Augustine. A fitting conveyance for your entrance into St. Augustine society."

That entrance was accomplished within twenty minutes. And the only thing that marred Governor Tonyn's introduction of Thomas and his officers was the way Artemis shouldered his way next to the captain and left Anne and Dinah to be lost amidst the crowd.

While people lined up to be presented, Dinah spied a friendly face and tugged Anne by the hand toward Mrs. Pilot, the wife of a regimental officer. The older matron took special pleasure in organizing balls, and her hand was evident in the decorations around the room.

"Mrs. Pilot," Anne said, "thee must have scoured the entire city to find so many lovely flowers."

"Oh, my, yes, Mrs. Hussey." The plump, cheerful lady chuckled, a deep, throaty sound, and her ruddy apple cheeks glistened in the ballroom's candlelight. "Roses, gardenias, lavender, honeysuckle. Everyone was eager to help with the preparations for these fine naval officers. Why, even my husband, who admits to enjoying a vigorous competition with his naval counterparts, awoke this morning with extraordinary enthusiasm for this event." She waved a pink-gloved hand at the middle-aged officer in question, who stood across the room in his red army jacket and white breeches. As he responded in kind, the lady continued to prattle on merrily about the supper she had organized for later in the evening. "And a large pig has been roasting over a pit outside the kitchen house since yesterday. And we have desserts that will delight the most discerning palate."

"The aromas are enticing," Dinah said. "How shall we make it until supper?"

Mrs. Pilot chuckled again. "Why, we must dance up an appetite. Which reminds me, Miss Templeton, I am sorry your handsome brother and his lovely wife are not in the city. Captain Templeton dances beautifully and could teach some of our locals a thing or two."

"Yes, he does." Dinah felt a pang of loneliness for Jamie. "Marianne made certain he learned the skill in London."

"Will he be returning to East Florida soon?" Mrs. Pilot tapped her chin. "We must have another ball when he comes to celebrate all the new wares he will bring us. Even if the governor will never countenance such an event, we can meet in another home."

"I have not heard from Jamie for five months, so surely he will return soon." Dinah's old fears resurfaced. "I pray he will not encounter that pirate, Nighthawk, and have his cargo stolen."

"Now, Dinah," Anne said, "thou knows that Captain Moberly's presence will surely put an end to the piracy."

"Indeed, it shall." Mrs. Pilot patted Dinah's hand, then gazed across the room. "Now if you will excuse me, I see we have some newcomers."

Dinah and Anne curtsied to the English lady, who scurried away to tend to her hostess duties. Mrs. Pilot had long ago made it her duty to see that those who had fled to St. Augustine because of the war found safety and welcome. Every time the watchtower bell rang to announce the arrival of a ship, whether merchant or military, Betsey Pilot could be counted on to ascertain its identity and the needs of its crew.

Anne smiled. "What would we do without her?"

"Endure great boredom, I am certain." Dinah peered through the crowd to see how Thomas fared and found him looking her way. Following Mrs. Pilot's example, she gave him a tiny wave, as though the two of them shared a good-humored secret. His wry grin and slight nod assured her that he had understood.

Thomas and Mrs. Pilot led the first dance, and young Mr. Richland claimed Dinah as his partner. She felt some relief, because dancing a country round with someone who was as provincial as she gave her the opportunity to reacquaint herself with her feet, silly appendages that seemed determined to embarrass her by failing to keep time with the music.

At the end of the set, she looked for the captain, hoping for rescue from Mr. Richland. But the senior Mr. Richland moved his son aside, took her hand and led her to the floor. As the next piece ended, Mr. Wayland bumped the older man aside, and after him, another officer sought her as a partner. Perhaps she smiled too generously. Perhaps Mrs. Pilot took pity on her for her pieced-together dress and sent the gentlemen to her rescue. To a man, they heaped praise upon her for her gown, which only caused her more discomfort. Or, more precisely, annoyance. Their effusive compliments seemed to border on insincerity.

At last, after countless rounds, she managed to hide behind a row of tall potted plants to catch her breath and watch the revelers from the shadows. Across the ballroom she saw Elizabeth Markham sipping punch with Mr. Wayland. To her surprise, her friend's expression held not a hint of her usual coyness, merely modest admiration. Could this young officer, the third son of a baron, have won her heart? Already?

A sudden rustling of the leaves nearby gave Dinah

a start, which quickly turned to delight. Thomas stood just beyond the plants, his blue eyes focused on her, a teasing smile on his lips.

"Hiding, are we?" He glanced over his shoulder. "Are you not enjoying all the merry matchmaking?"

She emerged from her refuge, feigning indignation. "Hmph. This ball was meant to be in your honor, not a matchmaking event."

Now he laughed out loud. "My dear Miss Templeton, every ball is a matchmaking event."

She rolled her eyes and shook her head. "I suppose."

He turned to face the room with her. "May I fetch you some lemonade?"

"Gracious, no, but I thank you, sir. This past hour, I have had lemonade enough to drown me." Nearly every gentleman with whom she had danced insisted on fetching her some refreshment between sets.

He regarded her for a moment. "Ah, to have an abundance of tasty lemonade available after months at sea. I believe my officers and I would very much enjoy drowning ourselves in it."

"Just as you are drowning in the admiration of our city?" She could not withhold a laugh. "Why, look over there at my friend and yours." She pointed with her folded fan. "I do think Miss Markham would be a fine wife for an officer in His Majesty's navy. Her father is wealthy, and her mother has taught her the proficiencies required of a gentleman's wife…or an officer's. The younger son of a baron could not do better, could he?" She lifted one eyebrow and smirked.

"I have no doubt the young lady is quite accomplished and worthy." The captain eyed Elizabeth and tilted his head as if considering the proposition. "Yes, I believe she will do wonders for Mr. Wayland. By the expression on his face, I do believe you have lost your chance with him."

"My chance?" Dinah permitted herself a ladylike snicker. She started to remind him of her vow not to marry a seafarer, but somehow the words would not form. "No, thank you. Elizabeth may have him."

"Ah." The captain gazed about the room. "Well, then, you do have your choice between Mr. Richland Senior or Junior. I recommend the lad, for the old fellow, while handsome enough, seems set in his ways." He spoke in a mock-serious tone, as if constructing a battle plan. "I do believe you could get Junior in hand with very little trouble."

Dinah bit her lips to keep from giggling. "Captain, I order you to cease matchmaking for me." A playful thought nudged her mind. "That is, unless I am permitted to serve the same office for you."

He gave her a slight bow. "Fair enough. Make your selection and present me to the lady."

She stared around the room, seeking a likely candidate. "Hmm. Well. How about…no, not her. And then there's…but no, she would not suit." She released a dramatic sigh. "I fear not a single match can be found for you in our city, sir."

Kindness would not permit her to tease about pairing him with any of her acquaintances. Kindness? Or perhaps something far more selfish? If only for the rest of this evening, she wanted Thomas to herself. With brotherly concern, he had sought her out and now stood beside her like a sentinel during this short intermission between dances. And how kind of him to indulge in nonsensical banter that lifted her heart and caused harm to no one. How generous of him to ignore the plainness of her makeshift ball gown. Yes, she would gladly have this gentleman standing beside her, if only for this evening.

Thomas had never felt such respite from duty and obligation as he did in Dinah's company. The fragrance of a single gardenia, so artfully placed in her thick, upswept blond hair, wafted up to delight his senses. He saw a resemblance to her brother in her well-formed countenance, especially in her dark-brown eyes, which met his gaze with good humor and friendly understanding. Her straight, narrow nose had a pert little upturn at its tip, a perfect complement to the upturned corners of her full, rosy lips. Her simple but pretty pink frock cast a healthy, honest glow upon her ivory cheeks, so different from the excessive blushes of the giddy girls who had earlier clamored for his attention. In fact, he had yet to see this young lady blush, although it could not be attributed to a lack of modesty. She merely seemed oblivious to her own loveliness, and actually rather shy and confused by the admiration heaped upon her by every man in the room, whether young or old, unattached or married.

Even the governor himself had remarked on her beauty, nudging Thomas's arm as he said it. Thomas had refrained from asking what the man meant by that gesture. They had exhausted their discussion of Nighthawk's piracy and the unpredictable East Florida weather. No doubt the governor, for all his austerity and grousing, was a matchmaker, like everyone else in attendance. And for this night, Thomas could find no one he would rather be matched with than his dear young kinswoman. Yet even as he thought it, he reminded himself that they were not truly related, at least by blood. No legal or moral matter would prevent their being permanently matched.

Belay that line of thinking, man. No, he must not think of her as anything but his sister-in-law. Must not think of marriage at all, especially to a colonial, especially to a young lady who did not wish to be shackled to a naval officer. His duty was to protect her from unwanted suitors…and that disagreeable Hussey. In fact, he must investigate that situation further as soon as he returned from the coming week's patrol of the East Florida coast.

He glanced down to see her hands clasped together almost as if she were wringing them. Had something distressed her? He scanned the room and noted that couples were lining up for the minuet. And approaching fast on their starboard side was young Richland, his eyes fixed on the lady like a pelican's on a fish. The young pup had nearly tripped her half a dozen times when they had stood up together. In her defense, Thomas moved in front of his companion and bowed.

"Miss Templeton, will you do me the honor of this dance?"

Relief and gratitude glowed in her radiant smile. "Why, yes, Captain Moberly." She placed her gloved hand in his. "I thought you would never ask." There it was again. That delightful smirk that conveyed a world of good humor.

Thomas's heart soared. As often happened in her company, all he could think was *what a delightful creature.*

But, as always before, an inner voice cautioned *Avast!*

Chapter Eight

The southeasterly wind swept over the *Dauntless*, bringing with it the salty scent of the ocean and cooling Thomas as he paced the quarterdeck in the blazing sun. Five days of patrolling the coast and inlets from Amelia Island down to Turnbull's New Smyrna plantation had turned up nothing. Just as he had expected, the presence of the British fleet in the West Indies and the three frigates here had served notice to Nighthawk. Unless the man was a fool, he would cease his piracy.

Yet, despite Thomas's reassurances to Dinah, he worried about her brother. Templeton did not lack courage, as he had proven four years ago when he rescued Thomas's young nephew from drowning in the manor lake in Hampshire. Of course, courage was required of any sea captain, especially during a time of war. But Templeton's reluctance to fire on a ship that threatened him made him the perfect target for repeated plundering by Nighthawk.

Thomas would feel no small relief when he laid eyes on his friend again. During their last meeting in London some fourteen months earlier, Templeton had seemed preoccupied, distracted, almost morose. Thomas had attributed it to his forced separation from Marianne. Lord Bennington had disowned her, but he still served as a patron for her husband and conducted business with him. Thomas had never comprehended his father's eccentricities, and now that the old man was dead, he would never know what had driven him.

Ah, such ponderings did nothing to soothe his mood or calm his restlessness on such a dull day. What would brighten his disposition was sailing back into St. Augustine harbor and seeing Dinah again. Her company was more refreshing than these brisk Atlantic breezes.

He might as well admit it. He was weary of the war. Weary of the service. He had no doubt his father's death had ended any influence in his favor with the Admiralty. His eldest brother, the new earl, seemed to have his own favorites whose careers he could advance. But Thomas found himself strangely unalarmed about the matter. In fact, if not for this rather independent assignment of guarding St. Augustine and the challenge of catching one more pirate, he might consider resigning the Service entirely.

All his life, he had done his duty. But with Father's death, it seemed he had done enough, for he would no longer have to face the old earl should he happen to fail. And like some of his fellow officers, he was beginning to agree with Charles Fox and his cronies in Parliament. Perhaps it was time to release the recalcitrant colonies to their own devices.

"Sail ho," the watchman called from the crosstrees. "Three points off the larboard quarter. Looks to be a merchantman."

At last. Something to alleviate the boredom. "Mr. Wayland," Thomas called to his lieutenant, who stood below him on the main deck, "as soon as the vessel is near enough, signal her to heave to." If he could fill out an inspection report, however mundane, it would prove to his superiors that he was doing his duty *and* that his presence was required on the East Florida coast.

At the thought of being reassigned, he chafed against his woolen jacket, which was scratchy in the heat. A lighter uniform would be more suitable in these climates, and many times he felt the urge to throw off his frock coat and let the wind blow through his linen shirt. A fine example that would set for his men.

Within the hour, the *China Swan,* which flew the Union Jack above its merchant flag, bobbed alongside the *Dauntless,* and Mr. Wayland was preparing to take a small patrol to deliver Thomas's greetings to the merchant captain…and to inspect his papers. While the men lowered a cockboat and rowed over to the other ship, Thomas observed the action through his spyglass. Once Mr. Wayland boarded the other ship, Thomas noted that the gentleman, a plump, scruffy fellow, displayed an odd nervousness. Snatches of his animated conversation with Mr. Wayland wafted on the wind, proving the man to be English, so the man should welcome the frigate's presence in these waters.

After more conversation, Mr. Wayland returned to the *Dauntless.* "Captain Moberly, Captain Thatcher offers his compliments. He, uh—" he cleared his throat "—he asks if he may send over a gift. Some silk or a fan for your lady, or a sandalwood box."

"Huh." Thomas snorted. "That's blatant bribery, Mr. Wayland." He glared across the water at the merchant captain, who stood on his quarterdeck tugging at his collar and fussing with his shabby coat. "Take over another ten men and find whatever it is this Thatcher does not want us to see."

"Aye, sir." Wayland saluted Thomas, and the gleam in his eyes revealed his eagerness for the task. The lad was bored, too. No doubt about that. And this bit of excitement might turn up some interesting contraband. Guns or powder for the rebels? Opium? Slaves?

"Mr. Brandon," Thomas called to his first officer. "Sharpshooters to the tops. Man the swivels." Against his better nature, he almost longed for a confrontation. He could even feel the heat of battle rising within him.

There it was again, that unreasoning anger. And this merchantman made a convenient scapegoat. Although the Almighty promised to forgive such lapses, Thomas would not like to experience excessive guilt the next time he recited the general confession in church. He drew in a deep breath to regain his senses. What he needed was an hour spent in Dinah's soothing company. An hour or two or—

A commotion aboard the *China Swan* drew his attention. Two of Thomas's crew escorted a dark-haired woman from below. The exotic beauty broke away and ran to the quarterdeck into the arms of the captain. After much communication back and forth between the ships, the situation became clear. Somehow that unkempt merchant had secured the love of the young lady, and he feared that if discovered she might be sent back to her cruel father. If they could but sell their cargo in St. Augustine, they could sail quietly to England and find safety and happiness.

Poor chap. Did he actually think this pretty Oriental lady would find acceptance by England's middle class? Clearly, love had blinded him to the realities of his home country. Yet the fierce devotion and protectiveness now blazing from the man's eyes suggested he would not care, as long as she was with him. What madness.

But Thomas found his heart welling up with sympathy for the couple. He would ignore the merchant's attempt to buy him off. In fact, he would purchase the very items the man had offered as a bribe. Thomas had brought many gifts from England to dispense to his family members in East Florida. Still, the silk from China would do nicely as an additional gift for Marianne. Would Dinah think him too forward if he offered her a fan or a sandalwood box? Well, he would purchase both and then seek Mrs. Hussey's advice before making a fool of himself.

After choosing his purchases and permitting his crew the same privilege, Thomas gave Thatcher a stern warning not to keep secrets from His Majesty's officers and not to offer bribes. Then, as the *China Swan* tacked away from the *Dauntless,* Thomas saw Mr. and Mrs. Thatcher on the quarterdeck waving to him. Throwing dignity to the winds, he waved back.

Would that he could find the same happiness they shared, a happiness that defied convention and rules and class. The kind of defiance that had led Marianne to forsake all she had ever known and stow away on Templeton's ship. If the man had not proved both his love for her and his honorable character by marrying her, she would have been disgraced forever. Thomas would require the same courage and defiance his sister had displayed in order to—

He quashed the thought straightaway. Before he let his heart rule his head, he would make certain Marianne had no regrets for her impetuous flight from their father's home four years ago. That would be the proof of the pudding as far as he was concerned.

But as the pilot boat towed the *Dauntless* over the bars into St. Augustine Harbor, Thomas still could not erase from his mind the picture of the uncombed but blissful merchant and his happy bride.

"And your wife's name is Alice?" Dinah sat beside a soldier's bed in the infirmary penning a letter for him. Ignoring the unpleasant odors of the sickroom, she dipped her quill into the inkwell on her lap desk and waited for his response.

"Aye, Miss." The man, who appeared to be in his forties, could barely speak above a croak, and his twitching eyes conveyed his concern. "Tell her I'm well, will you? I'll not have the lass worryin'…" A cough interrupted his anxious plea.

"Shh. It's all right." Dinah's heart ached with understanding. While her own loved ones lived a mere two-day ride away, it might as well be an ocean that separated them for the few times they saw one another each year. "I'll write only what you tell me to."

"God bless you, Miss." He gave her a quivering smile.

After adding some cheery details that the soldier dictated about life in East Florida, she spent a few minutes sketching his broad, pock-marked face in the corner of the foolscap. She softened the scars and the harsh lines of his illness, but the likeness was clear. This was her favorite part of preparing messages for the soldiers' loved ones at home in England.

"Here you are." She held the page out. "You can make your mark at the bottom."

"Why, Miss, that's a fine drawing." Tears filled the man's reddened eyes. "That's a special kindness to me and my Alice. God bless you." He repeated, "God bless you."

"You're very welcome." Dinah swallowed the emotion that rose up to threaten her composure. Being useful to these brave men gave her life purpose and a strong sense of satisfaction, but she must not damage their pride with her pity. "I'll put this in the post at Panton and Leslie for the next outgoing ship."

She gathered the letters she had written over the past two hours and carried the lap desk back to Dr. Wellsey's office, then made her way to the front of the building. Smelling as always of liniments and herbs, the physician met her in the entry carrying a small jar.

"A gift from Joanna." He held it out to her. "Honey." His wrinkled brow revealed some hesitation on his part. "I should tell you it is from her mother."

"Oh, my. This is a rare treat." Dinah accepted the jar with a smile, her mouth watering at the thought of honey on her morning bread. While Artemis might decline a gift from the Cherokee woman, Anne would be delighted. "Did Mrs. Ramsey gather it from her hives?"

Relief softened his features. "Yes. She and her sisters have become quite adept at the art of beekeeping."

"Ah, how grand. Please tell all of them we will enjoy this very much." Dinah moved toward the door. "And tell Joanna I am looking forward to our trip to Bennington Plantation. We do not have many opportunities to visit with each other." All due to Artemis's censure. But she would not say so.

"True." Dr. Wellsey followed and opened the door for her. "We're eager to go as well. Mr. Moberly is a good friend, and I often wonder if it was wise of me to leave the plantation. St. Johns Towne has many medical needs and only an apothecary to tend them."

"But you're needed here as well." His presence alleviated the burden on the sole military surgeon, Dr. Yeats, in caring for the sick military men. And she could not think of what she would do without her ministry to the soldiers, which could only be accomplished under this good doctor's watchful, protective eye.

He released a wry chuckle. "Yes, but Joanna would be happier if we lived closer to her family."

His words jolted Dinah. Twice in the past few minutes, she had been reminded of the longing in her own heart to be near family. "I understand." Indeed, she did. But what use was it to long for them when they insisted she would be happier in St. Augustine? If not for Thomas—

Another jolt. Indeed, she had been happier since he came. But then, true to the life of a naval officer, he was gone from the city again and frequently would be. Unreasoning resentment filled her heart. Like everyone else she cared for, he'd left her behind. Well, she simply would not permit herself to care that much for him.

"I wish you good day, Doctor." She tucked the honey jar and letters into her burlap bag, pulled her straw bonnet onto her head and stepped out into the sunlight to post the letters. With every firm step on the hot, sandy path toward the city, she pounded determination into her mind. She would not let her heart rule her head.

June sunshine beat down on her, even through her hat, as she reached the city gates and trod down St. George Street. The ocean breezes did not reach the narrower lanes, which became like ovens where the overpowering smells of horses, cattle and unwashed humans permeated the air. Dinah hastened her steps to escape the still, choking atmosphere.

She came at last to the bustling, open Parade in front of the governor's house, where she noticed a familiar couple in the shade of a live oak tree. Dinah thought the young lady leaned a bit too close to the naval officer, and as she came near, she was sure of it.

"Elizabeth," she called.

Her friend turned and waved. "Dinah, come greet Mr. Wayland, just back from patrolling the coast."

Dinah's heart leaped to her throat. The *Dauntless* had returned. Forcing down her ridiculous giddiness, she joined her friends. "How good to see you, Mr. Wayland. I hope your voyage was successful."

"Good afternoon, Miss Templeton." He swept off his bicorne hat and made an elaborate bow. Elizabeth gazed at him as if he were Adonis. In fact, Dinah also thought he was rather handsome, but he knew it as well, which spoiled his appeal, to her way of thinking. "I can say with assurance that St. Augustine is safer today because of our little voyage."

Elizabeth spread her fan open and tilted her head. "See what Mr. Wayland brought me?" The ivory implement was carved with delicate filigree and painted with rows of pink and blue flowers. "He was just telling me that the *Dauntless* accosted a pirate ship and confiscated a large cargo of contraband."

"Well, I—I—" Mr. Wayland's tanned face grew red.

"A pirate ship?" Dinah's pulse quickened. Now perhaps she could stop worrying about Jamie. "Was it Nighthawk?"

"Mr. Wayland actually boarded the ship himself," Elizabeth gushed, "with half of the armed sailors from the *Dauntless*. They had to go below—" she spoke in a hushed tone "—and you can just imagine how dangerous that was." She gazed at him with adoration beaming from her eyes. "I know *I* can imagine it. Think of all those pirates hiding in the dark hold waiting to attack His Majesty's sailors, and not a shred of conscience about doing it."

"But was it Nighthawk?" Dinah wanted to shake the information from Mr. Wayland, who suddenly appeared nonplussed. "You must not keep us in suspense."

"Miss Templeton." Thomas strode across the Parade, a warm smile gracing his lips. "I was on my way to call on you, but here you are."

Against the warning in her head, she rushed to meet him, coming just short of gripping his arm. "Oh, Captain, do tell us the pirate you accosted is Nighthawk. Did you arrest him? Is he imprisoned at the fort?"

He stopped, and his mouth hung open just a bit. "I beg your pardon?" A dark frown came over his whole face, and he stared beyond her. "Mr. Wayland, may I have a word with you?" Despite sounding like a request, it was clearly an order.

"Ah, yes, sir." The lieutenant's normal baritone voice rose to a tenor pitch. "Um, ladies, will you excuse me?"

While Dinah and Elizabeth watched, the two officers walked, or rather, marched some twenty feet away. Even in the busy, noisy Parade, Thomas's anger was evident in his low, rumbling, indistinguishable words and the way he bent over the shorter man. Mr. Wayland lifted his hands in a placating gesture, but Dinah had confidence the captain would not strike him. People walking by skirted the two men, eyeing them with curiosity.

"Whatever do you suppose is the matter?" Elizabeth gripped Dinah's arm. "Will they explain it to us?"

Dinah could feel her friend's trembling. She patted her young friend's hand. "I am certain they will. Otherwise, they would have gone to their quarters…or someplace more private to discuss it." Disappointment had already claimed her. No doubt they had not captured the infamous pirate.

After several moments, they returned.

"My dear Miss Markham." Thomas gave her a slight bow. "Mr. Wayland has something to tell you."

Beneath his tan, the young officer blanched. "Miss Markham, please forgive me. I took the liberty of… of *jesting* with you about the nature of our encounter at sea. 'Twas a mere merchantman, who gladly sold us some of his wares." He grasped her hands. "Please forgive me. I was preparing to tell you my report was all foolishness, but then Miss Templeton arrived and…" His smile was more of a grimace. "I rather lost control of the situation."

Dinah released a sigh. Of course he would have told Elizabeth the truth before the misinformation spread throughout the city, for otherwise he would have been branded a liar.

"Oh, Mr. Wayland." Young Elizabeth beamed up at him, every bit as adoringly as before. "To think that you would banter with me in such an amusing way." She tapped his forearm with her new fan. "I am certain *Mamá* would like to see my gift *and* you. Will you kindly escort me home?"

Looking like a lovesick puppy, Mr. Wayland offered his arm. "Miss Markham, I would be delighted. Miss Templeton." He bowed to Dinah. "Captain Moberly."

He gave the captain an informal salute, and the two of them sauntered away.

Dinah clapped her hand to her mouth and stared out toward Matanzas Bay. Beside her, she heard Thomas snort out a chuckle. They locked gazes and began to laugh in earnest. She felt her mirth clear down to her middle, and her eyes began to water.

"Oh, my goodness," was all that she could gasp out. Then the full import of the truth came home to her, and she exhaled with disappointment. Nighthawk had not been caught, and so Jamie was still in danger of being accosted.

"My dear Miss Templeton, may I escort you home?" Thomas offered his arm, and his twinkling blue eyes chased away her moment of worry.

"I would be delighted. On the way, I must post some letters." She lifted her bag.

"So you have been busy at the infirmary." The merriment in his eyes turned to a warm, kind look that further soothed her heart.

"Yes." She looped her free arm in his, and they began their trek. "It is the least I can do to show gratitude to the soldiers of the garrison, and your sailors as well, when they are ill and so far from home." The strings of her burlap bag, hanging over her other arm, began to pinch her skin, and she twisted her hand to ease the discomfort.

Without missing a step, the captain relieved her of the burden. "The people of St. Augustine are exceptional in their hospitality."

"We endeavor to see our protectors do not become bored. In fact, Mrs. Pilot has arranged for a picnic at Anastasia Island plantation. It will take place tomorrow after the church service. Some of the ladies have been baking all week. Will you come?"

"How could I decline such a thoughtful gesture?"

She smiled up at him. "Now you must tell me more about this merchant man Mr. Wayland mistook for a pirate!"

After a brief stop to post the letters at Panton and Leslie's mercantile, Dinah and the captain continued their walk across the city.

Thomas grinned and began his story, but as they chatted one thing struck her. Mr. Wayland had brought Elizabeth a gift, a clear indication that he meant to court her. In contrast, Thomas did not bring Dinah a gift, which said it all: He had no intention of courting her. She scolded herself for her flash of disappointment. Dinah vowed to redouble her efforts to gain control of her wayward heart.

Chapter Nine

On Sunday after the church service, Dinah and Thomas joined the other invited guests at the dock, where they all embarked on flatboats for their short voyage across Matanzas Bay to Anastasia Island.

The island, most of which was owned by Mr. Jesse Fish, boasted a vast plantation and verdant forests where cattle and horses roamed at will. In addition, it held the coquina quarries that provided the building blocks for many St. Augustine homes and official buildings, not to mention Fort St. Marks.

Dinah gripped the captain's arm as they climbed from their boat onto the small pier on the island's bay side. Above the embankment, canopies fluttered softly in the breeze above tables laden with the food prepared by the ladies of St. Augustine. White-gloved servants and volunteers stood by to serve the guests from the various covered dishes and to shoo away insects. Today, however, there appeared to be few bugs about the place. The day was bright and sunny, a good day for a picnic, even if the breezes off the ocean were a bit brisk. They gusted over the picnickers, carrying the aromas of fish, clams and beef cooked over an open fire. Feeling as carefree as the wind, Dinah clutched her wide-brimmed hat to keep it from blowing off. In today's heat, she would not need the shawl she had brought in her oilcloth bag.

"Shall we sit with Mr. and Mrs. Hussey?" Thomas's flat tone made his preference clear.

"Or Elizabeth's family?" Dinah looked for the Markhams, who had come over to the island on a different boat.

"Or perhaps we can take a short walk before we join anyone else?" A strange, almost vulnerable expression tightened the captain's face.

"Of course." Intrigued, she permitted him to lead her away from the crowd gathering at the serving tables.

He cleared his throat. "I took the liberty of speaking to Mrs. Hussey about a matter relating to you. I did not wish to do anything inappropriate—"

Dinah gave him an encouraging smile. This surely could not be a serious issue.

He reached into his indigo coat and pulled out a slender package. "May I offer you this small…gift…which I procured from the merchant—"

She stifled a gasp. He *had* bought something for her. "Why, thank you." Taking the parcel in hand, she carefully removed the string and paper and tucked them in her bag. "Oh, what a lovely fan." She spread it open, glancing briefly at the colorful pattern before focusing on him. "How very thoughtful, Captain." As confusion tumbled about in her mind, she demonstrated her gratitude by removing her old fan from her wrist and replacing it with the new one.

"You are most welcome." His face softened, and his posture relaxed. "Now, shall we join the others? I must admit I am famished after Reverend Kennedy's fine sermon."

As she placed her hand on his offered arm, all things came into perspective. If he had meant this gift to be more than a simple token of his friendship, he would not be so eager to join the throngs. She tried to laugh at her own foolishness in expecting more. If she did not capture his heart, Dinah would never be faced with an offer she would have to refuse.

Safe. That was how Dinah felt with Thomas, even when he appeared to have fallen asleep on this lazy afternoon.

In fact, these days she felt safer just walking the streets of St. Augustine, where off-duty drunken soldiers sometimes exhibited improper behavior, even around well-bred ladies. The city was not large, and everyone knew everyone else or at least knew who they were. In addition to the British military presence and government officials, the population held a mixture of American Loyalists, Indians, black slaves and Minorcans. At Dr. Turnbull's invitation, the Minorcans had come from their island homes to colonize New Smyrna. When Turnbull had tried to turn them into veritable slaves, many had escaped to St. Augustine. Yet, in spite of their rough manners and odd clothing, Dinah never felt threatened by them. And she could not fail to notice that people, especially Governor Tonyn and Colonel Füser, the commander of the garrison, treated her with even more consideration these days. Her family's relationship to Thomas Moberly had become common knowledge, somehow marking her as someone significant to her fellow citizens. She did not always appreciate the attention.

Many of the other picnickers now strolled up and down the sandy banks along Matanzas Bay or sat chatting under the half-dozen canopies. A group of boisterous young men had smoothed a tract of dirt and sand for a game of skittles, but the ball kept stopping in the loose earth before reaching the pins. After a while, they resorted to lobbing the ball as if shooting it from a cannon, to the amusement of all.

Dinah studied her exquisite new fan. On either side were delicate paintings of Chinese gardens. In one garden stood a young man and in the other a young lady. Each one wore a wistful expression while reaching out toward some unknown, unattainable object—no doubt the person on the other side. The message of the pictures could not be plainer. Thomas—how should she put it?—*cared* for her. But his social position and her own resolution separated them from any future together, and he regretted it as much as she did. Now that he had so gently dispensed with that concern, they could continue as friends, *safe* in each other's companionship. The finality of it threatened to dismay her, but she cast away such useless sentiments.

She glanced over at him. He was leaning back in a wooden chair like her own, arms folded over his broad chest, his long legs stretched out and his bicorne hat pulled over his eyes. His gold-braided blue wool coat, white breeches and shiny black shoes bore traces of sand that in no way diminished his dignified appearance. Like most of the men in St. Augustine, he did not wear a wig, but kept his black hair in a queue. Dinah wondered what it would look like unbound, a silly thought. Thomas was always perfectly dressed, perfectly groomed, perfectly mannered.

She plucked a blade of grass from a tuft growing

nearby and reached across to touch its tip to his upper lip. Not waking, he waved his hand, and she quickly pulled back until he relaxed. Again she tried her prank. Again he waved away the annoyance. At her third assault, he seized her wrist in a gentle grip.

"Belay that, miss, or I'll have you swabbing the deck." His deep chuckle contradicted his words.

Dinah retrieved her hand and sniffed. "Well, sir, if you would stay awake and offer better company, I'd have no need to bother you." In truth, this man provided far better companionship sleeping than other men who were fully awake. In fact, she had declined several gentle-men's invitations to stroll over to the quarries.

He slowly sat up and stretched. "Ah, neglecting my duty, am I?" He stared north toward the mouth of the bay, then south toward the slow-moving river that entered it. "Have I missed much?" He rubbed one eye and yawned, endearing gestures to Dinah. Clearly he felt comfortable with her, too.

"Just those darling children playing tag among the trees." Dinah nodded toward the forest, and a vague yearning struck her. Watching them reminded her of her own longing to one day have her own children, not just a growing band of nieces and nephews.

"Hmm." A lazy grin graced his lips. "You know, you can hardly blame me for napping after that excellent repast."

"We did serve a fine meal, didn't we?" She had made scones and put one on his plate herself, then watched him enjoy it with her fig preserves and cream.

He studied the woods as if searching for something. No doubt his duty demanded such constant vigilance, even on a rare day of rest. She followed his gaze, but nothing seemed amiss.

"Will you walk with me, Miss Templeton?" He stood, brushed sand from his coat, and reached out to her.

"That would be lovely." She placed her gloved hand in his and rose, but caught her foot on her chair leg and stumbled into him. Drawing in a quick breath, she inhaled his beguiling bergamot scent. As he steadied her, his sky-blue eyes searched hers with the same intense gaze he had trained on their surroundings. Her heart tripped over itself, yet she could not move back. He seemed to have the same affliction, standing so near to her with the corners of his lips curved slightly upward and his gaze now softened.

After several moments, during which Dinah could not gather a single coherent thought, the squeals and laughter of the nearby children broke their connection. They each stepped back and turned toward the water's edge, where a boy had waded in to retrieve a ball and been swept off his feet. Thomas stiffened and took a step toward the disaster. The father rushed in to save the day and fell into the water as well, but quickly regained his footing and rescued the lad. The riotous laughter of everyone involved put all in perspective. Thomas exhaled a quiet breath and relaxed.

"You must be thinking of your nephew's accident." Dinah's heart warmed as she remembered the story of Jamie saving the late Lord Bennington's grandson. The heroic deed had sealed the earl's affection for Jamie and assured his continued patronage.

"Yes." The captain offered his arm, and they began their stroll. "Before that incident, I fear I was less than courteous to your brother." He released a mild snort. "How arrogant of me. Yet such treatment of merchants is expected among the aristocracy. Templeton changed my thinking forever about the worth of a man."

And the worth of a woman? Dinah's heart once again tripped around in her chest. Perhaps she had been wrong. Perhaps this aristocrat no longer saw the disparity between their classes as a hindrance to his courting her. Should she also reconsider her opinions regarding marriage to a seafarer? No! Giving him her heart would betray everything she had ever longed for in marriage, for she could never bear the loneliness of a sea captain's wife. Like the hapless couple on the fan, she and the captain were destined never to be together. She must settle for friendship and that alone.

Thomas sent up a silent prayer of thanks for the noise of the unruly children. He had almost kissed Dinah right on her too-enticing lips, and he doubted she even realized that her eyes had held a warm invitation for him to do so. But such behavior in public would surely damage her reputation, making a lie of his secret vow to protect her from all harm. He thanked the Lord they had both returned to reality when the children began their rumpus.

Surely she had understood the message of the fan. Like the hopeful young lovers pictured on it, they both might long to enter a true courtship, but they must be cautious. If the objections each held could not be satisfactorily addressed, they must draw back before either suffered injury.

What was he thinking? It was too late for him. The moment she tickled him with that blade of grass, he had at last surrendered his heart to her. If he had admired her wit and good humor before, he now felt utterly charmed. Utterly captivated. Not since his childhood had anyone teased him that way. As a captain in His Majesty's navy, he represented all the authority of the Crown, a fact that usually worked in his favor. Yet Dinah had never been the slightest bit intimidated. Abiding in anyone else, that attitude would have been offensive. In her, it was the bait that drew him to the hook. Now she need only pull in the line, and he would be hers.

Today she wore her gardenia fragrance, his favorite, for it seemed to suit her more than lavender. When she placed her hand on his arm, he enjoyed the trust emanating from her eyes as they strolled into the woods, where other picnickers wandered about, taking in the scenery. Gusting through the trees, the Atlantic breeze blew strands of her blond hair free from beneath her hat to flutter across her graceful neck. He would not take the liberty of brushing them back in place. In fact, he would like to see all of her thick, lustrous hair unbound and thus blowing in the wind, just as he would like to see her free from any care.

She made no move to secure the strands. As always, her natural beauty was enhanced by her lack of concern for such details. She did not lack modesty, but always seemed more concerned for others than worried about her own appearance.

They reached a clearing that provided a view of the ocean a half mile away and found that the wind was much stronger here. To the east, gray clouds sat like wooly burls upon the horizon, and not one sail spiked over the wide sea. Instinct nettled within him. When he had awakened from his nap, he could feel that the atmosphere had grown heavy. And in the woods, no birds sang and no insects buzzed about them. A storm was coming, but he gauged that it would take some hours before it reached them. They must go back to the city soon, but surely they had time for a few more private moments.

He peered beneath the wide brim of her hat in search of that ever-present, winsome smile.

She looked up, and her smile broadened. "Yes?"

"Just checking." Checking to see if she regretted their almost kiss. To his dismay, she did seem to have a bit of tension pinching her cheeks.

"For what?" She held her hat while tilting her head to see him.

"To be certain you are enjoying our walk." Not a brilliant comment, but he could think of nothing clever to say.

"Oh, yes. Thank you." Her smile vanished.

Ah, she had moved back from him. What had happened? How could he amend it?

"I saw you speaking with Artemis earlier," she said. "He seemed a little…upset."

Thomas gripped his emotions. The perfect opening. "He asked me to use my influence with you to gain control of your money."

She grimaced, and worry creased her forehead. "What did you say to him?"

He would not express his own concerns about her fortune until he spoke with Frederick, with whom he had many issues to address. Why had his brother left this dear young woman under the care of such a greedy, perhaps dishonest man? But Thomas must encourage her now. "I assured him that you are a capable woman, fully able to manage your own affairs."

Her forehead smoothed, and her smile returned. "I thank you." The breathiness in her voice said even more than her words. "Sometimes I do not feel capable. Perhaps Artemis is right and I should let him invest my money in his business ventures."

Longing to reassure her with an embrace, Thomas

instead forced his footsteps over the sandy ground. "Yes, of course. And have the American pirates select his cargo, and his alone, to remove from your brother's ship." That incident had troubled Thomas for some time, for it made little to no sense. "Has Mr. Hussey mentioned political enemies? Sometimes this sort of thing happens when a man is employed in the government." Indeed, that might be a clue to Nighthawk's activities. Perhaps the pirate lived here in the city and sought to undermine efforts to maintain stability. Or perhaps the man knew Artemis and wanted to ruin him for some reason.

She bit her lip, then sighed. "I do not know about enemies, but he does have political ambitions. And as an employee in the state house, he is privy to important information. For one thing, you know, of course, that Governor Tonyn has forbidden the establishment of a colonial legislature because such bodies are the source of the rebellions in the northern colonies." She gazed toward the ocean, a thoughtful frown marring her smooth forehead. "But the loyalists here have proven themselves, and so the governor may permit the people to have an elected assembly in the next year or so. If this happens, Artemis plans to offer himself as a candidate to represent our district of St. Augustine. But I cannot see how those two things go together. Oh, unless someone wants to bankrupt him so he cannot purchase the five hundred acres a candidate is required to own."

They walked in silence for a short time, and Thomas weighed Hussey's ambitions against possible financial limitations, which would give ample cause for him to covet Dinah's money. "So, then, does he plan to buy a plantation?"

She shook her head. "He cannot become a planter

without slaves. And if I can say only one good thing about Artemis, it is that he refuses to own a slave. He has held fast to that part of his Quaker upbringing."

Thomas nodded his approval. So the man possessed at least one redeeming quality. "But if not a plantation, what then?"

"I do not know." She gazed up at him, her face brightened. "If you think it proper, will you ask him?"

"Indeed, I shall make a point to do so."

Thomas had not enjoyed his earlier discussion with Hussey, nor had he managed to extract any helpful information from him while others crowded around waiting for the servants to serve the food. Patience and further investigation would be required to learn why he persisted in his attempts to control Dinah's finances.

Another burst of high wind blew against them, followed quickly by more, each threatening to topple them. Thomas gripped Dinah's hand and in silent agreement they hastened back toward the woods, laughing like the children. In fact, the entire party moved toward the bay shore, seeming to understand that it was time to return to the city.

As they slowed to a walk, he gazed at his merry companion and remembered the moment scant minutes ago when he had almost kissed her. He pulled in a deep breath to secure his emotions which, before he met her, had never been quite so muddled and unruly. And now, to make matters worse, anxiety pressed into his chest as the atmosphere grew heavier.

"I regret that our outing must be cut short, but we should go back."

She stared up at him until her hat blew off her head and hung by its ribbons down her back. A tiny frown darted across her forehead—disappointment?—as she replaced it with a graceful gesture. "Yes."

Necessity forced them to keep holding hands on their way back through the sand to the canopies, which now flapped in the wind like sails trying to rip free of their lines. Servants hastened to gather picnic leftovers while the gentlemen bustled their ladies into the flatboats to return to the city. Thomas noticed with satisfaction that Dinah placed her new fan into the oilcloth bag she had carried on the outing.

He surveyed the scene to determine where he might be the most helpful. Mothers and nursemaids hurried about in panic and pandemonium, gathering their children and loading them into the flatboats. Gentlemen saw to the safety of their own families, while servants packed the food and furniture. Like Thomas, Dinah studied the situation with concern, but the citizens of St. Augustine seemed to have matters well in hand. His duty was to return her safely across the bay and then see that his crew had secured the *Dauntless*. While the rapidly approaching storm could be a mere squall, this was the season of hurricanes. Dangerous storms were common in his line of work, but he had never faced one in the company of a lady. He would not allow anything to happen to her, ever.

Chapter Ten

Like all St. Augustine citizens, Dinah had always been thankful that Anastasia Island provided a barrier for the city against the worst ocean surges. But these sudden, powerful winds could still damage buildings, and the excessive rains could turn the dirt streets into rivers of mud. The first large drops began to fall just as she and Thomas stepped from the flatboat onto the dock on the city side of the bay.

As they hurried across the Parade, he stared toward his ship, his jaw clenched. "I shall escort you home before seeing to the *Dauntless*. Mr. Brandon is in charge and will secure the vessel, but I should be there during the storm."

Dinah stopped. "Please tend to your duty. I will be all right." Her heart raced, but she did not want him to see her fear.

"Please do not argue with me." His tone was stern, and he gripped her arm to move her forward through the people scattering in every direction.

She tried to stop again, but he nudged her along.

"Captain, we can go to the governor's house. It is closer, and he will not turn us away. The house is made of coquina, just as the fort is, and will stand firm in the highest winds."

"Ah. Very good." He redirected their journey.

Another thought skittered through her rising panic, and she broke loose from his grasp. "I must fetch Macy." She lifted her skirts to run.

The captain again caught her arm. "You know of my affection for your cat, but you will not risk your life for him." The storm on his face matched the one now swirling around them. "I forbid it."

"You what?" She stared at him, her emotions rioting within her. "You have no say-so in the matter." She wrested her arm from him. "Now please go take care of your ship." *Your ship, which will always be the most important thing in your life.* As the realization struck, raw anger tore through her. Anger, yes, and fear of the danger he would be in just getting to the *Dauntless* in these violent, swirling winds.

"Miss Templeton." He retrieved her arm yet again and loomed over her while rain sheeted off of his black bicorne hat. "At this moment, I must assure your safety. We are twenty-five yards from the governor's—"

"I am *not* your responsibility," she shouted above the wind's roar. "Go to your ship. That is your *duty*." She did not intend to spit out her words, but her unreasonable anger had unleashed her natural restraints.

His eyebrows shot upward, then bent into a dark frown, and his lips formed a thin line. "I do not have time for this." He swept her up in his arms as if she were a pet cat and strode across the remaining distance to the coquina house. Too stunned to speak, she did not resist him. He deposited her at the wooden double doors and tipped his hat.

"Miss Templeton." He turned away but stopped at the

approach of another man. "Ah, Mr. Richland, would you please escort Miss Templeton inside and make certain she remains there?"

Dinah gaped, first at the captain and then at the eager young man now grinning and bowing in front of her.

"You can count on me, Captain Moberly." Mr. Richland gave him a poor imitation of a salute.

While she watched with dismay as the captain spun away toward the bay, Mr. Richland moved to shield her from the battering wind. "Miss Templeton, may I escort you out of this hurricane?"

The violent shiver that coursed down her back had nothing to do with the cold rain soaking into her light muslin gown. Anger and fear vied for preeminence as she peered around her would-be protector to watch the captain attempt to cross the Parade. His broad shoulders were hunched forward against the blinding walls of wind and water that kept driving him back. She managed a quick silent prayer, but felt no relief. Why had she been so angry with him?

"If you please, Miss Templeton." Mr. Richland's anxious tone cut into her thoughts.

She permitted him to guide her inside, where servants hastened about with towels and blankets for twenty or so people who had taken refuge in the entry hall of the large house. She dragged off her ruined hat and tossed it with others on the floor near the door.

A fire roared in the huge stone hearth and Dinah found a place among the people seated close to it. Her escort fetched a blanket and wrapped it around her... and held it in place a trifle too long. She shuddered, but not from the cold.

He jerked his hands away. "Forgive me." He sat beside her, seeming not to notice his own wet clothing.

"Mr. Richland, you must fetch a blanket for yourself." She pulled her own wrap closer and eyed the coffee now being offered by the servants.

He followed her gaze, then gave her a crooked, boyish grin. "Will you save this spot for me?" His words were punctuated by a shiver.

She patted his arm. "Go. Your grandmother will be distressed if you become ill."

He grimaced, and his grin disappeared. "And you? Would you also be distressed?"

Dinah snuggled into her blanket, willing her natural body warmth to return. "Of course. I am always concerned when my friends suffer illness." She forced a gentle tone into her voice and punctuated it with a cheery smile.

"I did not mean to suggest—"

"Please. Get yourself a blanket."

Hoping her manner of dismissal was not unkind, she turned and stared toward the fire. Movement beside her indicated that he had gone, but he returned all too quickly and held a cup of steaming coffee in front of her. Not wishing to look at him, she accepted the cup with a sigh. If nothing else, the young man was persistent. "Thank you."

"You are welcome." The deep male voice of the person who took the seat beside her held a world of authority.

Dinah gasped and turned to see an entirely different and much more welcome companion. "Captain Moberly." *Thank You, Lord. He is safe.* So her prayer had been answered, after all.

Like the clothing of everyone else in the room, his uniform was drenched and smelled of wet wool, but he seemed unaware of it. He held a pewter tankard of coffee and stared over its rim at her. "The wind drove me back."

To me. "I see." Her heart began to race.

"I must apologize—"

"Please forgive me—"

They spoke at the same time. Both stopped. Both laughed softly, self-consciously. At least Thomas appeared to feel as sheepish as she did, Dinah thought. She tilted her head and lifted her eyebrows, inviting him to continue.

"I am confident that Macy will be all right. Cats have a way of surviving."

Hot tears sprang to her eyes. She had never known a man who cared for cats. In fact, few people cared for them at all. Yet she found such comfort in her pet when Artemis made her life miserable. "Yes, they do." What could she say in return for his concern? "Your Mr. Brandon is a capable officer. I am certain he and your crew can manage."

"I have no doubt of it." A dark frown still marred his sun-bronzed forehead, and water streamed from his rumpled hair onto his uniform.

"Captain Moberly." Mr. Richland appeared in front of them, disappointment lining his face. "You've returned." He cleared his throat and adjusted the blanket wrapped around his shoulders. "I will be happy to continue to see to Miss Templeton's welfare."

The captain trained his frown on the younger man, and Dinah thought she heard the beginnings of a growl in his throat. "You have done enough, sir. Carry on." He waved his hand in a dismissive gesture.

"But—" Mr. Richland's frown matched Thomas's, but when the captain stiffened, he gave Dinah an apologetic shrug and moved away.

She eyed her companion. "You were rude to him," she whispered.

"Was I?" He shrugged. "I suppose. But I was not about to surrender my place to a lad whose attempts to court you are unwanted."

"Oh, dear. It's that obvious?"

He snorted. "As it should be." After draining his mug, he set it on the floor, then crossed his arms and stared into the fire. "Once this storm is over, the *Dauntless* must patrol the coast once more before our trip to St. Johns Towne."

"Yes, I assumed you would." *You will always be at sea. Always be leaving.*

They sat in silence for several moments while people milled around or huddled in groups. Some men puffed on cigars or pipes, clouding the air with smelly smoke. Dinah tried to wave it away, along with the odors of wet clothing and humanity that permeated the room. Outside the wind howled and rain slammed against shuttered windows and pounded the roof.

"But I will return." His words came so softly, so unexpectedly, that Dinah was not certain she had heard right. Then he directed an intense gaze into her eyes. "I will always return."

Warmth from somewhere deep within welled up almost like a fever rushing through her and reaching toward her cheeks. Such an odd, disconcerting sensation. A blush? Surely not, for she had never blushed in her life. But she could not deny that his words seemed like a promise, a pledge of some sort…to *her.* And that warmed her far more than the blanket wrapped around her shoulders.

Had she understood him? Had she understood that he could not say more at this time? Seeing an uncharacteristic blush fill her cheeks, he guessed…he hoped she grasped his meaning.

Unable to stare into those deep, dark eyes any longer without declaring himself, he forced his gaze toward the hearth. The dancing flames seemed to taunt him, for they blazed liberally and without restriction, unlike the fiery love burning in his chest that he somehow must contain.

He admitted to himself that the events of the past hour had stirred such feeling within him so as to push him beyond all doubt, and he fully comprehended the reason. When the high winds had first begun to lash the island, some ladies had screamed and dashed about in a frenzy. But Dinah had calmly hastened along, making certain the children were taken care of before she entered the returning boat with him.

Once across the bay, he observed that she had had a moment of understandable fear, which increased his determination to protect her at all cost. Yet she had harnessed her emotions and considered another creature's peril and would willingly have endangered herself for the beast. Frustration and fear for her had driven him to take charge of the situation, and he hoped she would forgive him for his ungentlemanly behavior. At the memory of her shocked expression as he carried her across the Parade, a smile tickled the edges of his lips. He prayed they would one day be able to laugh at the ridiculous situation, for they both had been doing their best in the midst of an uncontrollable crisis.

But now he must think of his ship, which should have been his first concern. His decision to keep the *Dauntless* anchored in the bay had turned out to be a wise one. These unexpected storms—and he was certain this was a full-blown hurricane—could surprise even the most seasoned captain. Because he was new to the tropical latitudes of East Florida, he had learned a bit more about the weather today. Instead of ignoring his instincts about the changes in the air so that he might walk a few more moments with Dinah on the beach, he should have acted immediately, seeing her to safety and then taking care of duty.

Until a few short weeks ago, nothing could have kept him from returning immediately to the *Dauntless*. He had no real fear for the vessel, for she had weathered much worse storms out at sea. But he had to admit a nagging guilt and concern. Should anything happen to his ship, he would have to answer to the Admiralty for not being aboard, for not going there straightaway when he realized the weather was turning bad. That thought stirred no little anxiety in him. Had he failed in his duty? Was he growing lax because his father was no longer there to condemn his every blunder, every miscalculation?

"Are you cold?" Dinah's soft words, filled with caring, caressed his ravaged emotions.

He shook his head, and water rolled down the front of his coat and splashed on his hat, which lay on his lap. "This is nothing compared to the drenching one can experience at sea." He swept both hands over his hair, pulled it back and secured it with the ribbon tie he had managed not to lose.

As for his lovely companion, his earlier wish to see her hair unbound had been granted. The next time he wished to see it thus, he would specifically wish it would not be wet, for she looked a bit bedraggled. Beautiful, but still bedraggled, he amended. And utterly charming. The thought brought forth a chuckle.

She responded with a laugh, as she always did when

he expressed his amusement. "And what do you find so humorous, Captain?" Mischief lit her eyes, and he knew all was forgiven.

At last the tension in his chest loosened, and he laughed in earnest. Throughout the room, heads swung in their direction and raised eyebrows questioned his outburst. He swiped his hands down his face and shook his head again. To answer the still-curious crowd, he shrugged. "Nothing like a little foul weather to equalize humanity."

Thomas conferred with the governor and other knowledgeable men cloistered in the house and they pronounced the storm a true hurricane, although not the worst one Thomas had ever seen. Fortunately, the coquina building held strong. After some sixteen hours, the calm eye arrived and Thomas thanked his host for his generous accommodations, bid Dinah adieu and made his way to the *Dauntless*. The frigate bobbed about in the bay, but with sails lashed to the yards, she would not be driven into the docks by the winds.

Thomas inspected the ship and gave his approval to Mr. Brandon's and Mr. Wayland's reports of all that had occurred in his absence. He once again reviewed his own choices in the drama and knew he must not let his feelings interfere with duty again. With all in order, he took to his cabin, where Hinton awaited him. Another reminder of his failure. If his steward knew to get to the ship immediately at the hint of calamity, Thomas had no excuse.

Despite his seven and twenty years—a relative youth—Hinton tended toward the maternal. After he made certain Thomas donned a clean, dry uniform, nothing would suit the steward but to dispense tonics and hot toddies. Thomas endured all but the plasters Hinton wanted to apply after he cleared his throat and his man declared it a cough presaging pneumonia. Thomas promised Hinton he would submit to the treatment should more serious symptoms appear.

But the only symptoms of something amiss that he could detect within himself were an irregular pulse and the inability to think clearly. His equilibrium returned only after he evaluated his feelings for Dinah and declared the complete surrender of his heart. But he could not run up the white flag until he was certain neither of them would suffer regret.

The back side of the hurricane struck with greater force than the first half, but still the *Dauntless* was not driven aground. Thomas found himself praying more fervently than he ever had, this time for the safety of those in the governor's house, especially Dinah. He felt a fair amount of confidence that all would be well. But hurricanes were always unpredictable, and they frequently threw off tornadoes that caused more damage than the high winds and pouring rain.

At last the violent weather moved away over the land, followed by clear skies and hot winds, which despite their humidity dried St. Augustine within two days. The *Dauntless* had ridden out the storm safely anchored in the protected bay. And Governor Tonyn assured Thomas that the services of his crew were not required to return the city to orderliness. Nothing prevented Thomas from making plans to sail out on patrol.

Sensitive to Dinah's main objection to his livelihood, he had taken care to include the hint of a promise when visiting to bid her goodbye.

"I expect this voyage will be short." Seated in her parlor, he had noted the guarded look in her eyes and enlisted every shred of self-control he possessed to keep from going down on one knee and declaring his regard for her. Surely once he was out of her presence, out to sea, he would be able to think clearly. Did she see his feelings in his eyes? "I look forward to our journey inland next week." How had he managed to say that in an even voice? To distract himself, he petted Macy, who had ridden out the hurricane safely tucked in Dinah's clothespress. The creature had curled up beside him on the settee and seemed determined to leave copious amounts of gray fur on Thomas's indigo coat.

"Yes." The lady spread open her fan, his gift, and waved it before her lovely face, which took on a soft pink shade, as it had during their confinement during the storm. "I am eager to see our dear ones again." She stared at the fan and suddenly blinked as if surprised, then snapped it shut. After a moment, during which consternation filled her eyes, she gave her head a brief shake. "Will you tell me about growing up with Frederick and Marianne? You must have been very close."

Her question seemed like a challenge. Or perhaps a diversion. Had something about the fan alarmed her? He marveled that it had survived the rain, even tucked as it was in her oilcloth bag. But if he asked her what was amiss, her response might lead to dangerous waters. She had given no indication that she understood his message worked in silk and ivory, and for now, it seemed wise for him not to explain it.

Forcing his thoughts back to her request, he had told her about Marianne's birth and the joy it brought all of her brothers to teach her how to ride, trying as always not to interject his anger toward his brother Freddy into his conversation. But the sympathy emanating from her eyes told him he had not deceived her.

This understanding, this wisdom in one so young, was yet another reason to love her. Somehow he must find a way to soothe away her misgivings about…what? Why, nothing less than becoming his wife.

Chapter Eleven

"I love Captain Thomas Moberly." Kneeling beside her bed, Dinah whispered the words in a prayer. "And I am convinced that he loves me. Yet I dare not ask You to grant us joy."

Requests such as this seemed too large, too personal, even selfish. And perhaps the captain would be required to ask permission of the Admiralty to marry at all. Would those men of exalted rank scorn him for marrying a colonial miss whose small fortune was not sufficient to advance his naval career? And what of his aristocratic family? His brother Frederick had married Dinah's cousin, but she sensed Frederick lived outside the approval of the other Moberlys. And even after four years, she still could not grasp the complexities of Jamie's marriage to the captain's sister, who had been disowned for her choice. Family and position seemed to be of the utmost importance to Thomas. How could Dinah ask him to give them up for her?

And what of her own objections? Yes, he had promised in his gentle way always to return, but what if he received orders to join the British fleet in the West Indies, where they waited to take part in the war to the north? Surely that would prevent his keeping the promise. She would not even consider the inherent danger of his sailing on the unforgiving ocean. Battles, storms, mutinies, sickness—all could take him away from her forever. Oh, why had she not guarded her heart more fiercely?

Did the captain battle his own objections? Was that why he did not speak of the ardor so evident in his eyes? And what secret message had he intended with the fan? When they sat in the parlor yesterday and she held the fan before the sunlit window, she had seen for the first time a new configuration of the characters painted so expertly on the silk. What a shock it had been. But she dared not trust what she had seen. Difficult as it was, she must wait for his spoken declaration, for if it never came, neither of them would be put to shame.

Dinah rose, took her Bible from the bedside table and sat in the wooden chair by her window. Opening to the place where she had left off the day before, she read the verses from Jeremiah twenty-nine, stopping at verse eleven. "For I know the thoughts that I think toward you, saith the Lord, thoughts of peace, and not of evil, to give you an expected end."

Peace. An expected end. Was this a coincidence, or could she seize upon it as a promise from the Lord? She dare not think He was promising her a future with Thomas.

She slumped in her chair. Would that she could find some wise soul to advise her, some older woman, friend or mentor. Elizabeth was sweet but empty-headed, and only seventeen, not old enough to provide the support and wisdom Dinah needed.

Anne had always been her friend, but in recent years she had rightfully kept no secrets from her husband.

Of course Artemis could not be trusted to know of Dinah's dilemma, and especially not of her love for the captain.

Next week's journey to Bennington Plantation offered no hope of finding a confidante there. Cousin Rachel and Jamie's wife, Marianne, were kind and good, but they always seemed to hold something back from her, always grew quiet when she entered a room while they were talking, then brightly introduced some trivial topic. Moreover, Dinah must consider Marianne's delicate condition, along with the grief they all would experience once the news of Lord Bennington's death was announced.

Dinah shook herself. How selfish of her. Just as she withheld pity from the soldiers to whom she ministered, she would not pity herself. Instead, she should be praying for these dear ones. She read the verses in Jeremiah again and committed verse eleven to memory, letting its one clear meaning sink deep into her soul. God knew His thoughts toward her, thoughts of peace and not of evil. She would choose to have hope that the future He planned would be far better than any she could plan for herself.

That settled, at least for now, she knelt in prayer again, pleading for Marianne to safely deliver her child. For Jamie to avoid the pirates who plagued the coast and stole his valuable cargo. And for Thomas to catch Nighthawk…and to return home safely…to her.

"Captain Moberly? Sir?" Mr. Brandon's voice carried more than a little apprehension.

Jolted from his deep musing, Thomas wrested his gaze from the western horizon and directed it toward his first officer. "Yes, Mr. Brandon."

"Sir, did you not hear the lookout?" The man's furrowed brow held a hint of…understanding?

Perturbed by his own lack of focus, Thomas stared up at the man on the crosstrees. "No, I did not. What was his call?" Regret pummeled him. He would never excuse a breach of duty in his crew, and certainly not in himself. He must keep his mind on the task at hand, not on the lady awaiting him on shore. Why had he thought that sailing out on patrol would clear his head? Instead, it had visited upon him an uncharacteristic disquiet that he could not settle.

"Sails ho." Brandon pointed toward the east, where dawn had broken a scant half hour before and the sun tossed gold and silver bunting over the rippling green sea.

Thomas pulled his spyglass from its pouch and extended it eastward. Just coming into view were the tips of the white sails of two ships that appeared engaged in some sort of parley. Fighting? No, for no cannon smoke filled the air. Still, he had the unsettling feeling that all was not well. Neither ship flew their colors, so he had no way of discerning their loyalties.

"Make all sail." He eyed Brandon. "Let's find out what these two are up to."

Mr. Brandon faced the main deck and cupped his hands about his mouth. "All hands about ship! Topmen aloft. Set the royals!"

Thomas turned to the helmsman behind him. "Bring her up two points to starboard, Mr. Smith. Right on their tails."

"Aye, aye, Cap'n," the man returned with a grin.

Thomas felt a smile edge across his own lips. He enjoyed nothing more than the thrill of giving chase. And if this was Nighthawk and he caught him, perhaps that would vindicate his presence in St. Augustine and he would not be ordered away. But then, perhaps if he ended this audacious pirate's activities, the Admiralty would decide his larger frigate was no longer required in the colony. Hardly a reason not to catch the man, but the thought did give Thomas pause. He could not think of leaving the colony with his feelings for Dinah in such upheaval.

With all canvas spread toward the favoring breeze, the *Dauntless* sped over the mild sea toward the other ships. One of them broke away and caught the same wind in its massive sails and swept like a diving seagull toward the nearby Florida Current. Once in that north-bound stream, the vessel could easily gain a lengthy head start.

"Do you think it's Nighthawk, Captain?" Mr. Brandon stared ahead, his eyes bright with eagerness.

"Only one way to find out." Thomas's own pulse raced with an anticipation he had not felt in some time. But then another thought struck him. The departing sloop might not be the pirate ship. Or the two could be allies. He had best check the near one, lest he miss the real culprit. She was not moving, which could mean any number of things.

"Mr. Brandon." Thomas's first officer possessed a tactical mind worthy of being consulted.

"Aye, sir?"

"We'll check this first sloop before giving chase. But it may be a trap, so assemble the gun crew and load and run out the guns, if you please. She sits high in the water. Either she's just been raided, or she's lightened her weight to make it easier to flee inspection."

Mr. Brandon studied the ship in question. "Aye, Captain, but the other one will be lost to us. If this one's a pirate, wouldn't she run?"

Thomas grunted. "Not if she wished us to chase the wrong ship. If I were a pirate captain—and as smart as this Nighthawk is reputed to be—I'd play dead to feign my innocence whilst I sent my enemy on a fool's errand. But she's not flying colors. Let's find out why."

"Look, Captain." Mr. Wayland joined them on the quarterdeck and waved toward the merchant ship. "They're hoisting a distress signal."

Thomas glanced at the three multicolored flags lining the ropes, signaling "need immediate assistance," and clenched his jaw. He had begun to taste the success of seizing the pirate, but now he had no choice but to go to the aid of the sloop. "Mr. Smith, bring us athwart her stern." If Thomas could be assured the other ship was Nighthawk's, he would be obligated to follow. But with this uncertainty, he must see what this other ship was about.

Determined to find the answers, Thomas joined Mr. Wayland and twenty of his sailors to row over to the *Courier*. Climbing the rope ladder and swinging over the bulwarks, he eyed the small sloop's crew of perhaps eighteen men, ragtag sorts of varying ages, all of whom avoided his gaze. Several of them clustered around a bearded older man lying on the deck, his head cradled by a lad with the same face some thirty years younger.

"Captain, sir." The young man reached out a hand toward Thomas. "Have you a surgeon aboard? My father—" He broke off with a sob that Thomas thought sounded forced. But perhaps his opinion was colored by his reaction to his own father's demise. Still, a man should be able to contain his emotions.

"Mr. Wayland," Thomas said to his lieutenant, "signal for Mr. Stark to come aboard." Seeing no blood on the fallen man, Thomas felt some satisfaction. If the fleeing culprit was Nighthawk, he had kept to his reputation for not inflicting fatal injuries. While Thomas might one day have to see the pirate hang, he nonetheless could respect his humanity.

A quick study of the main deck revealed no evidence of a struggle. None of the men appeared afraid or distressed. Did this mean they were Loyalists? Or was it all an act?

The afflicted man seemed to rouse a little. "Let me up, boy." His weak voice sounded legitimate. Once he sat up, he scrubbed one hand over his face while gripping his chest with the other. "Lost it all, lost it all. He took every last barrel. What about the crew, lad?"

"All well, sir."

Too well, to Thomas's way of thinking.

The young man eyed Thomas. "Father, the British Navy is here." The gentleness in his voice struck Thomas, and he swallowed away sudden emotion. The tenderness between these two...so unlike—

Duty shoved away personal thoughts, and he stepped closer. "Sir, I demand to know why you are not flying your colors. We are at war with the American colonies, and every ship is required to declare its loyalties."

The captain still clutched his chest, and he moaned. This time, the moan did not ring true to Thomas, and the hairs on the back of his neck rose. Something was amiss, but he could not discern what. He signaled his men to go below to inspect the vessel.

"Your flag, sir," Thomas demanded. "Where is it?"

The old man coughed, and his son's widened eyes conveyed a fear that seemed otherwise absent from his demeanor. "Sir, the pirate captain demanded our Union Jack." His pleading eyes reddened. "I think it was Nighthawk," he whispered as he accepted a flask from one of his crewman. "Here, Father. Take a drink," he murmured. "You'll be all right soon. The surgeon is coming."

Somehow this all had the feel of a well-rehearsed play as good as any Thomas had seen at London's Theatre Royal. But without proof, he could do nothing. He released a long sigh of frustration and ground his teeth together. How could he have been so foolish?

His gaze shot toward the bright, *empty* eastern horizon.

Chapter Twelve

"The house will be quiet whilst thou are gone." Anne folded Dinah's pink frock and tucked it into the brown leather portmanteau. "But I shall console myself with the knowledge that thou will be having a grand time."

Dinah's heart skipped at the thought. "I shall miss you, too." She glanced around her room and tapped her chin with one finger. "Now what am I forgetting?"

Anne laughed. "I do not think anyone can leave home without thinking much the same." Her eyes twinkled. "What a blessing that thee will have Captain Moberly for additional protection *and* for company."

To keep her friend from seeing her foolish grin, Dinah turned to her clothespress and pretended to search for forgotten items. "Hmm. Perhaps I should take a winter night rail."

"For summer? In East Florida?" Anne's teasing tone almost broke Dinah's resolve. "Oh, Dinah, if thee could but see thy expression when I mention his name."

"Nonsense." She continued to move clothes around, unfolding and shaking them out, then refolding.

Anne sat on the bed and sighed. "I do understand thy feelings. Was it only six years ago that Artemis first came calling?" Her gaze shifted toward the window, and her lips curved in a soft smile. "Ah, such sweet memories. Seeing thy joy as thee awaits the captain reminds me of my own courtship."

Dinah watched her for a moment, stunned by the peace and…was that joy on her friend's face? Shame needled into her mind and heart. Of course Anne loved Artemis, not because he was good, but because *she* was. In fact, when Dinah had been a young girl watching her foster sister fall in love and marry, she had admired Artemis, too. Back then, he had been kind to her, as to a younger sister.

"I do long for those days sometimes." Anne's smile disappeared, and her forehead furrowed.

Dinah sat beside her and grasped her hands. "Dear one, how I wish—"

"Can thee imagine how hurt he was when his childhood friends turned against him?" Anne blinked, and a single tear rolled down her cheek. "Thee knows that I hold no king in honor above any other man, but to Artemis, monarchs are God's designated authority for all to obey. To him, the young men of Nantucket are traitors to King George, and he holds no small degree of bitterness against them for their threats to tar and feather him for his loyalty to the Crown." She shuddered.

Dinah mirrored her reaction and then pulled Anne into her arms. "In this I agree with Artemis. Romans thirteen, verse one, tells us that we are to be subject to our God-ordained rulers, and when we resist their power, we commit sin. How can mankind live without the order provided by kings and governors?" And naval officers, too.

Anne pulled back and gazed into Dinah's eyes, her smile returning. "But in Luke twenty-two, our Lord

Jesus says that while the kings of the Gentiles exercise lordship over them, we, His children, are not to live in that manner."

"But—" Dinah released an exaggerated sigh. "Oh, Anne, we always say the same things when we have this discussion. Let me add that if everyone lived for the good of others, as you do, we would not need rulers. But many people are cruel and greedy and evil. Someone must prevent their wicked deeds, and therefore we must have rulers. How else shall evil be contained?"

The clopping of horses' hooves sounded beyond the window, and Dinah jumped to her feet.

"He's here." She rushed to the window. "I mean, *they're* here."

Anne joined her, laughing. "Yes, *they* are here." The uncharacteristic teasing grin on her sweet face showed Dinah that she had not been the slightest bit fooled.

The moment Dinah emerged from her house, Thomas's anxieties disappeared. There would be time enough when he returned from this trip to think of chasing pirates and quashing revolutions. He had been granted leave by the Admiralty before sailing here from England so that he might visit Bennington Plantation. Perhaps this would be the last favor his father's influence could purchase for him.

She wore a simple brown traveling dress with a white underskirt and her wide-brimmed straw hat. Around her shoulders rested a lacy white shawl, enhancing her delicate appearance.

As quickly as dignity permitted, he hurried through the rough iron gate to assist her. With an Indian guide, two soldiers from the fort's Sixtieth Regiment of Foot and four of Browne's East Florida Rangers riding with their party through the wilderness, he could not very well completely relax his military bearing lest he lose the men's respect.

"Miss Templeton." He doffed his hat and bowed. "You are as radiant as today's sunshine that heralds a successful expedition." *Bother.* What a clumsy compliment. And here he fancied himself a poet. Did the verses he had already penned sound as foolish as what he'd just said? Whom could he ask to critique them before he made a fool of himself? But then, the smile Dinah directed his way held no censure, only generous acceptance. Perhaps his worries were without foundation.

"Good morning, Captain Moberly." She accepted his offered arm. "Your presence in our expedition ensures an enjoyable time, not to mention how safe we will be."

Once again she had responded to his efforts in an approving manner. Once again his only thought was *What a delightful creature.*

He handed her into the covered coach, where she settled across from Dr. and Mrs. Wellsey and greeted them.

"Will you join us, Captain?" She glanced down at the space beside her.

"Perhaps later." Thomas felt a pang of regret over the arrangements he had made, but nothing could be done to change them. "I must ride with the soldiers for now."

She gave him a gracious nod. "Yes, of course. I understand."

With Dinah's baggage loaded onto the coach, Thomas mounted his borrowed steed and took his place at the front of the party with the other men on horseback. The coachman directed his team to follow them northward through the narrow streets to the city gate. Behind the coach, a wagon rattled along conveying Hinton, a serving girl and Dr. Wellsey's medical supplies. Thomas noted with satisfaction that his steward took to the trip with the same unruffled composure he always exhibited aboard ship, whether in storm or battle or becalmed waters.

The thirty-six-mile journey would take two days, if conditions remained as pleasant and favorable for speed as they were presently. Wellsey had assured Thomas that accommodations might be procured along the way, whether in the solitary Temple Inn some eighteen miles away or through the hospitality of some plantation owner.

Once the party passed through the earthen walls that protected St. Augustine, they began their journey along King's Road, which led northwest toward St. Johns Towne and Cowford on the St. Johns River.

Mrs. Wellsey's brother Charles, the guide who rode beside Thomas, pointed toward the countless alligators sunning themselves in the marshes beyond the city gate. "If we keep to the road and the bridges through the swamps, they should not bother us. But sometimes one will come out of the water looking for a meal, so keep watch."

As if to affirm the guide's words, one of the giant beasts lunged from its perch on a log and clamped its massive jaws around a hapless blue crane that had wandered too close. The rest of the immense flock took flight with a thunderous flapping of wings while several more of the reptiles joined the feast, thrashing about in a watery melee.

As he took note of the guide's words, Thomas withheld a shudder. These creatures were as vicious as sharks and posed more danger because they came onto the land. He eyed Charles.

"Those hides look like armor. Is it possible to kill them?" He tapped the musket sheathed in a scabbard on his saddle.

Charles shrugged. "If you shoot well." Were he a sailor in Thomas's crew, his bold grin would have constituted blatant insubordination. "You'll need to use your sword on the snakes."

Thomas caught onto his game. The lad was trying to unnerve him. "So we'll see many snakes?"

"Not if they see you first."

Thomas returned a smirk. "Duly noted." But his stomach clenched over the uncertainties of the road ahead. As if facing his brother were not enough, his first priority of protecting the ladies might prove more difficult than he had thought. Used to lengthy voyages aboard his ship, he would learn something new on this journey into the jungle wilderness.

"How kind of Mr. Moultrie to give us the use of this handsome coach." Dinah ran her fingers over the red velvet upholstery and mahogany paneling. Wide windows provided a grand view of the passing scenery and permitted fresh forest air to breeze in. The coach drove over the smooth, wide road, rarely jarring the travelers. And although the wheels flung bits of heavy, sandy earth, very little dust flew up to hamper breathing or soil clothing.

"His generosity could be political," Joanna Wellsey said. "Captain Moberly and his brother could prove to be important allies for Moultrie in the future, should Dr. Turnbull decide to start his trouble again."

"Ah. Perhaps so. But still, it is a lovely way to travel."

Dinah and her friends often lamented the disagreements among the East Florida leaders. Was it not enough that the northern colonies fought against their king? These men should do everything possible to be in accord. The thought reminded her to pray for Thomas's upcoming meeting with his brother.

She had never felt it appropriate to inquire about his obvious dislike of Frederick Moberly, whom she found to be the kindest of gentlemen. Staunch loyalist John Moultrie and his rebel brother, Alexander, had seen their family shattered by the war. Surely Thomas and his brother could reconcile whatever differences divided them. Dinah beseeched the Lord that it might be so.

Leaning back on his bench, Dr. Wellsey read his *Philosophical Transactions of the Royal Society* through spectacles that kept sliding down his nose. From time to time, he would read a paragraph aloud and voice his agreement or disagreement, but most of the time he appeared absorbed in the medical journal.

Dinah had hoped to pass the travel time in pleasant conversation with Captain Moberly, so she searched her memory for something to discuss with Joanna. The dark-haired woman was amiable enough, but she did not engage in idle chitchat like Elizabeth or discussions of spiritual matters like Anne. Perhaps she obtained her reserved demeanor from her Cherokee heritage, but sometimes her father's Scottish wit showed up in her blue eyes. Dinah decided a companionable silence would suffice until they stopped for their midday meal.

Shortly after noon, the party reached a clearing deep in the forest and left the roadway. The doctor helped his wife from the coach, and Thomas assisted Dinah.

"I thank you." Dinah took his hand and stepped down, feeling strength in his grip. She gazed up at his handsome face for as long as she dared before forcing her eyes to take in their surroundings. "How beautiful. Wild, but spectacular." A canopy provided shade from the sun, and the breeze fluttered the ever-present Spanish moss hanging from the trees.

After the men checked the area for dangers, Thomas led her to a fallen log and they sat side by side.

"Are you comfortable in the coach?"

She wanted to tell him she would be more comfortable if he were riding inside with her, but good sense prevailed. "Oh, yes. It is a grand conveyance."

"And you do not mind this—" he waved his hand toward the forest and lifted one eyebrow "—*jungle,* for lack of a better word?"

She laughed. "I suppose I've grown accustomed to it. If I must travel this road to see my dear ones, then it is a burden I gladly bear." Never mind that the captain's company lightened that burden considerably.

He leaned toward her, his shoulder almost touching hers. "Tell me, Miss Templeton, is there anything that does not please you? For I never hear you complain."

The humor in his voice and gaze sent a pleasant feeling through her. As warmth began to rise within her, she forbade it to reach her cheeks. She would not, must not blush, for that would betray everything. Until the captain declared himself, she must hold on to her heart. The heat brought perspiration to her face, but she refused to lift her fan to wave it away. It was too soon to ask him if the images meant what she had guessed.

"Hungry?" Again his eyebrow arched, and he tilted his head toward the wagon, where his steward and the serving girl were laying out a repast of bread, cheese, fruit and lemonade.

She nodded. "You?"

"Indeed." He patted his stomach, an informal gesture that stood at odds with his elegant uniform. But it only added to his pleasing presence. "I'll see if I can hurry things along." He rose and executed an exaggerated bow. "I shall return." Suddenly serious, he straightened. "I shall always return." Then he strode away.

A lump formed in her throat. With his repeated promise, or seeming promise, could she forget her own lifelong vow never to marry a seafarer? A bittersweet pang stretched through her soul as she realized what she truly longed for from Thomas. He might promise always to return, but could he promise never to leave?

Chapter Thirteen

The two-story Temple Inn turned out to be less commodious than Thomas had hoped for, but then, one could not expect the amenities of an English inn here in this wilderness. The proprietor was a jolly Scot, an uncle of the guide and Mrs. Wellsey, and one of their Cherokee relations ran the nearby livery stable. Several other guests were already ensconced in various common rooms, but Thomas managed to secure private quarters for Dinah and Mrs. Wellsey to share, while he and the good doctor would sleep in a large chamber filled with other men.

As his steward and the serving girl unloaded baggage, two servants hurried out of the wood-frame building to assist with other tasks, and soon all were settled into their rooms. Shunning the inn's noisy tavern, Thomas, Dinah and the Wellseys gathered in the small tearoom to enjoy a tasty supper of squirrel, alligator, wild boar and several exotic vegetables.

Thomas would have preferred to dine privately with Dinah, but propriety forbade it in this remote setting. While the four of them chatted about mundane matters, he studied her solemn countenance, trying to discern what had changed during their midday meal. In that wild forest setting, he had felt it necessary once again to promise always to return to her, no matter how often he must leave. Yet when he'd come back with a plateful of food for her, her merry mood had vanished, which threw his hopes into doubt. What more could he do to persuade her of his good intentions other than resign his commission and leave the navy?

A lightning bolt could not have struck him with more force than that thought. Leave the navy? In the middle of a war? Although he had pondered his own feelings of weariness with the war, he now knew resigning was impossible. Duty counted for something. For *everything* to a man of honor. Like a long-ingrained habit, the question reemerged, *What will Father think?* The idea spoiled his appetite. But why? He no longer needed to try to please the patriarch, always an impossible task in the best of times. He should probably consider what the Almighty required of him. Yet, at this moment, the only person he wanted to please sat across from him pushing her supper around on a pewter plate.

"Do you not care for alligator, Miss Templeton?" Thomas wondered if she could hear the emotion in his voice.

She looked up, and a hint of a smile graced her lips. "Oh, yes. I have become well accustomed to it. And, as everyone in East Florida says, I would rather eat the alligator than have it eat me."

In response, Thomas offered a shuddering wince that earned him a broader smile. At that moment, locked in each other's gazes, they seemed to be the only two people in the room. He could easily spend the rest of his life ending each day in her sweet company.

A tiny frown dashed across her forehead, and she

looked down at her plate. What random thought had broken their connection? Were they alone, he would ask. For now, his appetite having fled, he could only stare down at his own half-eaten meal.

Dinah glanced around the room once more, making certain she had left nothing behind.

The serving girl, who held a small leather satchel, paused by the door. "No need to worry, miss. I packed everything."

"Yes, of course. I thank you, Nancy." Dinah had never employed a personal servant, and she felt a bit unnerved having this girl hover about trying to anticipate her needs. But Thomas's steward had insisted she must have someone in attendance, and so it was done. In St. Augustine, where many poor loyalists had fled along with wealthier ones, servants for hire were easy to find. Nancy had turned out to be an agreeable girl who was eager to please her.

Dinah looked out the front window to check the progress of those who were packing the coach and wagon. Captain Moberly stood beside the coach, talking with the driver. He glanced her way and she ducked back, feeling foolish and angry at the same time.

Last night she had lain awake arguing with herself, at last coming to the conclusion that no matter what happened or did not happen between them, she would lose. If he professed his love, she would not be able to deny her own feelings for him. They would marry. He would leave. And leave and leave. And each time he left, her heart would break. But if his now-obvious affection for her cooled and he never spoke of it, her heart would break then, too. She could not win. Nor could she rein in her feelings to save her life.

Another look out the window revealed a mild uproar about the baggage. The usually placid Dr. Wellsey seemed to be at odds with Hinton about how things should be packed. Dinah sighed. She could not wait to get back in the coach and complete the journey. While her cousin and her sister-in-law might treat her as a something of a featherbrain, at least her niece and nephews would be glad to see her, and she could sketch their portraits to show how they had changed since last she'd seen them.

She went downstairs and, to avoid the captain, walked out the back door to view the landscape. A kitchen house was set apart from the inn, some distance from the trees. She wandered close and, through the open door, saw several black servants busy at their work. Were they slaves or free? Their friendly banter with the Indian cook suggested they were among those who had escaped their bonds and fled one of the rebelling colonies amidst the chaos of the war.

The early-morning air carried the scent of pine trees that mingled with the aromas of pies and meat roasting for the inn's guests. Dinah had taken a cold breakfast of bread and cheese in her room, but the bread had been freshly baked and delicious.

From the front of the inn came shouts announcing that all was in readiness for the trip. Dinah walked around the building through the tall grass and past a large woodpile. As she neared the front corner, the unmistakable angry rattle of a viper reached her ears. Instinct shouted within her *Stop. Do not move.* Her Uncle Lamech had nearly died from a snakebite four years ago, and his description of the event had burned into her memory.

Fear brought beads of perspiration pouring down her

face and stinging moisture dripped into her eyes, but she dared not wipe it away. Her hands itched from brushing through the grass, but she could not scratch. Her legs shook, but she could grasp nothing to steady herself. Daring to look from the corner of her eye, she saw the beast's tiny, hooded eyes set in a swaying triangular head, a gray and black diamond-patterned back and a small, beaded tail that shook its angry warning at her. Her throat constricted. She could not cry out, could not even whisper.

Lord, save me.

Ahead she saw Thomas by the coach, and in that instant, all became clear. She might be bitten at any moment, might die, never having experienced the joys of marriage. Her heart raced with fear and love.

I love you, Thomas Moberly. If God grants me life, I will be happy to be your wife, no matter how often you must leave me.

With that thought, an odd peace settled over her.

"Sir?" Hinton's voice shook with uncharacteristic emotion, and his eyes were focused toward the side of the inn.

Thomas turned to see Dinah standing oddly still. Her expression stunned him, for the gaze she fixed on him bespoke love and trust and—

He saw the snake. Not four feet from her, it rattled its warning, and Thomas's heart seemed to stop.

You'll need to use your sword on the snakes, Charles had said.

Thomas had thought it a jest, but now his sword was the only weapon he had at hand. He slid it from its scabbard and moved slowly toward the serpent. *God, help me.* If he could draw the creature's attention—

As if comprehending the drama, the others in the party stood still. All except the innkeeper's dogs, which ran toward the snake, barking furiously. They darted close, then backed away, then darted close again. With each movement, the snake's attention swayed between the dogs and the lady. Thomas understood. The shaggy mongrels were providing him with the opportunity to come behind the viper and kill it.

Easing into the brush beside the woodpile, he inched closer, not taking his eyes from his target. But then it swiveled its head his way, and its rattles vibrated in a fury. If he should be struck, so be it. He would gladly die for this woman.

The dogs increased their noise and, like swordsmen, thrust and parried, attacked and feinted, demanding the snake's attention. Before it could remember his presence, Thomas slashed his sword downward with all his strength, severing the menacing head from the body. A second violent cut sliced the writhing body in two pieces.

Thomas would have struck again, if only to vent his heightened emotions, but the inn's Indian cook ran toward him, waving her arms. "No, no. We will eat it. Do not damage it further."

A whimpering laugh emanated from nearby, and Thomas dropped his weapon and rushed to catch Dinah as she fell forward. For the second time in their brief acquaintance, he scooped her up in his arms and carried her to safety. This time, she flung her arms around him and buried her face in his shoulder.

"I knew you would save me." The hot breath of her whisper fanned his neck.

He held her close and rested his chin on her head as

a wild and giddy feeling swept through him. "My dear Miss Templeton." It was all he could manage to say.

But now he knew with certainty that he could give up anything, *everything*, to spend his life with her...*if* she would have him.

Chapter Fourteen

Throughout the morning as Thomas rode alongside the guide at the head of their party, he considered what lay ahead. After this morning's near disaster, his priorities had shifted, and he found himself eagerly anticipating at least part of the visit to Bennington Plantation. He would take great enjoyment in approaching Dinah's uncle and asking permission to marry her. He had some questions about why this Lamech Folger had not provided a home for Dinah. But having heard only praise about the man from Templeton, Thomas would assume the best. Of course, his first choice would be to address her brother, but Templeton might not return from London for some time, and Thomas was not willing to put off the matter until his arrival.

Of course his first task would be trying to establish a tolerable relationship with his brother. If not for their sister Marianne, he would have no qualms about reporting their father's demise immediately. No, that was not true. As a gentleman, he must show some sensitivity for Freddy's wife, whose life would be affected as much as the rest of theirs would. Furthermore, Thomas would not wish for Dinah to think him unfeeling. He had no intention of wearing a mask or hiding anything from her. But perhaps he should have told her clearly what she no doubt had already guessed: That he and Freddy had grown up as enemies.

The idea did not sit well on his mind. He had never worded it quite that way, but he entertained no doubts that it was true. Yet until now, Thomas had never felt compelled to examine the whys and hows of the situation. While their eldest brother had enjoyed all the privileges and protections of his rank, Thomas and his brother Robert had fended for themselves. Their mother had died shortly after Thomas's birth and neither of them had any memories of her. He'd never considered how tragic her death had been until his own wife died, and the realization had doubled his sorrow.

But all too soon after his mother's demise, his father the earl had found a new countess, a pretty young thing in whom Thomas never found fault. Still, she and Father indulged their firstborn boy, dear little Freddy, who always denied he was the favorite. The whiny little brat who always ran to his *mamá* rather than standing up and fighting like a man.

Thomas groaned inwardly. He was no longer a boy and should not entertain such petty thoughts. He ceased being a boy when Father sent him off to the navy at thirteen. He'd always felt somehow that his forced naval career had been Freddy's doing. Or perhaps it was the countess's way of protecting her son. All he could recall was his own sense of being utterly bereft. He alone had been sent away from the family, he alone cast out into the harsh world of military service to learn his duty to his king and country.

Yet he had enjoyed one bright spot in those growing-up years. All four brothers doted on Lady Marianne, their pretty little sister. Thomas's stomach clenched at the thought of her giving birth a second time. Would she, like his mother and wife, succumb to the lethal dangers of childbearing? Or would Mrs. Wellsey prove to be a competent midwife and deliver both mother and child safely through the valley of the shadow of death? Thomas prayed that God would be merciful.

As the day advanced and grew hotter, the party passed wagons, riders and foot travelers on King's Road, enduring the odors of man and beast and occasionally the aromas of fresh fruits and vegetables. From time to time, they turned out at a clearing while a wagonload of products from a plantation rumbled past on its way to St. Augustine. Still, the horses managed a fair pace on the busy thoroughfare. Along some stretches of the highway, hard-packed dirt made good progress possible, but in others deep, sandy ruts slowed the coach and wagon. But with the abundant oak and cypress trees forming a cooling canopy for the travelers, and with a fresh breeze carrying the varying scents of pine and magnolia to delight their senses, no one complained.

In fact, Thomas could not recall a single time he had ever heard Dinah complain, not even about the snake. And he still marveled at the way she had shaken off her fright this morning and insisted they must begin their journey without further delay. Admiration and love welled up in his heart and he longed to complete his poem extolling her many virtues. Perhaps Marianne could advise him. If she branded it rubbish, he would burn the page. But his sister would likely praise his efforts, however poor they might be. Doubt surged through his mind. He never had this sort of dilemma in tending to his duties. But then, since meeting Dinah, nothing in his life had been the same.

"This is our turnoff." Charles pointed to the right, where a byway broke from the main road.

Thomas's chest tightened. Every happy anticipation forgotten, he decided that riding into Bennington Plantation felt much like sailing into battle, and he must place all guns in readiness.

"I would say it was at least eight feet long and a good twelve inches around." Dr. Wellsey formed a circle with his hands as if trying to gauge the size of the snake, then wrote something in his journal.

"No more than six feet." Joanna tapped the page. "But a fat one. My uncle will have a special item of fare to offer his guests tonight."

With a small shudder, Dinah lifted her head from the pillow where she had reclined since they left the inn. "If you please, I would not wish Captain Moberly to know I fainted." She pulled herself up to a sitting position on the cushioned seat. Indeed, she felt nothing but embarrassment for behaving in such a weak manner in front of these friends.

"Not a word." Joanna patted her hand. "You were very brave. Most white women I know would have become hysterical. They would not have had the good sense to stand still, as you did."

"Do you require smelling salts?" Dr. Wellsey reached for his medicine bag.

"No." Dinah brushed a hand over her forehead, finding grit mingled with perspiration. "But I thank you for your kind ministrations." She looked out the window. "Have I slept long?"

"Most of the morning." Joanna glanced outside. "We turned off on Bennington Road a half hour ago."

"Ah!" Her lack of sleep last night must have contributed to her exhaustion after her ordeal. She reached into her small traveling bag and pulled out a linen hand-kerchief. "Do we have water?"

Dr. Wellsey produced a flask, and she poured a small amount onto the cloth. After wiping her forehead, she checked the soiled fabric.

"My goodness, the deeper inland we travel, the more dirt flies up from the road to cover us."

Joanna reached for the handkerchief. "May I?" She brushed it over Dinah's face, then gave it back. "That's better. But he will think well of you even with smudges on your face." Her gentle smile made clear of whom she spoke.

Dinah lifted her fan and waved it to dry the mois-ture…and to cool the heat trying to fill her cheeks. Never again would she criticize Elizabeth Markham for blushing, for if the heart was sufficiently engaged, surely any lady would surrender to the phenomenon.

The party wended its way through the dense forest and finally came around a thick stand of palm trees. In the distance, some fifty yards away, Thomas saw a tall, well-formed man raising an ax over a fallen oak tree. His hair had loosened from its queue and his soiled white shirt flapped in the breeze as he hacked into the wood much like how Thomas had hacked into the snake that morning. The sight surprised him.

Freddy. Working. At hard labor. Why had he not assigned one of his many slaves to such a chore? Several of them worked within yards of their master and could have been ordered to cut the wood. Thomas could taste his revulsion as keenly as he could taste the dirt from the road that filled his mouth and covered his clothes.

Slaves. The bane of the Christendom. And his family was as guilty as any.

As Thomas rode nearer, Freddy turned and saw him. And did not move.

When Thomas reined his horse to a stop and dismounted, his brother at last set down his ax and lifted one hand in a brusque greeting.

"Tommy." He swiped a sleeve across his forehead. "What a surprise."

Thomas nodded. It was all he could do not to blurt out his message about their father, just for the satisfaction of seeing how Freddy would react. Once again, guilt sliced into his gut at such a thought. But he could not help himself.

"So, what has it been? Nine, ten years?" Freddy reached down and picked up a finely carved cane. Then, with great care, he stepped over small limbs and branches and limped toward Thomas, leaning on the walking stick as if he would fall without it. With each touch of his right foot on the ground, his jaw clenched.

Shock slammed into Thomas's chest. The pain twisting his brother's face was real. He had seen enough malingerers to know whether a man's suffering was false or genuine. Yet Freddy appeared to be trying to hide it.

"What happened to you?" Thomas could not stop the question or its breathless delivery.

Freddy shrugged. "A little disagreement with a musket."

"An accident?"

"No." He looked beyond Thomas and grinned. "Wellsey. Good to see you. Who else is with you?" His greeting was hearty, free, not guarded as when he had addressed Thomas.

Thomas watched as the surgeon and his wife returned Freddy's welcome like old friends. Like family. Even Dinah emerged from the coach and embraced him with enthusiasm. And they all traded jolly pleasantries.

"Frederick," said Dinah, "you shouldn't be out working in this heat on your wounded leg." She put her fists at her waist. "What do you think you are doing?" Her concern smote Thomas's sentiments. They were friends.

Freddy laughed, and Thomas heard the echo of his own voice in the sound of it.

"Now, cousin dear, my wife scolds me enough. Let it be." He tweaked her nose, a gesture not at all pleasing to Thomas. But she laughed and batted his hand away. "Who better than I," he said, "to remove the tree our last hurricane blew down? It provides me with some much needed exercise. Did you suffer from that storm?"

"Not terribly." Dinah sent Thomas a questioning smile, and his heart hammered. "And you?"

Where did he fit in all of this? In truth, he did not fit at all. Aching, self-preserving pride ignited a fire in his chest, but he dared not let it burn. Instead he focused on a matter of no little severity. Who had dared to shoot Freddy? He was the king's magistrate for St. Johns Towne and Cowford. Assaulting him was a hanging offense. Thomas surprised himself with this bit of family pride.

"God is merciful." Freddy's words refocused his attention on the present. "We lost a few trees—" he waved a hand toward the fallen oak "—but all of our people and livestock came through it safely." He looked around the group. "Well, come along, then. Let me take you to the house. We'll see that you shake off the dust of travel and have a good meal." He turned toward the white, two-story mansion and began his trek. The smile he sent Thomas seemed forced, but whether from pain or animosity, Thomas could not discern. "Come along, brother. We have ten years of separation to review."

During their silent trek, Thomas surveyed the grounds surrounding the house. Well-manicured lawns graced several quarters, much like the grounds at Bennington Manor, where they had spent their childhood. Perfectly shaped hedgerows enclosed flower and vegetable gardens. Outbuildings gleamed with fresh whitewash and dark-green trim. After his trip through the veritable jungles of East Florida, Thomas found the plantation a well-maintained estate, an orderly refuge in the midst of chaos.

The Indian guide, Charles Ramsey, bade them goodbye with a promise to return when the Wellseys were ready to travel back. The soldiers rode on to the nearby garrison. The Rangers were directed to a barrackslike building where they would stay for a few days as part of their volunteer duties to guard the area from rebels.

Hinton and the serving girl merged with the house staff to tend to their various duties. Thomas, Dinah and the Wellseys followed Freddy into the house, where they were met with a clamorous riot.

Three small, blond children chased two black-and-white spaniel puppies into the entrance hallway, with a slender black girl racing to keep up. The unruly moppets dashed among the adults as though through a forest, but their young nursemaid stopped and put her hands over her mouth.

"Oh, Mister Frederick, I'm so sorry," she called above the chaos. "We didn't know you had company."

"It's all right, Caddy." Freddy grasped the tiniest offender by his shirt but seemed to have trouble keeping his balance. His cane saved him from plunging to the floor. "Whoa, Davy, slow down. Kezia, look who's here."

At that moment, a pretty little lady dashed down the stairs. "Children, please hush. Aunt Marianne is sleeping. Oh!" She caught sight of Dinah. "Dinah!" As she started across the floor, a puppy scampered toward the drawing room with the older boy in pursuit, nearly tripping her.

"Nooo, Jamie, you can't have her," the oldest child, a girl, shrieked. "That's my puppy." She dashed after the dog and the boy, whose giggling was filled with mischief. Freddy managed to keep a grip on a struggling Davy.

Servants rushed in from all directions and tried to sort out the melee. Thomas realized he was standing with his back to the wall and his hand on the hilt of his sword, a reflexive reaction, to be sure.

"Enough," cried the little lady.

"That's enough," Freddy shouted at the same instant.

Everyone stopped. Except the pups. They had found a small rag and both tried to claim it, growling fiercely as each tugged on an end.

"Betty." Freddy addressed a white servant who reminded Thomas of a servant from Bennington Manor who had come to East Florida. "Please take the dogs outside."

The young woman curtseyed, then scooped up the wiggling pups and hastened out the front door.

"Caddy, take the children."

"Noooo," squealed the little girl. "No, *Papá,* I want to see the soldier." She rushed over to Thomas, stopping just short of his knees, her face filled with wonder. "Are you a soldier?"

Thoroughly enchanted, Thomas opened his mouth to

answer, but his brother cleared his throat…just as their father used to do, and all went quiet.

"Kezia, go with Caddy."

"Yes, *Papá*." The child's expression fell into a heart-broken pout, complete with trembling lower lip. But no tears came forth.

Thomas was tempted to scoop her up and defend her. And tell her he was in the navy, a service far superior to the army. But he permitted no insubordination on his ship and would not support mutiny in his brother's house. With difficulty, he resisted the child's charms. With even more difficulty, he resisted the laughter inside him that threatened to demolish his composure.

Kezia hung her head as she took the servant's hand, but she managed a winsome glance over her shoulder at Thomas. He thought his heart might burst. The lad called Jamie happily skipped along with them, while little Davy scampered to catch up.

For a full ten seconds, the adults watched the children leave. For Thomas's part, he felt utterly captivated by the moppets. A deep longing welled up inside him, a painful ache that he had no child of his own. Nor even a family. Not even a wife. Yet.

Freddy was the first to shake off the spell. "Well, that was entertaining. And now, my dear—" he held out his hand to his wife "—come let me present my brother, Captain Thomas Moberly."

"Captain Moberly, how nice to meet you." She came forward, moving as gracefully as her taller cousin, and her eyes exuded a welcome that supported her words.

"Tommy, this is my beloved wife, Mrs. Moberly." Freddy's stare dared him to…what?

Thomas bowed and placed a kiss on her hand. "I am honored, madam."

Her radiant countenance, so like Dinah's, bespoke a woman content with her life. "And we are honored to have you in our home."

Thomas gazed at her and then around the group of adults. And in an instant of shattering clarity, he at last understood his lifelong melancholy and hatred. Freddy, his spoiled younger brother, possessed everything that Thomas had been denied, everything he had longed for all his life. And if Dinah rejected his proposal, he would never have it.

Chapter Fifteen

Dinah watched Thomas exchange pleasantries with Rachel. Although she could not see her cousin's face, she did have a full view of the man she loved. Amidst the confusion of dogs and children, she had still managed to catch glimpses of his reactions, and she felt more than a little concerned. Her beloved, if she might call him by that endearment, had appeared ill at ease since their arrival. He had not embraced his brother, nor had he shaken his hand. In return, Frederick had not seemed compelled to offer more than an obligatory greeting. Yet when their niece and nephews invaded the room, she had seen a tenderness in the captain's face, revealing perhaps the same affection she felt for those adorable children. How she wished they could talk privately so that she might inquire about the deep pain so evident in his intense blue eyes.

"Now," Rachel said, "you must all freshen up from your journey, and then we'll have tea in the drawing room in an hour." She beckoned to the nearby servants, then sent them to prepare rooms. The young woman who had taken the dogs outside returned and looked to her mistress for instructions. "Betty, you will assist Miss Templeton."

The servant curtseyed and moved to take her place beside Dinah, but the girl from St. Augustine stepped toward Rachel, eyeing Betty the whole time. "If you please, ma'am, I'm to see to Miss Templeton's needs."

Betty's lips pinched and she sniffed, but she moved back.

Under other circumstances, Dinah would have laughed, but the last thing this household needed was dissension among the servants. Their employers faced sufficient friction to place this visit's felicity in doubt.

"Ah, I see." Rachel, always well-composed, smiled. "Well then, Betty, would you take charge of arranging tea? I'm sure our guests will need something substantial after their travels."

Betty's face brightened at this apparent elevation in her duties. "Aye, mum." She curtseyed again. Then, with an imperious glance at Nancy, she glided from the room with her nose in the air.

"Dinah, dear—" Rachel appeared to struggle against a smile "—please make yourself comfortable in your usual room. You can tell your girl what you need."

"I cannot go until you give me a proper greeting." Dinah bent slightly to embrace her shorter cousin. Rachel's firm responding hug felt welcoming indeed and did much to settle Dinah's misgivings. "There. That's much better." She looked across the large front entry and found Thomas watching her. His brief nod further lifted her heart. "Rachel, do you think it would be all right if I peek into Marianne's room?"

"Excuse me, Miss Rachel." Joanna left her husband's side and joined the ladies. "I would like to see Mrs. Templeton, too."

"Oh, yes, of course," Rachel said. "She has been tired of late, and I will gladly release her to your care."

An unpleasant feeling akin to jealousy surged through Dinah's chest. But of course she could not tend to Marianne's particular needs. In fact, being unmarried, she might not be permitted to attend her sister-in-law's lying-in. But as she began her trek up the front staircase, followed by Joanna and Nancy, she gulped back her old feelings of rejection. Perhaps if she proved useful enough during this visit, Rachel and Marianne would welcome her fully into their circle instead of keeping secrets from her all the time. But another thought trumped that idea. If she became the captain's wife, she would advance into that privileged company of married ladies. And perhaps Bennington Plantation could bear one more wife of a seafaring man while her husband went about his duties. Her heart lightened at the thought of living here with her family.

First, Thomas needed to reconcile with his brother. If only she could open his eyes to the similarities they shared. Why, they even looked alike: tall and broad-shouldered, with long black hair worn in identical queues. They had similar handsome features—except for minor differences in their patrician noses, and were separated in age by less than three years. But while Frederick's dark-gray eyes had a mellow, placid look, the captain's intense blue eyes could exude both ice and fire, cold steel and sunshine.

Dinah could see that the captain also held her in high regard, in fact, loved her. She lifted a silent prayer that he would not keep her waiting long before he declared himself…or made it clear that he found their match impossible.

At the top of the narrow staircase, she tiptoed across

the wide board floor and quietly opened Marianne's door. The beautiful English lady, who had forsaken the privileges of her title for love of Jamie, lay sleeping on her canopied bed. Her black hair was fanned across a white linen pillow, and her ivory complexion bore a slight flush, evidence of the day's heat. Beside her, a small slave girl pulled a cord to keep the woven straw ceiling fan moving silently. The child gave Dinah a sweet smile, and she returned a tiny wave.

"I'll wait to see her," Dinah said to Joanna.

The midwife nodded and slipped past her into the bedchamber.

"Come along, Nancy." Dinah felt strange ordering the girl about, but Nancy seemed pleased to be in her service. "We both need to be refreshed."

In her own bedchamber, Dinah gazed about at the familiar décor, a bit nicer than her room in St. Augustine. Like Marianne's chamber, this back corner room boasted windows on the adjacent walls. A pine-scented breeze stirred the mosquito netting that hung beneath the linen draperies. A canopied oak bed, a mahogany dressing table and chair, an upholstered wing chair, an oak bureau and a wash stand provided for Dinah's comfort. Even the woven carpet added a touch of luxury unknown in the house she shared with Anne and Artemis. If invited to live here, she could easily call this home, could easily enjoy the comfortable life afforded by the plantation's wealth.

Over these past four years, Rachel had encouraged her to stay in the capital city, where she had more of a chance to find a husband than in this wilderness. But now, having met Thomas, Dinah knew she would never wish to marry anyone else.

A longing to *belong* in this space, with these people, swept through her. What could she do to entice them to want her in return?

Thomas emerged from his appointed chamber refreshed. As always, his steward had quickly located water and towels and a clean uniform to make his master presentable. Thomas had considered donning civilian clothing, but that would put him on an even footing with Freddy, and he felt the urge to maintain his rank. After all, Freddy's position as the local magistrate should induce him to wear some sort of fine clothing. Otherwise, how could he command respect amongst his neighbors?

Downstairs, he encountered a familiar, slightly stooped man. Memories swept into his mind of childhood mischief and servants having to restore what Thomas and his brothers had demolished: vases, hedges, stairway balusters.

"Summerlin?" He reached out a hand to his brother's valet. The fragrance of mint drifted up from the man's black muslin coat.

"Master Thomas—" The elderly man stared at the offered hand a moment before shaking it. "Ahem. I should say, *Captain* Moberly. How good to see you, sir. You are looking well, if I may say so."

"And you, my good man." Thomas studied him up and down. "You haven't changed a bit in these past ten years. No doubt this East Florida weather agrees with you."

"It does, sir. The rheumatism I suffered at home has disappeared."

"I am glad to hear it." Thomas glanced toward

the empty drawing room. "Where might I find my brother?"

Summerlin stepped aside and waved down the house's center hallway, which ran beside the staircase. "In his office, sir. The last door on the left."

"Thank you. Carry on."

As Thomas moved down the hall, his pulse rate increased. Good sense had prevailed earlier in regard to the delivery of his message. He had yet to see Marianne and did not want news of their father's death known about the house lest a careless servant report it to her. But he could no longer put off telling his brother. As calm as he could be giving orders to his crew, even during battle, he now felt a pressure in his chest that threatened to explode. Was this grief? Anger? If grief, then he would much prefer to seek Dinah's comforting presence. But he must face the fact that only Freddy could share this tremendous burden.

He tapped on the oak door, feeling much as he had as a midshipman aboard Captain—now Admiral—Howe's ship, when he'd been called to the captain's cabin after managing an order badly. That had been the changing point in his life, the point at which he vowed never to make another mistake in his duty again, no matter how distasteful his assignment might be. And this was certainly one of the most disagreeable tasks he'd ever been given.

"Come in." Freddy's voice came through the door, sounding surprisingly genial.

Nonetheless, Thomas entered with all his senses heightened, expecting his brother's typical arrogance.

Seated behind an ornate desk, Freddy looked up and his eyebrows arched. "Tommy. Come in. Sit down." He waved toward a chair facing the desk. "You'll forgive me if I do not get up." His guarded expression made it clear that he did not welcome this meeting. "What can I do for you? Are your quarters adequate?"

"More than adequate." Thomas sat in the damask chair and ran a hand over the white wood. "Thank you." He stared at Freddy, who returned the look. It was almost like staring into a mirror, despite their different mothers. Obviously Father's blood had dominated in both of their geneses.

"You bring ill tidings."

Thomas nodded once.

Freddy's eyes narrowed, as if he were expecting a blow.

"Bennington." The word came out on a long, shaky breath, and with it, Thomas felt his chest sink.

"Ah." Freddy slumped in his chair, mirroring Thomas once again. After several moments, during which his expression worked through several emotions—grief, worry, a hint of bitterness?—he inhaled a deep breath. "How is my mother?"

"She is well. And sends her love."

Freddy's eyes reddened. "We must not tell Merry. Not yet, I mean."

"No." Thomas appreciated his brother's compassion for their sister. He seemed to have grown into a sensible man, and doubtless was more than competent in managing this plantation. A yearning opened in his soul to erase their childhood enmity. But how could he take the first step when he was the offended party? Twice offended, in fact. First for his own banishment, and even more so for Freddy's neglect of Dinah. "I brought letters from your mother and our brothers."

"Ah." Freddy grunted. "I suppose I must now kiss William's ring if I expect to remain in my present employment? How vexing to be required to call him Bennington." He shook his head. "Forget I said that."

Thomas felt the oddest impulse to comfort him. After all, he'd had almost four months to absorb the shock, during which time he had taken to the solitude of his cabin numerous times. "Grief can scramble a man's brain…and his tongue."

Freddy studied him for a moment. "Yes, it can."

"Would you like for me to leave you alone?"

Freddy straightened and pulled in another deep breath. "No. Let me give you a tour of the plantation. I'll show you how we make the indigo dye for that uniform you're wearing."

"I'd like that," Thomas said, "but I believe your charming wife invited us to gather in the drawing room."

Freddy grimaced. "Yes, of course." He brushed a hand over his eyes, then stood and retrieved his cane.

Thomas flinched. He'd forgotten about the injury, and his admiration for Freddy's stoicism increased. The whining brat appeared to have become a man. "You did not give me a clear answer regarding your injury."

"No, I didn't." Freddy limped past his chair. "Shall we go?"

At this brusque response, all the good will that had been growing within Thomas vanished. His sincere interest in his brother's well-being was an attempt to navigate their strained relationship into friendlier waters. Yet Freddy rejected his attempt. Well, even if his brother preferred to steer clear of such weighty discussions, Thomas would run out his guns and give chase. Before he returned to his ship, he would find out why he had been banished from their childhood home and why Freddy had failed to take care of their sister-in-law. They would hash out—or thrash out—their differences. And Father and the Dowager Countess Bennington would not be there to protect Freddy from his wrath.

Chapter Sixteen

Dinah walked around the edges of the drawing room, admiring views from the front and side windows. Outside in the late afternoon sunlight, workers in fields bent over indigo plants or cultivated the large vegetable garden. An elderly groom led a young horse around the shady circular front drive, and several spaniels joined them for their stroll. In the distant marshes, birds called to one another in melodic tones.

How easily she could live in this pastoral setting and find contentment. Of course she must find some way to contribute to the household. But surely there was something she could do to benefit her relatives.

The drawing room was elegantly furnished with two groupings of furniture and seating for at least fifteen or twenty people. In each area, mahogany coffee and side tables held vases of fresh wildflowers and roses, whose fragrances filled the air.

Dinah turned her attention to the pianoforte in the corner. Both Rachel and Marianne could play the instrument, but Dinah had never had the opportunity to learn. Would Thomas find her lacking in artistic skills? When she stood side by side with his accomplished sister, would he realize after all that Dinah would not make a suitable wife for a nobleman's son, a renowned captain in His Majesty's Navy? Oh, but she could learn if given the chance. Perhaps some time with Marianne would improve her talents and refine her manners.

Dismissing such pointless musings, she sat on a tapestry settee to await the rest of their party. Soon Rachel entered, followed by Betty, who was now dressed in a black muslin gown with a white apron. From the young woman's broad smile, Dinah surmised that she was pleased with her elevation.

"When everyone is present, I will ring for you to bring the refreshments." Rachel indicated a small bell on a side table. "Oh, Dinah, you're already here." She hurried over to sit beside her and grasped her hands. "We're so pleased to have you visit. How long can you stay?"

Dinah clutched her cousin's hands and searched her countenance in an effort to see if there were limits to her hospitality. But Rachel's dark-brown eyes exuded only welcome and affection.

"I have no obligations in St. Augustine." She tried to keep her expression bland, tried to keep hope from emanating from her own face. "I suppose I shall stay as long as you will have me."

"Oh." Rachel squared her shoulders. "Why…that's grand." Despite her words, her smile tightened.

Dinah's heart dipped to her stomach. "Well, of course, no more than a month beyond Marianne's lying-in. I must get back for Mrs. Pilot's next ball, which will be in early August. I am determined to have a new gown for this one and must have time to make it." Of course her cousin did not want another person living here. With an infant arriving any day, another guest would only add confusion. But perhaps she could find refuge with Uncle Lamech and Aunt Lydie in St. Johns Towne. Perhaps she could work in their mercantile to earn her keep.

"Dear Mrs. Pilot." Rachel's warmth returned. "How is my good friend? She was so kind to me when Frederick announced our engagement at one of those delightful galas."

Grateful for a diversion from a painful subject, Dinah forced out a laugh. "She is well, as always." She entertained Rachel for the next few minutes with the account of how the regimental officer's wife had convinced their stern governor to hastily arrange a ball for Captain Moberly.

"Yes," Rachel said, "Mr. Tonyn does require a special occasion for such an event, doesn't he? Of course, the sons of Lord Bennington are sufficiently important to break his usual practices." She leaned toward Dinah with a confiding air. "Tell me, cousin, what do you think of my handsome brother-in-law?"

Struggling to deny the heat climbing up her neck, she waved her fan with a casual air. "Why, he is all that one would expect of a Moberly and a British naval officer. As you said, handsome. And of course he has flawless manners, is skilled in every courtesy, courageous in his duty. Oh, and an excellent dancer." She gazed toward an open window and tried to concentrate on the increased breeze that had sprung up, seemingly for her benefit.

Rachel's responding laugh was more like a giggle. "Blushing is not a sin, Dinah."

"As you know, cousin, I do not blush…much." Somehow she must divert the conversation. It was too soon to talk about her...*interest* in Captain Moberly. Too soon to entrust her deepest thoughts to her cousin, who held her at a distance about her own concerns. "Do you suppose Kezia would permit me to take one of the puppies home?" Artemis would have apoplexy if she did that.

"How long did it take you to fall in love with him?"

"The puppy?"

Now Rachel threw back her head and laughed until her face grew red. "Oh, my dear, why do we refuse to admit to our hearts' fondest desires?"

Dinah stared at her, bemused. Until this moment she had not realized that one of her fondest desires was to receive her cousin's hospitality, a home where she did not have to answer for every action, every breath, every thought. But she was unlikely to be granted that wish.

Rachel drew up her own fan and waved it. "I believe I hear our gentlemen coming up the hallway."

Dinah smacked her hand lightly. "Stop that," she whispered. "He has said nothing to me."

"Ah." Rachel bit her lower lip, but her eyes gleamed with merriment.

Thomas had spent the last eighteen years controlling his thoughts and emotions, and he would not fail this time. He must turn all thoughts to Dinah and see to Freddy later.

His first task was to find out where her Uncle Lamech resided. For some reason, he had imagined Mr. Folger lived here at the plantation. But that made no sense. The old fellow owned a business in St. Johns Towne, a mercantile, if Thomas remembered correctly.

As he and his brother approached the well-appointed drawing room, well-appointed, at least, for a wilderness plantation, Thomas felt his heart lighten. Rounding the doorway, he spied Dinah seated by her cousin on an elegant settee. How graceful she looked in this setting, with her lavender gown and upswept hair. He liked to see her hair uncovered by a cap or bonnet, for her blond locks glistened in the daylight like gold.

"My dear." Freddy approached his wife and bent to kiss her cheek. "Where are the others?"

She gave her husband a cheery smile, and Thomas admitted to himself that Freddy had won himself a charming bride. Why had he ever thought these Americans common? Their English heritage was apparent at every turn.

"You knew, of course," said Mrs. Moberly, "that Dr. Wellsey would go to his old laboratory and begin work immediately. I advised him about some illnesses among the slaves, and he is determined to see that they are remedied, if a remedy is to be found."

"Ah." Freddy waved Thomas to a seat across from the ladies. "Of course. And I assume Mrs. Wellsey is with Merry?"

"Yes. And so, here we are." After ringing a bell on the table beside her, Mrs. Moberly set her gaze on Thomas.

He could not escape her piercing dark eyes, so like Dinah's, but with a matronly maturity. "Madam, I am grateful for the generous accommodations you provided for me at such short notice."

As her maid came forward and began serving refreshments, Mrs. Moberly eyed him with a playful scowl. "Thomas, if you do not call me Rachel, I shall refuse to respond."

Disarmed, he laughed. "Aye, aye, ma'am. I should say, aye, aye, Rachel." He glanced at his beloved, whom he longed to call Dinah aloud, then turned back to her cousin. Unable to think of any other strategy, he chose artifice. "Dear sister, you have a large, well-managed household. No doubt the credit goes to you, for Freddy—" he decided insulting her husband would not endear him to her "—is clearly taken up with managing the plantation."

Rachel bent her head graciously. "I thank you, Thomas. As a ship's captain, you know all about order, so your praise is appreciated."

"You are most welcome. And speaking of ships' captains, should I not soon be meeting your good father, a former whaler?" Along with some surprisingly tasty tea, he swallowed much pride with that bit of flattery. Like most other mariners, he despised whaling as a filthy, inferior seafaring occupation.

The lady's eyebrows rose. "Oh, he will be sorry to have missed you. Perhaps if he had known you were coming—"

"Uncle Lamech is not here?" Dinah's expression fell.

Had she guessed Thomas's plan and understood the implications of her uncle's absence? No matter. From her frown and furrowed brow, she appeared to need some sort of comforting. He would provide it as soon as possible.

"Why, no." Rachel turned to her cousin. "He and Lydie sailed to Jamaica a fortnight ago for both business and a holiday. They will not return for two or three months."

Now Thomas sat back in his chair, stunned. He would not wait that long to pay his addresses to Dinah, nor would he speak to her directly without one gentleman in her defense. He certainly would not ask that jackanapes Hussey for permission. That left only—

Freddy.

Chapter Seventeen

Dinah noticed the tightening in Frederick's jaw and the red tint around his eyes. She surmised that Thomas had delivered the sad news of their father's death, and Frederick was bearing it well. But she could not guess what was going on in the captain's mind. She knew only that when he entered the room, her troubled emotions settled into a comfortable assurance that all would be well. She did note that he and his brother seemed to lean away from each other, and they had chosen chairs some distance apart. She recalled a verse in Psalm 133 that she had read just days ago: "Behold, how good and how pleasant it is for brethren to dwell together in unity." She had lifted a prayer that these two brothers would soon resolve their differences.

But she could not expect others to tread a spiritual path when the news of Uncle Lamech's trip to Jamaica had quickly stirred her anxiety again. Now she would have to wait until he returned to ask if she might live with him and Aunt Lydie. As hard as it would be, she must choose to trust that God would take care of her.

Taking a bite of biscuit and jam, she forced her attention back to the conversation, which Rachel skillfully managed to keep on light subjects. Was that because she knew her husband and his brother were not at peace with each other?

"And so *Papá*'s mercantile now has competition, not only in St. Johns Towne but also in Cowford. This area is growing so rapidly that Frederick may require assistance in his duties as magistrate."

Thomas gave his brother a slight bow. "My compliments to you for your proficiency in your duties. With that rotten rebellion going on in the northern colonies, it is encouraging to see solid new English settlements growing on this continent."

Frederick and Rachel traded one of those husband and wife looks that Dinah envied, a gaze that bespoke shared beliefs, goals and hearts united. How she longed for such a relationship.

"Thomas!" Marianne walked, or rather, lumbered into the room, arms extended toward the captain.

"Merry." He set down his teacup and met her in the center of the room, gently pulling her into a fond embrace. "My dear sister, are you well?"

"Oh, yes, and better still because you have come." Marianne moved back a step. "Look how handsome you are in your uniform." She sniffed back tears, then reached a hand toward Dinah.

"Sister." Her sweet, welcoming smile held no lack of love.

Dinah hurried to embrace her, glancing briefly at the captain as he returned to his chair. "Marianne, you are the picture of health." Indeed she was, and from the size of her abdomen, it appeared the child would arrive very soon. Dinah wanted to ask when, but feared her status as a single woman would make the question improper. "Will Jamie be returning soon?"

Marianne's smile dimmed, and she looked away. "He has been gone only three months, not enough time to sail to London, conduct his usual business and return to East Florida." She sat next to Rachel on the settee and patted the space next to her for Dinah. "And so, Thomas, since my husband lingers across the ocean, you must give us all the news of home."

Dinah kept her eyes focused on Marianne, kept her expression placid so as not to give a hint of the family's sorrow. Her sister-in-law must be shielded from grief. It was enough that Jamie was away so often, the never-ending burden of a seafarer's wife. Could Dinah bear such separations from the man she loved? Her gaze strayed to Thomas, and her heart ached to see the tenderness in his eyes. How would he keep the bad news from Marianne?

"Where does one begin?" He glanced away and frowned as if considering his response. "William and Mary now have six in their brood. Robert and Grace are doing well and expect their first child in September. They all send their love and fond wishes, as does your mother."

"Thank you." Marianne seemed to drink in the captain's report. "Dear Grace deserves much happiness for her constancy to our family." Then her eyes reddened. "I would not expect Father to—" she shook her head "—never mind." Then she laughed. "I must say this, however. Father once complained about not having enough progeny. It seems to me that he should be well satisfied now." She patted her abdomen, shocking Dinah, but Rachel chuckled.

Even Frederick and the captain managed to find humor in the situation, which caused her to wonder exceedingly. And her admiration for the captain increased for the way he had managed to avoid distressing Marianne. Now she would do her part to keep the conversation diverted from grievous matters.

"You may all be interested in hearing about our trip here from St. Augustine." Hoping she had sounded sufficiently detached, she took a sip of tea to convey nonchalance.

All eyes swung to her, but she most enjoyed the captain's fond gaze.

"Why, yes, of course," said Rachel. "Forgive me for not asking."

"It was a pleasant trip, not too hot, and the roadway is surprisingly smooth. We enjoyed our stay at the Temple Inn. The food was excellent, and the accommodations comfortable. And, oh yes, Captain Moberly saved me from a rattlesnake just this morning."

The ladies gasped, and Frederick sat forward in his chair. "You must tell us everything, Dinah." He glanced at his brother. "A hero on sea *and* land, eh?" Mild admiration colored his tone.

Dinah described her ordeal, and Captain Moberly interjected a few things she had not noticed during her terror. Their relatives watched with mouths agape, murmuring "oohs" and "ahhs" and "thank the Lord" in all the appropriate places.

"I fear," she said, "that my courage at last gave out, and I began to faint. Captain Moberly caught me and carried me safely to the carriage, where—" she decided to confess all "—I did indeed faint." She saw the mild alarm in his eyes, but no censure for her weakness. "Of course, Dr. Wellsey and Joanna made certain I was all right."

"Oh, Dinah." Marianne hugged her awkwardly.

"Good gracious." Rachel stood and stepped around Marianne to embrace Dinah, too.

Her lips close to Dinah's ear, Rachel whispered, "You are mistaken, cousin. From the look in the good captain's eyes, I believe he has indeed *spoken*."

Thomas glanced around the group, all of whom now stared at him. It was all he could do not to shift in his chair and tug at his collar. "Freddy, I think it is time we took that tour of the plantation you offered me." He rose and bowed to Rachel. "Will you excuse us, dear lady? After riding all day, I feel in need of a good walk."

"Yes, of course," Rachel said.

"May I go, too?" Marianne struggled to her feet. "Joanna tells me my time is near and that I should walk every day. Her advice led to good results with my son."

Thomas glanced at Freddy, who seemed not to mind their sister's request. Although he would not have thought of it, she would surely provide a buffer between them, as she often had when they were children. With her along, however, he would have to temper his anger toward his brother lest he cause her distress.

Bother. Dinah was frowning, as if she might feel slighted. Now he would have to invite her to come, which spoiled all his plans.

"Dinah, dear." Rachel looped her arm around Miss Templeton's waist. "Will you come with me to see what the children are doing? Caddy is an excellent nursemaid, but I feel better if I check on them myself."

Dinah's countenance lifted. "I would love to."

"Marianne, we'll give you a report on little Jamie."

"Thank you, dear."

The two ladies walked toward the drawing room door

arm-in-arm, but as Rachel passed Thomas, she gave him a conspiratorial wink. It was all he could do not to burst out laughing, for his little sister-in-law was a true delight. How had Freddy ever managed to win such a charming lady?

At the front door, Freddy strapped on a saber and picked up a musket. "We have snakes here, too. And a few other creatures we prefer not to encounter." He handed the musket to Thomas and leaned on his cane. "Shall we go? I have something special to show you."

Thomas hesitated, wondering if he should retrieve his own saber from his room, then decided against it. All thoughts about thrashing Freddy now seemed juvenile, and they certainly would not engage in a duel with swords. Perhaps his anger over childhood matters would have to be forgotten. No matter how much pain he carried, how could he hold bitterness against someone who had changed so much? From everything Thomas had seen here at the plantation, Freddy had become a competent, admirable man, so unlike the boy he had been.

They walked on either side of Marianne, helping her down the front steps and along the shaded pathway to Freddy's mysterious destination. Merry seemed to know Freddy's plan, and so Thomas decided to enjoy waiting for the surprise. With every step, he observed that both his sister and brother endured with courage their different limitations. No word of complaint. No allusion to the pain each must be feeling. But every few steps, one or the other exhaled or inhaled sharply enough to show some serious discomfort. Thomas would have insisted that they turn back, but they both appeared eager to reach their destination.

"Here we are." Freddy waved his hand to indicate a large, covered springhouse. "Merry, will you sit?"

She laughed a bit breathlessly. "Yes, and none too soon."

Thomas watched her with concern. Perhaps they should not have brought her along. Still, after she eased herself down on the low coquina wall of the cistern, she smiled as she brought up her fan to wave before her face.

The simple gesture, something every lady did, reminded Thomas of the fan he had given Dinah. They had yet to discuss the message he had intended, but soon he could tell her everything.

Freddy sat beside their sister and pressed one hand down his wounded leg. This expedition had cost him dearly, a fact that Thomas would not overlook.

"Well, Tommy, how long will you be with us?" Freddy dipped his hand in the water and patted some on the back of his neck. "And while you answer, be a good lad and fetch us a drink." He pointed to a dipper beside the spring that flowed into the cistern.

An annoying bit of pride nettled Thomas. He was used to giving orders and being waited on. And now his little brother's spoiled side was reemerging.

"Oh, yes, please," Merry said. "I would appreciate a drink. This water is the sweetest and purest you'll ever taste."

"Of course." Thomas chuckled at his own foolishness. He would do anything for her. But for Freddy—

He filled the pewter dipper under the water flow, then carried it to his sister. "To answer your question, I cannot stay more than a week. Last time out on patrol, I nearly caught the pirate they call Nighthawk. I'm determined he will not escape me again."

"Oh." Merry's eyes widened. "Oh, my." She pressed a hand to her chest and appeared to be truly frightened.

Her alarm on his behalf moved him deeply, but he also chided himself for bringing up such a topic. "Never fear, sister. These are small matters you need not concern yourself with."

She looked at Freddy.

"We will make it a matter of prayer, will we not, Merry?" Freddy patted her hand. "Remember, fret not."

She nodded and then gazed across the landscape.

Thomas rejected the jealousy that threatened to invade his heart. Of course these two would be close, as they always had been. They shared a mother and had been raised under her loving direction. Still, being the outsider pained him. Best to speak his request now and be done with it. He leaned against a nearby pine tree and crossed his arms, trying to decide how to begin.

"I say, Tommy," Freddy said, suddenly cheerful, "take a look at that arbor over there." He pointed to an alcove made of woven live oak branches and covered with wild red roses. Inside the recess sat a small wrought-iron bench with a cushion on it. He grinned at Merry then back at Thomas. "I had that made for a special occasion a little over five years ago."

Thomas studied the structure, trying to imagine its purpose. He could picture Dinah seated on the bench. His brother's meaning suddenly became clear, and he grinned. "You proposed to Rachel there."

Freddy and Merry laughed, and the sound of it made for a cheerful duet. "Indeed I did. And there it sits, languishing for want of a similar use. Do you suppose I could rent it out?"

In this moment of understanding and camaraderie,

Thomas felt as if the weight of two tons of ballast had been lifted from his chest. He exploded in laughter that rivaled his siblings'. "Am I that transparent?"

Merry waved her fan. "Why, whatever do you mean?" But she could not contain her mirth, and soon had to bring out a handkerchief to dry her watering eyes. "Oh, Tommy, I am so happy for you. Dinah is the dearest girl, and we do love her. Will you propose to her here?" She put both hands on her round abdomen. "Umph. Even my child finds the situation delightful."

Thomas experienced a moment of concern, but his sister's expression did not indicate any pain. "I cannot think of a more enchanting place to address a lady in regard to marriage." He plucked a pine needle from his sleeve. "I am disappointed that neither Jamie nor Mr. Folger is here. In their absence, I must assume it is acceptable to ask you, Freddy, if I may indeed propose to our Miss Templeton."

Freddy's wide grin softened to a crooked smile. "You will perhaps be surprised to know what we have all known for some time that you two would suit each other well. You share many common interests." He glanced at Merry, who gave him a rueful smile, which struck Thomas as odd in light of the approval he was pouring out. "While we had no idea you would be transferred to St. Augustine, we did try to think of a way to put the two of you in each other's paths. And look, the Lord has done it for us. No machinations necessary."

His heart lightened beyond all previous hopes, Thomas studied his brother and a surge of affection rolled through him. At this moment, he could forgive Freddy any fault, any offense. "Shall I speak to her this evening? Before dark, of course."

"If you wish. If you're anything like me, you do not

want to postpone it. And if it grows dark before it can be managed, we can light lanterns." Freddy pointed to the string of lamps hung around the springhouse. "And one of us can accompany you."

"That is well pleasing to me," Thomas said. "Now, may we return to the house and my fair lady's company?"

Merry folded her fan and clutched it but did not rise. "I do have a matter to discuss with you both."

Thomas questioned Freddy with a look, but he shrugged.

"What is it, dear one?" Freddy touched her shoulder.

She bit her lip briefly. "You two are keeping something from me, but I am stronger than you think. Tell me now. I demand it." Her eyes flashed with resolve.

Thomas sat beside her, took her hand and again sent Freddy a questioning look. Freddy nodded once.

"Our father now rests in peace with the Almighty."

She swallowed hard. "I knew. Somehow I just knew it." She drew in a sharp breath and again rested her hands on her abdomen. Her eyes widened, and she gave out a long, broken moan of pain that sent fear coursing through Thomas. Ariel had begun her doomed delivery just like this. Freddy gaped at their sister and Thomas seemed unable to move. Merry's face scrunched into a red ball, and she gulped for air as if there was none to be had. "Dear brothers," she squeaked out, "will you please escort me to Mrs. Wellsey?"

Chapter Eighteen

"It's so quiet." Dinah sat with Frederick and Thomas in the dimly-lit drawing room. When her neighbor in St. Augustine had given birth last month, her screams had echoed through the narrow streets of the city. But for the past hour, not a sound other than an occasional footstep had emanated from the upstairs.

Even in the soft candlelight of the drawing room, Dinah could see mild tension creasing Frederick's face. But every muscle on Thomas's face was taut, making him appear nothing short of stricken. When he had carried his sister into the house and up the stairs, the entire household hurried to help. The children had already been put to bed, but the nursery door at the far end of the hall was covered with blankets to keep out any possible sounds. Servants carried linens and water to the bedchamber. And Joanna, Rachel and a slave woman with birthing experience cloistered themselves with Marianne. Before closing the door, Rachel ordered Dinah and the gentlemen downstairs, where they continued to sit in silence.

After some time, Thomas rose and paced about the

room, then stared out a window and swiped his hands down his face. "We should not have told her."

Frederick stood and limped to his side. "You know she's too perceptive to deceive. And for goodness sake, do not blame yourself for—" He glanced at Dinah, then murmured, "Listen, brother, here on the plantation, I've observed this sort of event more times than I can count. It was clear to me it would happen very soon."

Captain Moberly shook his head and massaged the back of his neck. "Whereas my one experience..."

Dinah picked at the hem of her long sleeves until stitches loosened. She understood the captain's concern. Having lost his wife and son, he must think every birth posed mortal danger. She cast about in her mind for a way to comfort him and could think of only one.

Slipping down on her knees before the settee, she bowed to pray. Soon she felt a presence beside her, and then another on the other side. Tears clogged her throat, making it impossible to pray out loud. Yet surely God would hear what her heart cried out. *Dear God, have mercy on Marianne and her baby. Have mercy on my brother and do not take his beloved wife from him. Have mercy on dear Thomas. How could he bear it if his only sister dies?*

"Almighty God," the captain prayed beside her, "grant safety, grant life, grant..." He groaned and said no more.

"Father in heaven." Frederick's voice came strong and true. "We pray on behalf of our beloved sister and her child. We know You love them and Jamie. We know You have a plan. Your ways are not our ways, and You never make a mistake, so help us to trust You, no matter what the outcome of this night." He paused but made no move to stand. Soon he continued. "In Scripture, You promise that where two or three are gathered in Your name, You will be there in the midst of us. We gather here to ask that all will go well and Marianne and her infant will—"

"She's here, master." The slave midwife stood in the drawing room doorway with her hands clasped, and a hint of excitement filled her soft alto voice. "Miss Marianne had a baby girl, and all is well."

Thomas slumped face down on the settee and exhaled a long, ragged sigh, while Frederick laughed and pulled himself to his feet, wincing as he grabbed his cane. "Praise God!" He put one hand under Dinah's elbow and helped her up. "I suppose you'll want to go up and see her…them."

Dinah could see the relief in his face. In fact, his whole countenance seemed to beam in the candlelight. "Yes, I'd like that."

She hesitated, waiting for Thomas to stand. When he did, she saw brightness on his face, too, but it came from a damp sheen on his cheeks. This dear man, so strong and brave in his duties, had wept with joy for his sister, and perhaps in sorrow for his own lost wife and child.

"Well," he said, straightening his uniform, "that was remarkably…fast." He cleared his throat. "Miss Templeton, please do not delay in bringing us a report."

Merry mischief swept into her and she gave him a sharp salute. "Aye, aye, Captain."

His responding laughter echoed throughout the room. What a pleasing sound, so filled with unreserved relief and unbounded joy.

She hurried out toward the stairs, but not before she heard the two men congratulate each other on being uncles once again. This truly was a night of miracles, and her heart lifted in praise over the goodness of

God. Not only had Marianne delivered her baby safely, but despite the mysterious animosity that had existed between the brothers, they seemed well on their way to reconciliation. In fact, she herself had felt God's hand upon the three of them as Frederick had uttered his eloquent prayer. She had always admired the faith he and Rachel exhibited, but now she felt her own faith bolstered and confirmed.

She tiptoed into the room and, at Joanna's nod, approached the bed. Someone had brushed Marianne's thick black curls away from her weary but peaceful face. She wore a fresh night rail, the bedding had been changed and the fragrance of pine and roses filled the room. But Dinah's gaze quickly settled upon her new niece, a tiny doll with a rosy, perfectly formed face topped by a sprinkle of downy black hair. Warmth and joy flooded her heart, and tears sprang to her eyes.

"Oh, Marianne, she's so beautiful."

Rachel approached and put an arm around Dinah's waist. "Isn't she? Little Jamie will be pleased to wake in the morning and find he has a sister."

Marianne chuckled softly. "And your daughter will be delighted her new cousin is a girl." She sighed deeply, and her smile disappeared. "The Lord giveth, and the Lord taketh away. Blessed be the name of the Lord."

Rachel moved to the head of the bed and gently embraced her. "Oh, dear one, may we not say that the Lord has changed our sorrow into joy? And think of this—your beloved father might not have forgiven you in this life, but now that he is in heaven, he at last comprehends the true grace of our heavenly Father."

Marianne laughed softly through her tears. "Thank you, dear one."

While the two mothers murmured over the infant,

Dinah found herself moving toward the end of the bed. Their friendship was far deeper than any she had ever known, and she had not been invited into their circle. A familiar cavern yawned wider within her, but she refused to let bitterness fill it, nor would she fall into self-pity. She resolved to count it sufficient that Thomas and his brother had settled their differences and that a new life had been brought forth into the world. If God chose for her to dwell in loneliness, so be it.

Her reverie was broken by Marianne's tired but serene voice. "I must get some rest, sisters, but Dinah, would you like to hold her?"

Dinah's heart lightened and she moved close and reached out her arms. With the baby firmly nestled against her, she looked at her kinswomen and experienced a moment of peace and belonging. These moments were rare and she savored it, basking in the warmth of Marianne's smile.

Chapter Nineteen

Thomas awoke at first light to see that Hinton, as always, had risen before him. While his steward quietly brought in hot water and laid out his razor and strop, Thomas lay abed planning his day. If all went well, by supper he could overcome every obstacle to his happiness, save one. Dinah would accept his proposal and he and Freddy would put to rest their childhood quarrels. The smattering of comradeship he and his brother had enjoyed portended good things, and Thomas would do his part to demolish the final barriers. After that, only one thing remained to complete his success, but catching Nighthawk would have to wait until another day. For now, a cool, fresh breeze blew pine scents in through the window's mosquito netting and foreshadowed success in all his ventures. Energized by these thoughts, he climbed out of bed and began to dress.

"Coffee, sir?" Hinton held out a steaming cup, just what Thomas needed.

"Thank you." He sipped the hot liquid and found to his surprise it tasted quite good. Then he submitted himself to Hinton, who stirred up a lather in his shaving mug, applied it liberally to Thomas's face and began to scrape away the heavy black stubble. During the process, he found himself examining the events of last evening.

He had struggled to find the words to pray for Marianne, yet Freddy spoke to the Almighty as if to a friend, a compassionate benefactor. Neither of them had ever addressed their father in such a familiar tone. None of Thomas's crew, even his officers, dared to address him that way. And Thomas certainly would never address a superior with such self-assurance. How could Freddy not tremble in the face of the ultimate authority of the universe? Perhaps before Thomas spoke to him about other matters, he should inquire about this bold and personal form of prayer. In fact, he found himself a bit envious of the relationship his brother seemed to have with the Almighty.

He chuckled inwardly. Someday he must address this issue with Freddy.

But first things first. Thomas must look in on his sister and new niece before he broke his fast. After basking briefly in the warmth of the hot towel Hinton applied and the refreshing sting of the shaving balm, he finished dressing.

"The house is quiet, sir." Hinton sniffed, as he did when things did not meet his approval. "Mr. Moberly does not have a breakfast room, but breakfast is laid out in the dining room."

"Ah, very good." Thomas wanted to laugh at his steward's snobbery. He himself might have found the plantation lacking in other circumstances. But today, everything pleased him, even delaying his visit to Marianne. Of course she would want to sleep late after last night's ordeal. Again, he marveled at her easy delivery and sent up a silent prayer of thanks.

Downstairs a servant presided over the breakfast buffet and upon inquiry informed Thomas that Mr. Moberly had left at dawn to make his rounds of the plantation. A small thread of disappointment wound through him but he dismissed it. Tomorrow would be soon enough to ride out with Freddy.

After an excellent repast, Thomas carried a cup of coffee as he took in the grounds surrounding the house. At the back corner, he found himself tripping over the spaniel pups and their mother, who no doubt were looking for a human playfellow. Charmed by the little rascals, he lifted one by the scruff of its neck only to have it scrape damp, dusty paws down his favorite blue uniform. Hinton would have to clean off the dirt before Thomas presented himself to Dinah.

He stared off toward the east, where countless slaves were already at work in the rice and indigo fields. An uncomfortable thought nudged his conscience, one he often considered but never resolved to his own satisfaction. It was one thing to employ servants, another thing altogether to own slaves. Even Father had once refused to purchase Africans as if they were livestock. That is, until His Majesty granted him these lands and he realized he must have laborers to cultivate it, cheap laborers, so profits could be maximized. So the old earl had set aside his objections and bought workers to increase the wealth that had come with his title.

Thomas took some satisfaction from knowing that his commission in His Majesty's Navy had been purchased long before Father acquired Bennington Plantation. Thus Thomas's service was untainted by human bondage. And now, after eighteen years in the navy, he could rightfully say he had gained his own small fortune and could offer Dinah a comfortable life.

They could live in St. Augustine until this infernal war was over, then perhaps return to England and settle in the house he owned between Southampton and Portsmouth. He could picture Dinah growing roses and hydrangeas in the garden and filling the nursery with little blond children. If not for the war, he would take her home as soon as they wed. But then, without the war, he might not have met her.

With no one about to engage his interest, Thomas extricated himself from the spaniels, wandered back to the house, and made his way to Freddy's study. Noting that all the issues of *The Gentleman's Magazines* were over a year old, he perused the surprisingly well-stocked bookshelves behind the door. Between two large tomes—Shakespeare and Milton—he noticed a folded broadsheet, and curiosity demanded a reading.

He opened the large page…and felt an invisible force smite his chest. This was that treasonous document those rebelling colonists had penned just four years ago, making excuses to the world for their violent rejection of their God-given authority. Thomas's lip curled into a sneer at its title: Declaration of Independence.

But why did Freddy have this?

Dinah enjoyed waking up to hot water in her nightstand and fresh clothing laid out for her to wear. Nancy seemed more than eager to please her, and Dinah had overheard the girl asking Thomas's steward how she might improve in her duties. While it was not an expense Dinah could maintain after they returned to St. Augustine, for now she would gladly submit to being pampered.

"Good morning, Nancy. I suppose everyone is up and about." She sat still before her dressing table while her maid brushed her hair up into a charming coiffure. The captain had complimented her hair more than once, and she hoped he would like this arrangement.

"Yes, miss. That is, the gentlemen and Miss Rachel. Miss Marianne is still abed."

"I see." Another good thing about having a lady's maid. Dinah did not have to go in search of such information. Perhaps Thomas and Frederick had gone out together, a good sign of their improving relationship.

Once Nancy had secured her hair with pins, Dinah left her chamber and moved toward the front staircase. But a tiny mewing sound coming from Marianne's room stopped her, and the temptation to see her niece won out. She quietly opened the door and peered in to see Joanna tending the infant while Marianne looked on with a glowing smile.

"Dinah." She beckoned her and patted the bed. "Come sit with me and hold the baby."

Seated with her back against a pillow and the precious child in her arms, Dinah thought she might melt into a puddle of bliss once again. "How wonderful to hold a baby." She felt a sudden ache to have one of her own. "What will you name her?"

Marianne rested her head on Dinah's shoulder, a gesture that further warmed her heart. "Maria, after my mother. And perhaps Grace, for my brother Robert's wife."

"Maria Grace Templeton." Dinah kissed the sleeping baby's pink forehead. "Welcome to the family." *And may you always feel welcome wherever you go.* A familiar hollow sensation opened within her, but she chided herself for such self-centeredness in the midst of this joyful occasion.

"You would like Grace," Marianne said. "She is the

dearest Christian lady." An indefinable look passed over her fair face. "Perhaps you will meet her some day."

"Perhaps." Dinah could not guess what Marianne meant, nor why she thought it necessary to suggest such a thing.

"Miss Dinah," Joanna said, "I should put her in her cradle now."

With reluctance, Dinah surrendered the sweet bundle and, seeing the weariness in Marianne's eyes, took her leave and went downstairs. She found Rachel feeding the children in the dining room, with Caddy helping. She filled a plate with eggs, ham and muffins, then joined them at the long oak table.

"Cousin, what can I do to help?"

"I thank you for asking, dear, but we have more than enough hands for every task." Rachel lifted a spoonful of porridge to little Davy's lips. "Now, Davy, you cannot grow up to be big and strong like your *papá* if you don't eat your breakfast."

Dinah bit into her muffin to hide the emotion that threatened to erupt. While holding her niece had brought joy, the old feelings of rejection returned all too quickly after Rachel rebuffed her offer to help.

"Want muff-im." He eyed Dinah's bread and reached out a chubby hand.

Mother and son argued for several moments before she called for a compromise. "Three more bites of porridge, and then a muffin."

From his bright grin and easy compliance to the terms, one would think he had won. In watching the dispute, Dinah had learned a nice lesson in mothering. She sighed, wondering if she would ever need to apply it to a child of her own.

But as that old, dull pain of loneliness wove into her

heart, she began to think she'd made a mistake to come here where she clearly was not needed.

Thomas spread the broadsheet over Freddy's desk, then sat in one of the chairs that faced it and crossed his arms. If his brother did not come soon, he would go in search of him and demand an answer for the presence of this traitorous document. The idea that someone in his family might be in sympathy with the rebels was more than he could comprehend. It was one thing to think the colonies should be released, another altogether to support their rebellion. Freddy was the king's magistrate. His influence could sway others to join the insurgency. East Florida could even be brought into the war.

Thomas might have found Governor Tonyn a little stiff and overly formal, but the man had been wise not to permit an election in this colony. The elected assemblies in the northern colonies had brought together men with traitorous ideas, and hence the violent struggle that had cost countless English lives, along with their Hessian allies. Thomas slammed his fist on the edge of the desk. Didn't Freddy realize what it would cost them both if this paper were found by the wrong person?

The door opened and Freddy limped into the room. "Good morning, Tommy. Did you rest well? Have a good breakfast?" His warm gaze shot to the broadsheet, and he smiled. "Ah, I see you've found some interesting reading material."

Thomas rose to his feet and glared at him. "Interesting? Don't you mean treasonous?"

Freddy had the gall to laugh. "It all depends on your perspective."

"And what does that mean?" Thomas could feel the

heat of rage rising within him, a strange yet familiar sensation from long ago.

"You know, do you not," Freddy said, "that we've had two battles in this area, one in '77 and the other just last year. Browne's East Florida Rangers managed to drive back the rebels both times."

"Of course I know. But what does that have to do with this?" He grabbed up the sheet, crumpling its edge in his fist.

Freddy shrugged. "How can you win a war if you do not understand why your enemy is fighting you?"

Thomas's grip loosened and the paper fluttered back to the desk. "Indeed, that is true. I see your reasoning." Relief poured through him like rain on parched ground, and he dropped back into his chair. "You had me worried in the extreme. Thank the Almighty your thinking is straight."

Gripping Thomas's shoulder, Freddy sobered. "We do thank Him for all His mercies." He moved to his chair behind the desk and laid his cane on the floor beside him.

His response seemed odd, out of place, but Thomas decided it was the very thing to open the discussion he had planned.

"I was deeply moved by your prayer for Marianne last night."

"The credit goes to Dinah for kneeling by the settee. I had prayed for her silently, as I am sure you did as well. But of course it was all over by the time we knelt together." Freddy chuckled. "The scriptures say 'Before they call, I will answer, and while they are yet speaking, I will hear.' The Lord had already safely delivered her, yet I believe He heard and honored our unified prayer."

He smoothed and refolded the broadsheet and tucked it into the center desk drawer.

"Where do you get such faith?" The question came out before Thomas could consider what he was saying.

Freddy's eyebrows rose. "Are…are you not a Christian, Tommy?" His hushed tone resounded with concern.

His first instinct was to be offended. But in an instant that reaction was replaced by gratitude for his brother's fear on his behalf. Something new was happening between them, and Thomas did not wish to impede it. Was that not why he had come to speak to Freddy? "I believe in the depths of my being all the words of our catechism. Christ Jesus is the only Savior of the world, and my belief in Him assures me of salvation."

Freddy's eyes reddened. His jaw worked, and he stared out the window, at last returning his gaze to Thomas. "I'm pleased to hear the affirmation of your faith." His unsteady voice underscored the depth of his sentiment, and once again Thomas felt a positive shift in their relationship.

"And so, I must ask you again, how do you summon the faith to speak to the Almighty as if He were… were—" He stared down at his hands.

"A friend?" Freddy's smile held no censure, no triumph or superiority, as often it had in their childhood.

"Yes. No. More like…" Thomas ran his hand through his hair, pulling several strands from his queue. Irritation swept through him. Here he was a renowned captain in His Majesty's Navy, a man of means, the defender of St. Augustine and all of East Florida. But at this moment, he felt like a boy at Eton being schooled by an underclassman.

"A father?"

Thomas snorted. "No, not at all. I never would have spoken so familiarly with Bennington."

"I understand." Freddy leaned forward and rested his forearms on the desk. "I'm sorry Mr. Folger is away. My father-in-law explains this so much better than I." He chuckled. "He lives it so much better than I do."

An uncharacteristic humility resonated in his voice, so Thomas tamped down his own vague surge of pride that suggested he should know more about everything than Freddy. Untoward competition had reared its ugly head once again, but he would have none of it. "I'm listening."

Freddy toyed with his quill pen for a moment before continuing. "We call God our heavenly Father, but you and I haven't had a living example of a good father, so no wonder this doesn't mean anything to us. In the scriptures, Jesus asks, 'If a son shall ask bread of any of you that is a father, will he give him a stone?'" Freddy emitted a wry laugh. "Our poor old father seemed to enjoy giving all his sons stones." He shook his head. "No, that's not right. What I mean is—"

"I think I understand." Thomas sat forward with his elbows on his knees. "So Rachel's father dotes on her like Father doted on Marianne?"

Freddy shook his head. "Daughters are a different story, as I have just begun to notice myself. But what I'm referring to is this—Mr. Folger raised Jamie Templeton as if he were his own son. Jamie's told me the old man was hard on him, but he was also fair. And Mr. Folger has become like a father to me. Then, in becoming a father, I have learned where our father failed and how different our heavenly Father is." He ran a hand over his jaw and stared above Thomas's head as if pondering his next words. "I think the old earl separated faith and duty and rank. He believed in God and salvation through Christ. But duty to king and country came first. And he considered the peerage a holy institution ordained by God for keeping mankind in order."

Thomas leaned back in his chair, nodding. "Of course. The Great Chain of Being. How can one argue that? The Almighty God is above all, and we each have our place in the hierarchy."

Freddy frowned briefly, then gave his head a quick shake as though to dismiss whatever troubled his thoughts. "Be that as it may or may not be, Christ came into this world to show us a new image of God. Not a distant, angry patriarch, but a tender, loving Father."

Thomas studied his hands. Perhaps one needed to be a father to comprehend these things. But then he recalled a young midshipman who had failed dismally in his duties. Thomas could not bring himself to order a flogging for the lad, but chose a lesser punishment. In gratitude, that young officer, now Lieutenant Wayland, had become devoted to duty *and* to Thomas. If the old earl had ever once shown mercy to him, he would have walked through fire for the man. "You've given me much to think about."

"And do not forget the value of praying." Freddy's mild smile conveyed only acceptance. "We can talk again before you leave." A hint of mischief lit his eyes. "Too bad you didn't have a chance to take Dinah on a walk out to the arbor last evening."

Thomas laughed, welcoming the change of topic. "Ah, yes. Well, perhaps you can help me with something." Fully aware of how he was exposing himself to mockery, he patted his coat near where the pup had left a muddy print. "I have in my pocket some verses I've been composing since shortly after I met Miss Templeton."

He cleared his throat, surprised at the high feeling this admission caused.

Freddy swiped his hand across his chin. "Verses, eh? You do recall that no Moberly has ever been a poet."

Thomas chewed the inside of his cheek. "But perhaps my mother's side of the family…"

Freddy blinked several times, and his lips quirked to one side. "One can only hope." He coughed into his fist. "By all means, let me hear what you've written." He waved one hand carelessly, an invitation to proceed.

In times past, the gesture would have annoyed Thomas. Now he was grateful to be heard. With much trepidation, he pulled out the sheet of foolscap and cleared his throat. "Fairest beloved lady that I love…" He eyed Freddy, who was holding his lips firmly between his teeth. "A gentle Athena, a pure Aphrodite, Diana's fair sister—"

"You used 'fair' in the first line."

"Ah, so I did." Thomas sighed, long and deep. "Truly rotten, eh?" He could see Freddy was trying hard not to laugh, and he blew out another long breath. "You have my permission to mock me."

Freddy had the grace to shake his head and merely smirk. "As Shakespeare's Benedick would say, we were not born under a rhyming planet."

Thomas ran a finger down the carved chair arm. "I suppose not. But what does a man do when his heart fairly bursts with—" Was he making himself too vulnerable? No. Freddy knew of his devotion. "—with love for his lady?"

"I understand how you feel. My Rachel…well, I never imagined such happiness as I now enjoy as her husband." Freddy rose and limped to the bookcase, pulled out a thin, leather-bound book, and placed it in Thomas's lap. "Page thirty-three."

Thomas read the cover: *Shakespeare's Sonnets, 1609.* He opened the collection and found the page. This time, the sigh that escaped him was filled with relief and admiration. "Shall I compare thee to a summer's day? Thou art more lovely and more temperate. Rough winds do shake the darling buds of May, and—"

"Yes, yes, that's what you want to use." Freddy pulled at his ear. "I am certain, if you must recite something to express your admiration for the lady, this is the best way to do it."

Thomas chuckled at his own foolishness...and vulnerability. In all his life, he had never felt as in harmony with another man as he did now, not even with Jamie Templeton when they had last met in London in '79. Even more than the night before, he felt ballast lifted from his heart and replaced by a soothing balm of friendship. "Thank you, Freddy. I shall go immediately to find Miss Templeton and ask her to marry me without any foolish attempts at poetry."

"A wise plan, brother." This time the humor in Freddy's expression served only to bolster Thomas's courage for the pleasant task before him.

Chapter Twenty

Since no one required her help or companionship, Dinah retrieved her hat from her room and wandered out onto the wide front porch. The morning air was fresh with the scent of pine, but would soon become too hot for much activity. Still, if she stayed under the trees, she could enjoy a pleasant walk.

In the distance, she saw the four East Florida Rangers practicing marksmanship, a reassuring exercise when one considered how close the plantation was to the border with Georgia, where much fighting occurred. She might find that unnerving except for the presence of the garrison, where the two soldiers who had traveled with them had reported immediately after their arrival.

Nearer the house, several black grooms worked with the horses in a fenced yard. Directly in front of the house, two gardeners knelt over the flowers planted inside the circle drive. Petunias, violets, pansies and zinnias blossomed within a border of tall gardenia bushes whose blooms had already fallen for the season.

Dinah ambled down the front steps and around the corner of the white mansion toward the kitchen house, where the aroma of fresh-baked bread filled the air. Nearby, several women bent over wooden tubs, scrubbing clothes. Everyone had a task except her.

Walking across the grassy back lawn, she glanced toward the house. Through a window, she could see Frederick at his desk and, as she moved farther, Thomas. Her heart leaped and her loneliness vanished, if for no other reason than that she knew he desired her company, even if no one else did. Indeed, at that moment he chanced to look out and see her, and his entire countenance brightened. He rose and moved out of her sight.

Her heart hammering against her ribs, Dinah waited and was soon rewarded when he emerged through the small, enclosed back porch. He wore his uniform, as always, but there was a smudge on the front of his blue coat. Several strands of hair had escaped from his queue and draped down his cheek. She had never before seen a single flaw in his grooming and found it charming... and disarming.

"Miss Templeton."

He hurried toward her with long strides, stopping just two feet away, towering over her with all his military magnificence. At that moment, if he had embraced her or even kissed her, she would not have objected, despite their unsecured relationship. Was it possible for a heart to burst with happiness?

"Good morning, Captain Moberly." Her words came out in a breathy rush and she pulled up her fan to wave away the heat in her cheeks.

He looked at the fan, and his smile broadened. "Will you walk with me?" His voice also sounded a bit breathless.

Dinah glanced at the house and saw Frederick standing in the window wearing a wide grin. More heat rushed into her face. "I would enjoy that." She looped her arm around the captain's and let him lead her wherever he would. He chose the path to the spring house.

"A fine day," he said.

"A very fine day."

"'Twill be hot soon."

"A veritable furnace." She could barely hold in a laugh at this silly conversation.

"Oh, bother." He brushed his free hand down the front of his coat, removing only some of the caked gray mud. "I meant to change my coat before I…"

She gazed up at him, and her heart performed another wild leap. Could a man's eyes be any bluer? As blue as the summer sky above them now.

He looked away. "Ah, see all the cranes near the boat slips?"

"Before you what?"

"Hmm? Oh, before I…" He ran a hand through his hair, dislodging more black strands. He stopped walking and blew out a quick breath. "Double bother. I should return to the house at once and have Hinton put me back together."

Dinah longed to reach up and make the repairs herself, but that would defy propriety. Still, she was not going to let him out of her sight until she knew his purpose. If it was what she expected, what she hoped—

"Never mind, Captain, no one here will find fault with your appearance." She tugged on his arm.

Grimacing, he raked his hair over his ear and began to walk again. Soon they came to the arbor near the spring house. The red roses covering the woven oak branches filled the air with a rich perfume.

"Will you sit?" He nodded toward the wrought iron bench inside the half-enclosed space.

"Certainly." Her pulse had slowed during their walk, but it resumed its rapid pace, especially when he sat down not a foot away from her. She removed her hat and laid it beside her, then looked at him expectantly.

"Miss Templeton, have you…" He cleared his throat. "Have you ever held your fan up to the sunlight?"

A swell of happiness washed over her. So she had not imagined it. "Yes." She spread the fan and lifted it before them. Enough sunlight filtered through the oak and pine branches to show a scene she had come to treasure.

He inched closer on the bench and peered at the object. "What do you see?" His soft, deep voice sent a pleasant shiver over her shoulders.

"When you first gave it to me," she whispered, "all I could see was a lonely lady on one side and a lonely gentleman on the other, each standing in their separate gardens and reaching out for what seemed unattainable."

"But now?"

"With the light shining through, I see a lady and a man holding hands." Sweet agony filled her soul. For weeks she had longed for this moment, but feared it would never happen.

He bent his head near hers and took her free hand. "Miss Templeton, I should like to hold hands with you… for the rest of my life." He cleared his throat. "A clumsy way of saying…asking if you will marry me."

She leaned against his shoulder, swallowing hard to quiet her happy tears. "I will."

He bent closer and brushed his lips across hers. Such a simple gesture, but the feelings sweeping through Dinah in response were at once riotous and serene, passionate and tender.

"I do believe—" his voice rumbled low beside her

ear, sending another pleasant shiver over her "—I fell in love with you the moment I saw you."

"Thomas—"

He pulled her to her feet and into his arms, stopping her words with another kiss, a firm, eager kiss that made her knees weak. Just as she began to respond, he broke contact, stepped back and walked out of the arbor. As she began to wonder what she had done amiss, he returned and resettled the both of them on the bench. He leaned away from her and rested against the woven arbor wall, while a sweet, gentle smile graced his firm lips, a smile that beamed clear up to his eyes. "My dear Miss Templeton, you leave me breathless."

She fanned herself furiously and stared out into the forest. "I must return the compliment, Captain Moberly." Gracious, how could she contain these warm feelings of love and affection?

"I want you to know that I spoke to Freddy and Marianne, and they both approve of our match."

She stopped fanning and eyed him. "Would you have proposed without their approval?"

His forehead creased briefly. "Perhaps. But not without your brother's, or at least your uncle's. Freddy has assured me these gentlemen will have no objections."

She laughed softly. "They've all been planning our marriage for several years."

"I suppose so. Jamie sang your praises more than once when we last met. Now I understand why. But I find myself thinking someone else had a hand in the plan, too."

Dinah questioned him with one raised eyebrow.

"Who else but the Almighty...our heavenly Father... could have arranged our 'accidental' meeting?" He ran a finger down her cheek. "Your beauty attracted me from that first moment at the hospital. Your kind deeds to the sick deeply moved me, because I saw your generosity and goodness. But the thing that won my heart—" he gave her a little smirk "—was your delicious wit and good humor."

She laughed in earnest now. "I do love that best about you, too, Thomas. Oh! May I call you that?" Had he noticed her slip of the tongue just moments ago?

He bent forward and touched his forehead to hers, an endearing gesture that made her heart race once again. "Only if I may call you Dinah."

"Indeed you may." She thought he might kiss her again, but he moved back. She could not help the tiniest pout of disappointment.

He patted her hand, then squeezed it. "There will be time enough for many kisses, my beloved. My lady fair—" He stopped and bit his lip, and she wondered why. "If I could but put the feelings of my heart into words…but alas, I am no poet." His countenance fell, and he appeared truly disappointed.

She tilted her head and lifted her open fan. "If you continue to bring me such charming gifts as this, we may altogether forgo the dubious pleasures of poetry, for all I care."

"You do not care for poetry?" His eyes widened, as if he were mildly alarmed.

"Very little, I'm afraid." She searched his face. "Why?"

"Oh, nothing." He coughed lightly into his fist. "Good old Freddy," he muttered.

"What?"

Another smirk, or perhaps more of a playful grin. "Isn't this a delightful arbor? Did you know Freddy built it for the very purpose of proposing to Rachel?"

"Yes, I do. What romantic gentlemen the Moberly brothers are." Gladness filled Dinah's heart. Had the captain, her Thomas, reconciled with his good brother? "Handsome, charming, heroic. My, what other of your attributes may I praise?"

Thomas stiffened, but she could see it was a pretense for annoyance. "I cannot disagree with your assessment, except for 'heroic.' When has my little brother ever fought for king and country?" He lifted his chin and frowned, but his cross expression quickly dissolved into wryness. "I do not mean to be unkind."

Understanding swept through Dinah's mind. "So you did not know that Frederick was wounded fighting with Browne's Rangers against the rebels."

"Ah!" Thomas looked as if he'd been struck, and he gripped the hilt of his sword. "He did not tell me. No one told me." He exhaled a long breath. "All this time, I thought—" He shook his head. "God forgive me, I have judged him harshly. Now we both have much to discuss. Much to forgive."

"You will find him a most forgiving man." Dinah grasped Thomas's hand. "Let's return to the house. By now everyone is up and about. You'll want to see our new niece." She debated whether or not to tell him the baby's name, but decided to leave that to Marianne. "And we have our own good news to share."

She stood and tugged him to his feet, but before she could lead him to the pathway, he pulled her into his arms and claimed another lingering kiss.

"My beloved," he whispered, "you have brought me only joy. Stay well. Stay safe while I am gone away from you."

She rested her head against his broad chest. "You must sail out on patrol again, I suppose." She toyed with a brass button on his coat and brushed away some of the remaining mud. "I don't suppose you could simply keep your ship safely in the harbor."

She could hear his chuckle rumbling in his chest. "My dear, a ship may indeed be safe in its harbor, but that is not why ships are built."

Fear swept in and tried to steal her contentment, but she gazed up at Thomas, willing away her despair. "Then I shall repeat your orders back to you, Captain Moberly. Stay well. Stay safe while you are gone away from me."

Chapter Twenty-One

Thomas had learned early in his naval career that a captain must be able to manage any number of crises at the same time. The path to success began with prioritizing. At this moment, walking with his beloved lady along the pathway beneath the oak and magnolia trees, he must first ensure her peace of mind in regard to their coming separation. But even as they chatted about future matters—where they would live, the procuring of servants—his mind reeled from Dinah's revelation about Freddy.

Why had his brother refused to explain his wound when Thomas asked about it? He should have been proud to describe the battle in which he had participated. Defending the borders of East Florida was key to keeping the rebellion from spreading here.

Thomas thought back to his arrival and the cold way they had greeted each other. In less than two days, they had moved a short distance beyond childhood rivalries, prayed together for the safe delivery of Marianne's child and chatted about several important matters, not the least of which was how Thomas should court Dinah. Had Thomas blustered on with his ill-conceived poetry, she might have discovered a flaw she could not overlook. Now he realized what folly his attempts had been. Yet rather than feeling humiliated, he felt grateful for and humbled by Freddy's honesty in helping him. His brother's amusement at Thomas's ineptitude only added to the richness of the incident.

"Before you leave, you must meet Reverend Johnson, the vicar at St. Andrew's Church in St. Johns Towne." Dinah drew Thomas's attention back to their betrothal. "He has officiated at two of our families' marriages." She gazed up at him with a sweet smile that earned her a quick kiss. The warmth of her response reminded him that he must temper his ardor, for she appeared to have no idea how she affected him. Her innocence made his heart swell with admiration and protectiveness.

"Ahem—" She fanned herself, and he congratulated himself once again on giving her such an ideal gift that had communicated his feelings so perfectly. "As I was saying, perhaps we might consider asking him to perform our wedding ceremony, too."

"Why, certainly. Reverend Kennedy seems the obvious choice."

Dinah released his arm and stopped. "We've not been betrothed for fifteen minutes, and you have already ceased listening to me."

The merry glint in her eye made it clear she was not upset, yet Thomas chided himself. Perhaps his skill at handling multiple problems was confined to commanding his ship. These personal matters almost had his head spinning.

"Forgive me." He bent forward in an elaborate bow. "Your acceptance of my proposal has sent me into transports of unrelenting joy. I hear only the birds singing their congratulations above us."

She snickered. "So you are a poet, after all?"

He shuddered comically. "You have my permission to break off with me should I try to claim that talent." *Again.*

"Never. You are mine, and I shall not let you go." She took his arm again, and they continued their stroll. "Where would you like to be married? And by whom?"

"Hmm. I admire Reverend Kennedy, but if you prefer Reverend Johnson, I will not protest." Another thought along those lines came to his mind. "My dearest Dinah, let this be the rule for our lives together. In matters such as this, when neither of us has a strong opinion, you may choose what you will. I desire only your happiness."

She laid her head against his arm and sighed, apparently satisfied with his response. Deep contentment filled him, and he placed an arm around her waist. With this woman by his side, he could face any trial. He would gladly give her whatever she asked for, but she seemed to want so little.

Ah, but he knew one thing she desired: her brother's safety. Once again, Thomas vowed to see Nighthawk apprehended and hanged so that Jamie Templeton could sail to and from St. Augustine without fear of being accosted by the pirate. This Thomas would do not only for Dinah but for Marianne and her children.

And now he had a new weapon in his arsenal to ensure his success. He would not come before the Almighty as to a distant, angry father whom he could never please. Or appease. Although he did not yet grasp the entire idea, he would try instead to pray to a Father whose love moved Him to give His children bread, not a stone. Just as Thomas would gladly give Dinah anything she asked for and would never harm her, he would now come to God expecting acceptance, not judgment.

Father in heaven, grant me victory over this pirate. Help me to deliver Dinah's brother—Marianne's beloved husband—safely home to those who love him.

Dinah could not decide whether she would prefer to dash back to the house to announce their betrothal or to stroll back at this pleasant, leisurely pace to have more time alone with Thomas. Her emotions teetered between giddy happiness and sublime ecstasy. Somehow, from the first moment they'd met, she'd known deep inside they would come to this. Despite of her former doubts and fears, she knew now that he loved her. And oh, how she did love him.

Mrs. Thomas Moberly. Or was that Mrs. Captain Moberly? She must learn. And what else must a captain's wife know to keep from embarrassing her husband? During her occasional visits to the plantation over these past few years, she had observed Marianne's gracious manners and tried to emulate them. Even Rachel had polished her practical Nantucket ways to become a more accomplished plantation manager's wife. If snobbish Governor Tonyn should ever deign to visit Bennington Plantation, he would find nothing lacking in his hostess.

"Are you pleased with this Nancy who has been your lady's maid?" Thomas applied a light pressure to her waist.

In response, she moved closer to him. How interesting to find their nearness did not prevent a steady walking pace. She had never walked in such closeness with anyone, much less the man she would marry. "In truth, I don't know what to expect, so whatever she does pleases me." Would he find her lacking in this?

"Ah. Well, my man Hinton has much experience as a personal servant, and he can teach her, should you decide you like her."

Another giddy swell rose inside Dinah at the thought. "I thank you. That's very considerate. I will keep her here and decide by the time we return to St. Augustine."

"Very good."

Through the trees, she saw the white clapboard plantation house, and a mixture of happiness and regret filled her. Soon everyone would know of their betrothal. Soon Thomas must return to duty.

As they neared the back lawn, Dinah saw the children at play, with Caddy in attendance. Poor Caddy, a sweet slave girl who was devoted to Frederick and Rachel. But the job seemed a bit much for her. Dinah guessed the twelve-year-old was too young to manage such active children. Perhaps, being a slave, she feared to discipline the master's offspring, feared being sent to the fields. But that would be too cruel.

As always, Dinah could not reconcile her cousins' ownership of slaves with their Christian faith. But then, Frederick did not truly own the slaves. As manager of the plantation, he had the responsibility to supervise everything and everyone, while the real owner was Lord Bennington. She knew Frederick to be a kind man and had never seen him mistreat a slave or anyone under his authority as magistrate. Rachel often said he ruled with the wisdom of Solomon. Dinah must leave it at that, just as she must leave Thomas to his duty.

By the time the two of them had entered the yard, the noise of the children had reached a riotous volume. There on the ground, little Jamie rolled about with smaller Davy, each hitting and kicking the other, both crying, while Kezia tried to jump into the fray. Caddy managed to hold the back of Kezia's linen dress, but Dinah thought she heard the fabric begin to tear. The ever-present puppies yipped and yapped and bounced about as though encouraging the fight.

"Nooo," Davy screeched with all the passion of an indignant two-year-old. "Mine, mine."

"Gimme it," little Jamie ordered, as if he were the captain over all.

"Oh, dear." Dinah felt tears spring to her eyes. Taking sides was out of the question with all of these children so precious to her.

"Excuse me, my dear."

Thomas broke away from her and towered over the melee, receiving a sharp kick to one shin for his efforts. Only mildly deterred, he grabbed Jamie's shirt just as Frederick appeared and seized Davy. Each man had to subdue his prisoner by wrapping strong arms around a small body and giving sharp commands to "stop this instant." Both boys obeyed without protest. Davy nestled into his father's neck and wailed. Jamie stuck a thumb in his mouth and leaned away from Thomas, glaring at him.

"Now, see here." Frederick spoke in a stern voice to both miscreants. "What's all this about?"

"He took my gun." Jamie pointed to the carved wooden weapon on the ground.

"My gun," Davy cried.

"Well, neither of you shall have it." Frederick eyed Thomas and tilted his head toward the back steps. "We shall have no more of this." He set Davy on the bottom step, and Thomas placed little Jamie beside his cousin.

The two men loomed over the little boys, who stared up at them, wide-eyed. Jamie continued to suck his thumb, and Davy pulled at a lock of his own blond hair.

"Now," Frederick said, "you will sit here until you decide to share your toys and play nicely together." He wagged a finger at each one. "You are kinsmen, practically brothers. These fights will not continue. Do you understand me?"

Two pairs of eyes, one blue, one brown, blinked back tears. Two little blond heads nodded in unison. Dinah thought her heart would melt, but she dared not interfere. Indeed, Frederick did have the wisdom of Solomon.

"Very well." Frederick motioned to Caddy.

She hurried to him, with Kezia in her wake. "Mister Frederick, I'm so sorry."

Frederick ran a hand through his hair, loosening many strands from his queue. Now he and Thomas almost looked like twins, except that Thomas wore the darker frown. Dinah wondered if he disapproved of Frederick's discipline.

"Caddy," Frederick said, "you are to watch over the boys and make certain they do not move. You have my permission to use whatever means necessary to keep them here."

"Yes, Mister Frederick." Caddy put her hands on her hips and glowered at the children. They turned their wide-eyed attention to her.

Frederick pointed to the door above the boys. "Kezia, go to your mother."

As always, four-year-old Kezia pouted. "But, *Papá*—"

"Do as I say." The authority resonating through his voice also carried a certain tenderness.

"I'll take her." Dinah stepped forward. "Come along, Kezia."

Kezia brightened, as if nothing was amiss. "Aunt Dinah, I made a doll." She clasped Dinah's hand…and her heart at the same time.

"Oh, my. You must show me." Before entering the doorway, Dinah sent Thomas a rueful smile. His responding nod communicated his understanding. They would have to wait to share their good news. She wondered if his frown meant he felt as disappointed as she did.

Chapter Twenty-Two

Once again, Thomas scrambled to sort out the chaos in his mind over the happenings in his brother's household. On his ship, he would have ordered the brawlers flogged. Of course children could not be flogged, but surely a swat or two to their posteriors would have taught a more lasting lesson than sitting on a step with an indulgent servant overseeing them.

But as he stepped away from the scene, he suddenly felt bereft. His son would have been just a little older than wee Jamie, and holding this nephew—no matter the circumstances—had filled an empty spot that had long pained him.

Still, there was a bright moment in the middle of it all. Dinah had proven her pluck by stepping in and carting off their pretty little niece. And while that child could also use a bit of discipline, Thomas knew he would never have the heart to swat a daughter. As for his betrothed, he could well imagine her as a wise and gentle mother. The thought of her giving him a son brought him less trepidation than he'd felt before Marianne's safe delivery.

"Well." Freddy clapped him on the shoulder. "How did it go?"

Thomas stared at his grinning brother, wondering for a moment what he referred to. "Ah, you mean my walk with Dinah."

Freddy laughed. "Given that she is now Dinah rather than Miss Templeton, you have answered my question."

Thomas permitted contentment to sweep away his crossness over the situation with the children. "Indeed, she has made me the happiest of men."

"I understand." Freddy waved his cane toward the stable. "Shall we walk? I want to inspect one of my mares."

"Lead on." Thomas welcomed this chance to talk more with his brother. Although he no longer felt annoyed about the situation with the children, he felt compelled to offer a word of advice on managing them. "Do the boys fight often?"

Freddy's eyebrows rose as if he was surprised by the question. "Oh, that." He chuckled. "Yes, several times a day." He sent Thomas a sidelong glance. "They are very much like brothers." His lips formed a thin line, but whether from displeasure over the incident or pain from walking, Thomas could not tell.

Now he wondered which topic to bring up first. He decided on the most immediate one. "We did have a brawl or two, didn't we?" He tried to conjure up some amusement over the situation, but none came. Instead, a bitter memory surfaced. "And since I was usually the victor, I've long suspected that Father sent me away to protect you." As the words came out, they sounded petty, foolish, an unfortunate childhood memory any grown man should have dealt with years ago.

Freddy stopped and leaned on his cane. "Is that what you think?"

Honesty forced his response. "Yes."

Freddy stood there staring at him, but behind those gray eyes, he seemed to be deep in thought. After a moment, he resumed walking, and Thomas fell in beside him.

"I wish," Freddy said, "that I could laugh over that last fight we had, but in truth, I barely survived it."

Now Thomas grasped Freddy's arm and stopped him. "What? What are you saying?"

Freddy blinked and moved back a bit, as if he thought Thomas might attack him. "You gave me a concussion, broke my arm and nearly broke my back. I was in bed for six months." He shook his head, clearly and *rightfully* troubled by the memory. "Do you mean to say you don't know this?"

For a moment, Thomas could not breathe, could not think. Nor could he recall the rage he'd felt, as though he might justify such actions. But those feelings had long ago been eradicated from his character as he learned military discipline. At that moment, like the sun bursting through storm clouds, the reason for his banishment became clear. No matter the cause for his uncontrolled temper, Father had been right to send him away before he murdered his own brother.

"No, I did not know." Why had no one told him how much damage his temper had inflicted? He set a hand on Freddy's shoulder. "W-will you forgive me?" Emotion closed off any further words, but the horror of what his brother had just disclosed weighed heavy on his soul.

Freddy's troubled countenance softened, and he clasped Thomas's shoulder in return. "I forgave you long ago, Tommy." He grunted. "More for myself than for you. As my father-in-law says, holding on to bitterness can destroy a man. Best to forgive the person who has offended him."

"I must meet this man." Thomas had served under a captain like that, but for far too brief a time to absorb all the wisdom the man might have imparted to him.

Freddy nodded, but his smile was less than agreeable. "Perhaps one day." He broke away and started off toward the stables again.

The heavy smells of horseflesh and hay, intensified by the summer heat, greeted them at the long, low building. But it was no worse than the bilge water and unwashed men on his ship.

The six or seven busy grooms stopped their work and gave Freddy their attention. He spoke to the head groom about the horses, inquired of another about his family, complimented the youngest among them on duty well done—all the same sort of loyalty-inspiring gestures Thomas would execute as captain of his ship. And now he must admit that in less than two days he had gone from bitterly resenting his younger brother to discovering him to be a remarkable, nay, a superior man. And rather than chafing from this knowledge, he felt a wave of fraternal pride surging through his chest.

They inspected the horses together, and Thomas noted with satisfaction that the grooms had given great care to his mount, as though he were a part of this stable. And the mare in question was pronounced docile enough for Kezia's first riding lessons. Then they began their journey back to the house.

In this day of much drama, Thomas hesitated to approach another serious subject. But his brother's marked and clearly aching limp pained him, too. As they passed beyond the stable fencing, he noticed the Rangers in a field practicing their maneuvers.

"Fine lads, those Rangers." He waved a hand in that direction. "Taking time from their plantations and businesses to keep the rebels out of this colony."

"Governor Tonyn requires every citizen to serve in that capacity."

"Even a magistrate?" Thomas noticed a slight grimace in Freddy's profile.

"No. But then, I suppose it's been Father's influence that caused the governor to exempt me."

Thomas once again stopped his brother. "Stubble it, Freddy. Dinah told me how you were wounded. Why won't you admit you were serving the king's interests in fighting against the rebels in their last incursion over the Georgia border?"

Freddy swiped a hand over his eyes. "Dear Dinah. She's determined to get it wrong. I was delivering arms and ammunition to the battlefield." He shook his head and began walking again. "Not terribly heroic. Just didn't realize I was supposed to duck when the enemy began firing."

Thomas swallowed back another surge of emotions. Very well, he would let his brother manage his own feelings about the event. But in his estimation, Freddy's actions equaled any soldier's or sailor's for heroism. Why, His Majesty's Navy depended upon naval transport vessels for ammunition and other stores. Not every man could fight. Some must work behind the lines to ensure victory. But he would not press the issue with his brother.

Of all the offenses he had held against Freddy, only one remained. Why had he not brought Dinah to live here, safely away from that Hussey fellow? At the least, either he or that much-praised uncle might have managed her inheritance so that Hussey could pose no threat to her security. But all that was of no consequence now. He would marry Dinah soon and make certain her every need was met. Thus he could overlook his brother's failing in the matter.

They walked around to the back of the house and to Thomas's shock, his nephews were chasing their puppies and each other around in circles, giggling with childish abandon. He could not restrained a chuckle, which Freddy echoed.

"There," his brother said. "It works every time. They always decide it's better to share a toy than to fight over it…or have it taken away."

Thomas could only shake his head. When the time came, he knew where he would come for advice in how to raise his children.

Dinah sat cross-legged on the nursery floor and rocked Kezia's doll. It was nothing more than a small stuffed linen pillow held together with wide childish stitches. But Rachel had sewn on a smiling face and made a blue cotton gown, and Kezia clearly loved the thing. Dinah felt privileged to be entrusted with its care. In the meantime, Kezia fussed with the tiny sheets in the doll's cradle, a miniature of the one where the new baby, Maria, slept.

At last Dinah felt useful. When she'd brought her niece upstairs, they'd tiptoed to Marianne's room and spent several enchanted moments gazing upon the newborn infant and watching Joanna change her. Then they came to the nursery and reenacted the scene. Kezia treated her doll with a tenderness that foreshadowed good mothering skills, and Dinah felt her own arms ache to hold a new life made with Thomas. Until then, oh, how she longed to stay here, never to go back to St. Augustine. She would miss Anne, but she would not miss Artemis's constant badgering to give him control of her money. Of course, that problem would soon be solved. And no longer could he try to force her into an unwanted marriage.

Joy upon joy filled her heart and mind. Maybe after she and Thomas were married, she could stay here more often, for instance, during his longer voyages. As a wife, she would have more in common with her cousin and sister-in-law. Then maybe they wouldn't stop talking when she entered the room. Or send her off to be with the children, although that part did not entirely displease her. Still, she longed for the company of women who loved her and whose loyalties to their husbands would not be compromised by confiding in her, as Anne's were.

"Miss Dinah." Caddy entered the room carrying a tray of food and followed by little Jamie and Davy. "Miss Rachel says you should come down and eat a bite."

"Thank you, Caddy." She gave the doll back to Kezia and kissed her playmate. "Thank you for playing with me. And tomorrow, I shall sketch your pictures, all of you."

The child threw her arms around Dinah's neck and squeezed hard. "I love you, Aunt Dinah." The boys added their hugs and "luff you" and "wub oo."

With that sweet affirmation, Dinah's heart swelled with love. The children filled an empty spot within her that their parents knew nothing about. She made her way down the hallway to freshen up in her room, then descended the front stairs in time to hear a duet of male voices laughing in the drawing room. In the brief instant between reaching the door and being noticed by the men, her heart once again soared with happiness. Thomas looked so at ease, so at peace. All the reserve he'd exhibited toward Frederick seemed to have vanished. In its place, she saw genuine affection for his brother.

"My darling." Thomas crossed the room, took her hand and kissed her cheek. His warm breath fanned down her neck and gave her a pleasant shiver. "Come join us. We're waiting to be called for the midday meal. Are you hungry?"

Only for your company. "A little, I suppose." She saw Frederick's knowing smile and looked up at Thomas. "Have you told everyone?"

"Not Marianne. I'd hoped to see her and the baby, but no doubt I will have to camp outside her door until she wakes the next time." His blue eyes sparkled in the sunlight streaming in through the tall drawing room windows.

"It will be worth the wait. She's so beautiful, Thomas. A baby is truly a miracle. So tiny and perfect." She wondered what color their children's eyes would be, what color their hair. Brown and blond like hers, or blue and black like his? His warm gaze made her wonder if he was thinking the same thing.

"Dinah!" Rachel rushed into the room and pulled her into a fierce embrace. "I'm so happy for you, cousin."

Dinah returned her hug. "Thank you." She wanted to ask if she could stay here, but could not find the words.

"And now," Rachel said, "you can buy or rent your own home in St. Augustine so you'll be there when Thomas returns from his voyages."

"Oh. Yes. Of course." Dinah glanced at Thomas, whose benign smile gave no indication he knew of her struggle. But Rachel was right. After they married, she would want to make a home for him in his ship's temporary port. And after the war, they would go to England, an exciting prospect they had discussed this morning on the way back from the arbor. Yes, she would willingly sail across the wide ocean or wherever Thomas took her, as long as she could be with him.

Chapter Twenty-Three

"Tell me more about your house in Portsmouth."
Dinah walked with her arm looped around Thomas's,
treasuring the security his presence provided on this
walk through the plantation woodlands. "Will I have a
garden and a kitchen house?"

He patted her hand, as he did when about to correct
her. She did not mind, for she had freely confessed to
him that she had much to learn.

"Yes, you shall have your garden, for both flowers
and vegetables, if it gives you pleasure. But the kitchen
is inside the house."

"I see." She thought of her Boston cousin, whose
kitchen was indoors, and was satisfied with the picture.
"And how many rooms?" Once there, she would have
to set up a cleaning schedule and hoped that sweeping
and dusting once a day would be sufficient.

"Eighteen."

Dinah gasped. "Oh, my. Why, how shall I ever—?"
She clamped her mouth shut. Somehow she would
manage. Perhaps some of the rooms could be shut off
and the furniture covered when not in use.

He peered beneath her hat brim, and his pursed lips

seemed an attempt not to laugh. "My darling, you will have servants to help you. Our home is actually quite modest, but will be sufficient for our needs."

"I see." Eighteen rooms made a modest home? Frederick and Rachel's house had twelve rooms, yet Dinah found the plantation dwelling quite commodious. She could not imagine what could fill more rooms.

Thomas had already told her the house came into his possession upon his marriage to Ariel, the only child of a baron. At times, she felt a pang of sorrow for Thomas's first wife. But he spoke of her with mild detachment, and Dinah could see he had managed his grief, as every person must do in his or her own way. She had little knowledge of English laws regarding inheritance but would gladly hand over her own small fortune to his control upon their marriage. But the words "*our* home" had sent a wave of happiness through her. Whatever was his would now be hers. Whatever was hers would now be his.

In the shade of a spreading magnolia tree, he pulled her around in front of him and gently pushed her hat off so that it hung by its ribbons down her back. He traced her cheek with one finger, then lifted her chin and gave her a quick kiss.

"Dinah, my love, these five days have been the happiest of my life. Our visits to St. Johns Towne and our picnics on the river have done much to relax me and prepare me to return to duty." He gave her another quick kiss. "I like your Reverend Johnson and found his sermon yesterday to be thought-provoking. If you wish for him to perform our marriage, I will be pleased with that arrangement."

Emotion caught in her throat, and she laid her head against his chest. No one had ever cared about her preferences as Thomas did. He put a warm, comforting hand on her shoulder but did not pull her any closer. Even in that he took care of her. While his fervent love and affection showed in his intense gazes and tender smiles, he would not ask for more than sweet, chaste kisses. In return, she forbade herself to cling to him now that his departure loomed near.

"I know only," she said, "that I do not wish for a long engagement."

His chuckle resounded through his broad chest, tickling her ear. "Nor do I, my beloved. Nor do I."

Thomas felt himself a changed man. If duty did not demand his presence aboard the *Dauntless,* he cared not if he ever went to sea again. How easy it would be to live the life of a gentleman farmer, like Freddy. With Dinah at his side, he would never lack for contentment. He could build his own haven in Hampshire, but unlike Bennington Plantation, he would do it without slaves.

One regret was inherent in that plan. He would be an ocean away from this good brother. Thomas had never found his eldest brother, the new earl, to be anything but an arrogant idler who relied on his birthright to the peerage to designate him a man. His next brother, Robert, had often been his partner in childhood mischief, but those days were years in the past. With Freddy, he had at last found a friend whom he could respect and confide in.

He had greatly enjoyed dispensing the gifts he'd brought from London to his family members: new parasol and kid gloves for Rachel and Marianne, play swords for little Jamie and Davy, a gold thimble and child-sized sewing scissors for Kezia, Gibbon's recently published *The History of the Decline and Fall of the*

Roman Empire for Freddy. Thomas was gratified by the appreciation heaped upon him by one and all, even the moppets.

There remained only a few matters he needed to discuss with Freddy before he left on the morrow. But for now, in the precious moments they had remaining, Thomas enjoyed walking arm-in-arm with his beloved Dinah along the path back to the plantation house.

"How long will you stay here?" he asked.

The troubled frown on her brow surprised him. "I don't know. I'd hoped Rachel would help me with my wedding clothes. She is an excellent seamstress."

"Ah, very good. But why not stay?" He squeezed her arm against his side to reassure her. "I will be gone for at least two weeks, if not longer, for I am determined to catch the pirate this time. He shall not escape me. But that is another matter. I would prefer that you be with those who love you, not that Hussey fellow."

Her sweet smile did not agree with the sadness in her eyes. "I shall stay as long as I am welcome."

"But of course you are welcome here." Uncertainty clouded his thoughts. Surely the ladies did not exclude their cousin and sister-in-law. He had observed only warmth from Rachel and Marianne toward Dinah.

She stared down at their pathway. "Yes, of course."

Another matter to bring up with Freddy. His brother must protect Dinah in Thomas's absence.

"Oh, Thomas, do you enjoy the children as much as I do?"

He wondered if she was changing the subject to avoid unpleasantness, but decided to accept the happy new topic. "They are…what word says it all? Enchanting." When he had at last seen his sister and newborn niece, their glowing pink complexions had removed the last of his fears. Some women could bear children; others could not. When the time came, he would trust his Father in heaven to see Dinah safely through it.

This new view of the Almighty had given him a peace in his soul such as he had never experienced. These past five days, he had read the Scripture passages Freddy had suggested concerning the nature of God as a loving Father. Each night, he had lain awake contemplating the matter and praying, as his brother also had suggested. At first, he'd felt considerable resentment toward his father for being such a callous, unloving parent. But he recalled that the old earl had often boasted of his own father's harsh discipline and how it had made a man of him. With this in mind, Thomas found it easier to forgive his parent, for he had merely followed the path laid out before him.

Yet did not the very Gospel of Christ dispense with such methods of parenting? If all men bore the stain of sin on their souls, as Scripture made clear, then all men deserved everlasting punishment. But God sent His Son to atone for that sin. He did not beat or chastise His children, because Christ had already suffered beating and even death in their stead. A man need only believe in Christ and reach out to accept that atonement, as John 3:16 clearly stated.

Freddy had broken from their father's sort of parenting. When the time came, Thomas would endeavor to do the same.

But the greatest revelation from meditating on the scripture came when Thomas began to comprehend how they would change his own thinking. God, the Almighty Creator, was not an angry, distant parent. He was a loving Father who was always near to lead and guide his children. Thomas could rely upon Him in matters large and small. And he vowed to begin immediately to make that his practice. It would affect everything he thought and said and did. Truly, he was a new man.

That evening, Thomas joined Freddy in his study for a last meeting before he returned to duty. Seated across the desk from his brother, he treasured each moment as they settled the last of their business. "I trust you found Bennington's letter satisfactory?"

Freddy's wry chuckle held more than a hint of dryness. "He wrote all the proper greetings and felicitations. But the long and the short of it is that I have now—or should I say *again*—entered a trial period as manager of Bennington Plantation." He shook his head in apparent disgust. "If profits increase, I may stay. If not—" His shrug seemed a bit careless under the circumstances.

Thomas leaned forward. "But what will you do if he replaces you? What of Rachel and the children? And where would Marianne and *her* children live while Templeton is away?"

"My father-in-law's trip to Jamaica is for the purpose of expanding the business he shares with Templeton. He has always said he would like for me to join their company."

"Ah." Thomas glanced around the room, taking in the shelves of books and the fine furniture. His brother lived in a spacious, well-furnished house, yet it was not his own. "You must know that you can always find a home with Dinah and me in Hampshire. You know the land. There's room enough to build a second house. We could provide another base for Templeton's trade in England."

Freddy stared at him for a moment, then blinked and swiped a hand over his eyes. "I thank you for that,

Tommy. But—" he glanced out the window "—the colonies are my home now. I cannot think of leaving."

"I do not blame you." Thomas snorted. "Infernal war. If it would just end, we'd all be able to make sensible decisions about our futures. You could break loose from Bennington, and I—" He ran a hand over his chin. "Will it surprise you to know I have come to think His Majesty should release the rebelling colonists and let them go their own way?"

Freddy gaped. "I had no idea."

Thomas snickered at his comical expression. He could not yet read his brother well, but something was working in Freddy's mind. "Do not be concerned. I am not some renegade or traitor. Surely you know my thoughts are shared by influential men in Parliament. Nevertheless, I shall do my duty to the end." Why not confess it all? "Then I plan to resign my commission. Dinah does not know it yet, but this will be my wedding gift to her."

Freddy's face was a study in amazement. "I can think of nothing she would like more. She often said she would never marry a seafarer. Then the poor child met you. Despite knowing me these four years, she had no idea how charming we Moberly men are."

"No idea at all." This bit of camaraderie sealed Thomas's devotion to his brother.

"So you think the king should release the thirteen colonies?" One dark eyebrow rose to emphasize the question.

Thomas regarded Freddy. He had been wounded defending East Florida's border and no doubt felt strongly about the war. But an end of hostilities could mean commerce between this colony and the new country to the north, a boon to Templeton's merchant business. "Practically speaking, I cannot imagine that they can form a cohesive government. Who will rule? That Washington fellow? Is he some Charlemagne they will crown as king?" He waved his hand carelessly. "Despite his mythical immortality and cleverness, I've no doubt all would fall into chaos, and they would come running back to the protection of the Crown. But at least no more good English soldiers and sailors would die trying to keep unwilling children under control." His own analogy disturbed him, but he would think on it later.

"Yes, far too many have died during this war." Freddy stood and grasped his cane. "I want you to read something."

As he started around the desk, Thomas rose. "Sit down. What do you want? I'll get it."

Freddy waved him down. "Nonsense. I'm improving every day." He limped to the bookcase and withdrew a familiar object from between two large volumes. "Here. Take this. Read it and tell me if you think the northern colonies can manage on their own."

Thomas accepted the broadsheet, but felt a twinge of disloyalty. "Ah, well, all right." He folded the paper into a smaller square and tucked it inside his coat.

Freddy returned to his desk and, despite his protests, Thomas noticed his clenched jaw. The effort had cost him, and Thomas would honor it by reading the colonists' declaration. As Freddy had said, a man should know the thinking of his enemy.

"I have a letter for you to take to St. Augustine." Freddy brought a sealed missive out of his desk drawer. "This is to Mr. Leslie. He and Mr. Panton are reputable men who have kept me apprised of Dinah's finances. Her money is in safekeeping in their vault. This letter will give them my leave to deliver future reports to you."

Stunned, Thomas accepted the folded vellum sheet.

"Reports?" He studied the finely grained lambskin, an expenditure designating an important matter. "You have watched over her all this time?"

Freddy coughed out an indignant laugh. "Of course. Someone has to keep Artemis Hussey's greedy hands off of her money. Every time he approaches Leslie about the matter, I hear about it within a day or two."

Emotion welled up in Thomas's chest, and so he echoed his brother's indignant cough. "Yes. Well. I thank you for taking care of her."

Freddy gave him a crooked grin. "That's your job now."

The perfect opening. "But until I can officially take on that delightful duty, perhaps you will continue to extend your hospitality to Dinah. She would welcome Rachel's help in making her wedding clothes."

"Hmm." An invisible wall seemed to spring up before Freddy's formerly warm gaze. "I would not deny my wife's exceptional skill with a needle. However, with the house to manage and Marianne and her children to look after, I fear she will not have time to complete the work when Dinah needs it. There is a fine seamstress in St. Augustine, a widow named Mrs. Cameron, who surely can undertake the endeavor."

After a moment of smarting from this rejection on behalf of his beloved, Thomas understood. Freddy was looking out for his wife and did not wish for her to be overburdened. "Yes, of course. I will encourage Dinah to return to the city as soon as possible and engage Mrs. Cameron's services."

Yet in the back of his mind, he felt disappointed that Rachel would not extend herself for this short time so that her own cousin might have her help. Did they not have enough slaves to perform all the necessary tasks about this place? Did Rachel truly not realize how left-out Dinah often felt?

But, no, Thomas would not allow bitterness to enter his thinking. Not when he'd finally bonded so closely with this brother, the only one with whom he shared so many common interests and opinions. The one who had already done so much to take care of Dinah, without her even knowing it. He did not need to ask another favor of Freddy, for soon enough, he himself would ensure Dinah's happiness.

Chapter Twenty-Four

The entire family crowded onto the columned front porch to see Thomas off. Enfolded in his embrace, Dinah trembled in spite of her resolve not to cling to him. How could she let him go? How would she ever manage without him? But her determination won out, and she shoved him away.

"Go on, now. The sooner you go, the sooner you'll return." She forbade her burning eyes to produce tears.

His smile was as gentle as his finger tracing down her cheek. "Pray that I catch the pirate quickly. That will earn me some time off." He placed a lingering kiss on her lips and rested his forehead against hers. "I shall return to you."

Her aching heart warmed at his promise, more so than all the other times he had said it. This time, she believed him without reservation.

Hugs, kisses, handshakes, Davy clinging to his Uncle Thomas's leg and the ever-present wriggling puppies made a merry pandemonium. Even Marianne had come downstairs to see him off and now clung to him with a strange desperation. When she finally released him, he declared himself the happiest of men to have such a loving family. Frederick quipped that Thomas had become lazy and would have difficulty returning to duty after such a long respite. Dinah laughed with everyone else and found that it lightened her heavy spirit. At least a little.

At last, Thomas gave her a final kiss, descended the front steps, and mounted his horse. The four East Florida Rangers had completed their patrol duties and were returning to the city with Thomas. Hinton cast a lingering glance toward Nancy, and Dinah's maid blushed. The steward then climbed into Mr. Moultrie's coach, and the travelers commenced their journey.

Dinah stood with the family on the porch and watched the procession. Thomas turned in his saddle and waved, and everyone else seemed to take that as a sign they could disperse. Dinah alone remained to watch as the group neared the cluster of palm trees beside the road into the pine forest. There Thomas waved again, then disappeared behind the trees.

She stared toward the palm branches swaying in the warm summer breeze. Perhaps Thomas would emerge from the forest and return to her. The hollow ache in her chest reminded her of the folly of her hopes. After sitting on the porch steps for uncounted minutes—or hours?—she wandered to the side of the house and settled into the swing hanging from a branch of a spreading oak tree. The gentle motion lulled her into a hazy stupor from which she could not waken. But why bother? She had completed the sketches of the children, her one unique talent in this family. No matter how much she tried to stifle her self-pity, she ached to think no one needed her here. Perhaps she should have returned to St. Augustine with Thomas.

The noise of a small riot broke into her thoughts. The children and their pets ran toward her from the back lawn, with Caddy in pursuit. They all seemed to see her at the same time and stopped abruptly.

Kezia marched toward her. "Aunt Dinah, I think it's my turn to swing."

"Miss Kezia, don't be rude." Caddy sent Dinah an apologetic grimace.

Dinah shook herself. "Never mind, Caddy. Come here, Kezia darling." She stood and placed her niece in the swing, then gave her a gentle shove.

The remainder of the morning passed quickly, for the children would not let her go. After each one demanded a turn at being pushed in the swing, they decided on a game of tag, with their aunt in pursuit. Dinah had not run in years and found the exercise invigorating. And she found her spirits rising rapidly. Amid the usual giggles, falls, drying of tears and more giggles, she realized her life could not stop because Thomas was away. He would often be gone and for much longer periods than two weeks. Somehow she would endure it and be brave and smiling for him when he returned home.

Thoroughly winded from the last chase, she waved Caddy over and leaned on the girl's shoulder. "Let's try a game of hide and seek."

Caddy giggled, a child herself. "Yes'm."

"You take Davy so he doesn't get lost. I think little Jamie and Kezia will be all right."

"Yes'm," Caddy repeated.

They explained the game and the boundaries to the children, and off they all went.

Dinah sat on the back porch steps. Feeling a bit self-ish, she decided to give them plenty of time to hide… and herself plenty of time to rest.

"How is Marianne?" Frederick's deep voice, so like Thomas's, came through the open back window of his office.

Dinah listened with concern. She'd noticed Marianne's distress when Thomas left and the way she'd clung to him. No doubt she was missing Jamie very badly, a feeling Dinah now understood. And Joanna had confided to her that new mothers sometimes felt weepy, though Dinah could not imagine why.

"Very frightened." Rachel spoke softly. "As am I. To think my brother-in-law and my cousin might—"

"Shh. Do not fret, but trust in the Lord."

Dinah's heart jumped to her throat. She moved to the edge of the step, preparing to dash into the house and demand to know what trouble Thomas and her brother might encounter.

"But what if Thomas catches Jamie? Will he be forced to hang him?" Rachel's voice dissolved into soft sobs.

"Shh, my darling. We must continue to pray. Jamie is serving a cause much greater than any one of us, and he knows the dangers." His soft chuckle sounded forced, even strained. "Remember, Nighthawk never fails, never is caught."

Dinah sank back on the step, barely managing to stop an audible gasp. Jamie was Nighthawk? How could that be? Why, that pirate had stolen part of Jamie's cargo... *Artemis's* part of the cargo. Now that finally made sense. Jamie had never liked Artemis.

But Thomas would soon be in pursuit of Nighthawk... *Jamie,* his friend and soon-to-be brother-in-law. Her mind refused to settle on this bit of madness. It was not true. She'd heard amiss. Frederick and Rachel were playing some terrible game.

No. Worse than a game. They were in sympathy with the rebels. Otherwise, how could they countenance Jamie's piracy? And how could they have offered hospitality to Thomas, their brother and their *enemy?* An oppressive weight pushed down hard on Dinah's chest until she could scarcely breathe. It was no wonder Rachel and Marianne had seldom offered hospitality to her. Had encouraged her to live in St. Augustine. And wanted her to go back there as soon as possible. Her comments against the rebels heaped condemnation on them. And could it be? Were they involved with helping the rebels bring the war to East Florida?

Forcing air into her lungs, she rose from the step and crept around the back of the house. Under a bush, she saw Kezia's pink frock and heard her childish giggles. Farther away, little Jamie peered over a pile of hay. He ducked down when he saw her. Caddy peeked around the front corner of the house, a wide smile revealing her pretty white teeth.

Somehow Dinah managed to "discover" them all, managed to pretend gaiety when she caught them and swung each around into the air. But in truth, her world had just shattered into a thousand pieces, and she had no one to console her.

Thomas scowled at the broadsheet lying across his desk. Contrary to what Freddy might have hoped, this document written by the colonists reinforced exactly what he'd come to believe: the Crown should relinquish all claim to the thirteen colonies, something His Majesty would never agree to. But Thomas had revised his former concern that the rebels would not be able to form a cohesive government.

Why had he thought such a long-lasting war was

being executed by simple farmers? This well-reasoned declaration made it clear that the men leading the rebellion knew exactly what they were doing and why they were doing it. They were not mindless mutineers, but intelligent, honorable men ready to determine their own destiny…with the help of God. Not unlike himself. He was tired of being at the mercy of the Admiralty, being sent hither and thither to defeat a foe whose only objective was freedom, the watchword of every Englishman.

No doubt some of his thoughts were influenced by his personal desire to marry Dinah and return to his home. But who among his superiors would try to stop him? No one. And he no longer wished to be a party to blocking the aspirations of the colonists.

Thomas snorted out a laugh. Freddy would be appalled at the results of his generosity in giving him this paper. Thomas now understood his "enemy" all too well.

Unfortunately, such understanding did not invalidate his orders to find Nighthawk and visit the king's justice upon him. But once that duty was completed, Thomas would resign his commission, marry his beloved and sail home to Hampshire.

He tucked those pleasant dreams into the back of his mind and renewed his determination to leave His Majesty's Navy with honor. He would apprehend the pirate and see him hanged, a final victory to offer his sovereign as a parting gift.

Chapter Twenty-Five

"Dinah?" Rachel spoke through the bedchamber door. "Will you join us for our midday meal?"

Seated beside the window, Dinah clutched a small pillow to her stomach, as if it would settle the turmoil churning there. "No." Courtesy demanded a better answer. "No, thank you."

The door opened, and Rachel entered. "Oh, come now, cousin. Surely you're hungry after playing with the children all morning." She sat on the edge of the bed. "By the by, I thank you for that. They are thoroughly exhausted and did not protest taking their naps. And in Thomas's absence, they are proclaiming you the best of playmates." Despite her cheery tone, her swollen, reddened eyes gave evidence of many tears. Did she really think Dinah would not notice?

Dinah had never believed in deception, but she could not disclose what she'd heard. What could she say? And how could she endure the coming days before she returned to St. Augustine with Dr. Wellsey and Joanna? The good doctor was treating several sick slaves and wanted to stay until their health was assured, however long that took. She could not travel back by herself.

"May I have a tray here in my room?" She could barely manage to look at her cousin. Why was Rachel living here instead of in Boston with all the other rebels in their family? Was Frederick a spy disguised as a loyal Englishman? Why, he'd been wounded in battle! Who had shot him, Ranger or rebel? Such agonizing questions had assaulted her for the past three hours.

Sorrow emanated from Rachel's eyes. "Dear one, we understand your melancholy, Marianne especially, because Jamie must be gone so often on business." She rose and embraced Dinah, and the fragrance of her gardenia perfume sent a bittersweet pang through Dinah's heart. "The Lord will sustain you, as He does her, if only you let Him."

Dinah thrust away bitter thoughts about Jamie and his "business." A bit of dark humor smote her, and she almost laughed. Pirate or not, rebel or not, her brother did love her. Perhaps he'd stolen Artemis's cargo to avenge the way she was treated in the Hussey household. No, more likely he'd used the profits to help the rebel cause. How could Dinah have been so blind as not to notice their subterfuge? But she could think of nothing that would have given any of them away to her. Even Thomas had been fooled.

What had Rachel said? The Lord would sustain her if she let Him? That truly was her only hope. She raised a silent prayer, beseeching God to help her muddle through these next days without her family finding out what she knew about them. And against everything she had previously prayed for, she pled for mercy that Thomas and Jamie would never encounter each other at sea.

The sun sank over the western horizon, and Thomas retired to his cabin. In spite of the rough seas, he anticipated a good night's rest. His approaching marriage and his remarkable reconciliation with Freddy left only one matter unsettled in his life. And this time, he would stay on patrol until he caught Nighthawk and saw the brigand hanged. Then he could resign his commission with dignity and self-respect.

On this, their eighth night at sea, they sailed east without lamps and in the dark of the moon, navigating by the stars and hoping to come upon the pirate without being detected. Thomas had learned from victims of the marauders that in daylight the pirate had tracked them like a shark tracked blood, then seized them at sundown, unloaded their cargo in the night and sailed away before dawn. The last such raid was reported to have taken place over a month ago, giving Nighthawk plenty of time to sail up the coast and deliver his booty to a rebel port and return to strike again. Further, the pirate had a trim ship and, if the wind was in his favor, he could outrun the *Dauntless,* as he had done before. Yet if wind and waves were favorable to Thomas, the *Dauntless* could approach the scene of a raid and catch Nighthawk before he could hoist his sails and make his escape.

Thomas's mind tacked away from those hopes and back to his future. Perhaps he, like Freddy, could join Jamie in his merchant business. He certainly had sufficient wealth to purchase his own ship and hire a worthy captain to command it for him. Then if his farming endeavors did not support his family in the manner he hoped, this could provide a supplement to his income. He had plenty of time to decide on the particulars of the matter. And with his new comprehension of the Almighty as a loving Father, far different from his earthly father, he would make it a matter of prayer, just as Freddy urged him to do.

At the memory of his reconciliation with Freddy, when he had felt the ballast lifted from his burdened heart, Thomas wondered why he had ever considered his brother an enemy. He chuckled into the darkness of his cabin. Life was good. He surrendered to sleep, envisioning the imminent capture of his true enemy.

Just as he dreamed of the noose slipping over the pirate's head, a soft tapping on his door awakened him.

"Captain Moberly?" Wayland's hushed voice sounded through the boards.

"Come." Thomas sat up and pulled on his shoes. They would not have awakened him if his presence was not required.

Wayland entered quietly. "We have something, sir. Two ships in a parley on the horizon. Enough lanterns lit to show considerable activity."

"Ha!" Thomas fumbled for his coat in the darkness. "We've got him now."

"Shall we keep the lights doused, sir?"

"Of course." His pulse quickened as he buttoned his coat and found his hat. "Order all hands to their stations and prepare the guns."

Once on deck, he pulled out his spyglass, hoping to identify his adversary. If the man lived in St. Augustine or did business there, Thomas would recognize him. Then if he managed to escape, he could be caught on land.

The sea calmed briefly, just long enough for Thomas to see the scene. Ragtag pirates swarmed over the merchant ship, removing the cargo to their own vessel. Thomas drew in a sharp breath. The casks they carried were clearly metal kegs of gunpowder. The long wooden crates looked like those used to transport muskets. This rendezvous was no ruse, as his last encounter had been. Nighthawk was stealing British arms and ammunition from a naval transport ship whose Union Jack waved proudly in the wind.

His first officer approached Thomas. "Orders, sir?"

"Dark and quiet, Mr. Brandon," he whispered. "The wind is behind us, and any sound will carry. If any man speaks without good cause, he'll receive a dozen lashes when this is over." He would catch the pirate tonight or die trying. But oddly, this time that vow did not settle into place with the same determination as before. Was he growing soft? A vision of Dinah came to mind, and he could only surmise that he had grown less willing to die for duty, for that would validate her loathing of the seafaring life. Worse, it would break her heart.

He shook off such thoughts and raised his spyglass again. Good. The pirate's sails were furled, and the two ships appeared to be grappled together as they bobbed on the uneven waves. Even if the pirate's lookout saw the *Dauntless* now, he would not be able to hoist his sails in time to get away. Victory was within Thomas's reach, but he could not fire yet. A misplaced shot could blow up both ships.

When the *Dauntless* sailed within a hundred and fifty yards, the pirate lookout did indeed appear to call down, and many heads snapped in Thomas's direction. Abandoning their booty, some fifty men scrambled like rats back to their ship, while others held firearms on the transport crew to keep them at bay. One pirate broke open a cask of gunpowder and spread it around the transport deck, but when he tried to throw a lantern into it, a crewman endeavored to knock him down with a belaying pin. A second pirate shot the crewman, and the merchant sailors ceased their attempts to resist. The British crew spied the *Dauntless* and a cheer went up.

"Thank you, Lord." Thomas nearly shouted the prayer, no longer concerned about making noise. The men in the top yards of the pirate ship scrambled to unfurl sails while other pirates released the grappling hooks. "You have delivered my adversary into my hands."

As the *Dauntless* closed in on the scene, the pirate ship broke loose at last and her sails billowed out in the wind.

"Make all sail, Mr. Brandon." Thomas could taste the victory now. Despite the rough seas, the wind was in his favor, and dawn would break in minutes. "Have Mr. Baynard run out the guns, if you please. At my order, fire a warning shot across his bow. He'd be a fool not to stop with all that powder on board."

"All hands aloft. Loose topsails and topgallants," Mr. Brandon shouted across the deck, then turned to the gunner waiting orders by the main hatch. "Ready the guns, Mr. Baynard."

"Aye aye." The man saluted and dropped below.

Thomas watched with satisfaction. In minutes, they'd be within firing distance. The seas granted them favor, and the *Dauntless* sailed with ease over the waves toward the action.

But the adversary seemed determined to prove his mettle. A flame burst from the stern chasers of the pirate ship. Smoke curled in the air.

"All hands hit the deck," Thomas yelled as he plunged to the boards. The shot splashed harmlessly into the dark waters. So this Nighthawk meant to fight. Well, Thomas would make it worth his while.

"Mr. Brandon."

Brandon's eyes gleamed with anticipation. "Aye, Captain."

"Tell Mr. Baynard to aim for his rigging and fire at will."

Within minutes the sky exploded with a thunderous boom that sent a quiver through the ship. Gray smoke blew back upon Thomas, and he coughed and swatted it away.

He raised his spyglass once more and saw his shot splash down near the pirate. The returning volley answered in kind, and a modicum of respect swept through him. The pirates wore nondescript, ragged clothing, but their seamanship was a well-oiled machine. In the rapidly brightening skies, he scanned the ship, searching for Nighthawk, wondering if he would recognize who held that office. There at the back of the quarterdeck, a tall, broad-shouldered man in dark breeches and a billowing white shirt shouted orders to his men. As if sensing he was being watched, he turned toward the *Dauntless*. The blow his look delivered almost felled Thomas.

Templeton.

My brother. My friend.

My *enemy*.

"Should we keep firing, sir?" Mr. Brandon called.

Thomas forced out the word, "Yes."

While Brandon relayed the order, a blazing ball from the pirate ship arced through the morning sky toward the transport vessel.

Mr. Brandon cursed. "Hot shot, sir."

The red-hot ball slammed into the deck of the looted ship, and within seconds an explosion shattered the roiling sea, sending boards and rigging in a thousand directions. The *Dauntless* continued to fire on the pirate ship, but he was fast slipping away. Too soon, the transport began to sink.

"Captain, sir," Mr. Brandon yelled, "we'll have to save the survivors."

Thomas trained his spyglass on men thrashing about in the water. British men. Loyal sailors who had done their best not to surrender their cargo. Many were waving toward the *Dauntless,* clearly desperate to be rescued. The blood of the injured and dead streaked the glistening gold water with red.

"Do it."

Thomas thought he might vomit. Yet in the back of his mind, he knew he would have done exactly the same thing as Templeton. By forcing Thomas to stop and save his fellow Englishmen, he could now escape.

But there was another casualty to his actions. Nighthawk's reputation as a benign thief had just gone up in flames with the transport ship.

But then again, this was war. And for the first time since 1776 when King George had declared the colonists in rebellion, Thomas experienced firsthand the extent to which they would go in order to sever their ties with the Crown.

But Father in heaven—Thomas lifted his eyes to the blue-gray sky—*why did it have to be my friend?*

Chapter Twenty-Six

Charcoal stick in hand, Dinah sat beside her bedroom window and faced a blank piece of foolscap resting on her small easel. She'd planned to sketch the vase of violets on her table but, for some reason, could not make the first mark.

Since returning to St. Augustine two weeks ago, she had found it difficult to resume her former habits. Without her nieces and nephews to bolster her spirits, she spent far too much time thinking about her adult relatives' betrayal. Even Macy, curled up on the floor beside her, failed to soothe away her pain with his soft purring. And now, over a month had passed since she had seen Thomas, and she could not stop worrying about him. What if, despite her prayers, he and Jamie had encountered each other? What if he'd caught her brother and hanged him at sea and now could not face her? Indeed, she had no idea how she could bear such a tragedy. Oh, if only Jamie had not joined the rebellion! What madness had compelled him to do such a thing? Further, she could find no sense in her family's renunciation of their allegiance to the Crown.

Her hand began to move, as if it had a mind of its own. The form coming into shape was her beloved's face, but she could not get the eyes right. Alarm filled her. Was she forgetting his visage? Thomas had never stared at her with such a cross expression.

Another startling thought brought forth a gasp. Had Thomas known all along that Jamie was Nighthawk? She searched her memory, examined every word, every conversation. Had he been using her in hopes of catching Jamie? No, that could not be. They had both been betrayed by their mutual relatives. And Thomas's reconciliation with Frederick had surely been genuine. But the doubts she tried to dismiss would not cease.

Her head began to ache, as it often did when she tried too hard to sort out all the clutter in her mind. With no one to confide in, sometimes she thought her brain might explode or her heart burst from the unending pain. To add to her misery, Artemis had refused to accept the announcement of her engagement to Thomas, saying the British captain was dallying with her. On the other hand, dear Anne had gently chided her for her despondency, insisting she must not waste into a shadow before her wedding day. Dinah's wedding clothes lay partially finished in her clothespress.

The jangling of the bell on the front gate did not excite her interest. This could not be Thomas, because the harbor bell had not rung to announce a ship's arrival for several days. Any other visitor to the house would be for Anne, who was quilting with friends, or Artemis, who was working at the state house. Cook had gone to market, so Dinah would have to face the visitor. She put down her charcoal stick and wiped black dust on a linen rag. Perhaps it was Elizabeth, back in the city with her parents after visiting Mr. Turnbull's plantation at New Smyrna.

Instead of Elizabeth, a tall man in rough Minorcan clothing stood outside the gate, a brightly colored woolen cape thrown carelessly over one shoulder and his face shadowed by a wide-brimmed hat unique to that group of settlers. Dinah supposed he was a shoemaker seeking work, although she usually recognized the men in that trade.

But as she drew closer to the gate, her pulse began to race.

"Jamie." She breathed out her brother's name on a sob, then hastened to unlock the latch.

"Dinah." Laughing, he strode through the entry and swept her up in his arms and swung her around as though she were one of the children. The odor of many days at sea clung to him, stinging her nostrils. The rough wool of his cape scratched her cheek. "My dear little sister, it's been far too long."

Ignoring his unwashed scent, she clung to him, sobbing, unable to speak.

He set her down and held her shoulders, his brown eyes round with curiosity. "Are you not pleased to see me?"

"Oh, Jamie, oh—" She grasped his hand and dragged him toward the house. "I did not hear the harbor bell. Where is your ship?" She glanced toward the street, which was bustling with passersby. "We cannot talk out here." She could feel his hesitation in the way he pulled against her leading. "You must come now."

Once they reached the dim parlor, he swept off his hat and gripped her shoulders again. "What is it? Marianne? The baby?" Alarm tightened his sun-browned countenance, fear filled his dark eyes.

She pressed both hands to her lips and shook her head, struggling to regain composure. "They are well. You have a beautiful, healthy baby daughter."

"Thank the Lord." Relief softened his features, but now he gave her a gentle, sympathetic frown. "Then what causes your sadness, dear one?"

He pulled her into his arms, and at last she released the full flood of tears she had held inside these many days. Of all the people in the world, he should bear the weight of her long agony. It was all his fault! She sobbed until her headache flared again. When at last she was forced to pull in deep, gulping breaths to keep from fainting, she was surprised he had let her weep so long.

He led her to the settee, sat beside her and took her hands in his. "Now, what was that all about?" His teasing tone, which had always gladdened her heart, now stung.

Sniffing and dabbing at her tears with a handkerchief, she tried to level a harsh look upon him. But his dear face, so warm with sympathy and brotherly affection, kept her from despising him. *Lord, how shall I begin?* She lifted her fan and waved it before her face. "You will be pleased, I hope, to know that I have met your brother-in-law, Captain Thomas Moberly." A giddy laugh, punctuated with a hiccough, escaped her at the shock…and *worry?*…that spread over his face. "I should say, more than met him. We are engaged to be married."

Jamie's face contorted into several expressions she would have found comical in any other circumstance: amazement, confusion, happiness, bewilderment.

"Engaged." His mild laugh sounded a bit strangled.

"Well, imagine that. I go off for a short voyage and find out someone has stolen my baby sister's heart."

"Oh, stop it, Jamie." Rage fired up within her, and she stood and paced the floor, gripping her folded fan with both hands. "You are Nighthawk, and my beloved fiancé is out to see you hanged. Oh!" She stamped her foot on the hard tabby floor, and pain shot up to her shin. But that discomfort was minor compared to the agony in her soul.

Just as Jamie stood up and stepped toward her, she strode across the floor and slammed her fan against him. As the ivory sticks cracked, so did her heart. "You traitor. You rebel. You thief!"

He did not move, nor did her strike seem to inflict any pain on his thick, broad chest. She swung away from him, sobbing again. A sound from the back of the house reached her ears, and she forced down her emotions. Jamie stared in that direction, and caution filled his face.

Dinah waved her hand dismissively. "Cook returning from the market." Cook, who had lost everything she'd owned in Virginia due to the rebellion. Wouldn't she like to know her mistress now entertained a traitor?

But the thought stabbed deep into Dinah's soul. She could never betray her brother, in spite of his betraying all she believed in. Only one consolation came to mind. At least her prayer had been answered and he had not encountered Thomas.

"Ah." Jamie slumped back down on the settee. "I'd best leave soon, but first you will hear what I have to say." He motioned her to sit beside him.

Clutching her broken fan, she sat in a chair some distance away. "Why are you dressed like this? Where is your ship? Why did we not hear the harbor bell announcing your arrival?"

He waved away her questions. "We have more important things to discuss."

"Very well. What excuse will you give me for your piracy?"

His wry chuckle reignited her rage, but she managed not to explode upon him again. "Little sister—"

"Stop calling me little. I am a woman of one and twenty years, the same age that Marianne was when she married you." She tried not to spit the words out, but she tasted the bitterness in her mouth.

To her satisfaction, his agreeable nod held no condescension.

"Dinah, why do you honor a king who would drain the very life out of his colonists, to make them into veritable slaves?" The soft intensity of his voice underscored the fire in his dark-brown eyes. "Why would you willingly pay exorbitant taxes to an unjust tyrant who will not listen to your most reasonable complaints, nor cease to force an oppressive military presence upon you and your neighbors?"

She glared at him, knowing and hating that he could outwit her in any argument. "The garrison at Fort St. Marks protects us, as do His Majesty's ships, one of which is commanded by your wife's flesh and blood— my own betrothed. There is nothing oppressive about it." The broken fan burned in her hands. Would she ever be able to fix it?

"But the colonies have been taxed—"

"Stop." Dinah stood, thrusting her palm toward him to emphasize the command. "I am not in sympathy with your rebellion, and I never shall be."

"Very well." He stared down and casually brushed

a hand over his coarse vest. "Will you call for the soldiers?"

She huffed out a hot breath. "Oh, the very idea. Of course I should. But—" her voice broke "—how could I bear to see you hanged?"

He gazed at her so gently, so gratefully, that something settled within her. Her only brother, her enemy, her friend. No, she would never betray him. But neither would she lie for him.

"I love you, my sister." His eyes glistened. "I know you and Moberly will be happy." A chuckle. "Did we all not say the two of you would suit each other very well?"

She nodded, unable to speak.

The front door opened, and Dinah gasped. "Anne."

"Yes, just me." Anne swept in, a basket on her arm. "Why, Jamie Templeton, what brings you here?"

He rose and bowed to her. "Good morning, Mrs. Hussey. How good to see you, dear lady." He stepped over and kissed her hand. "To answer your question, I'm going to see my newborn child, but thought I should visit Dinah on my way."

Dinah eyed Anne. They all knew the plantation would have been easier for him to reach by way of the St. Johns River and should have been his primary destination. Her mind raced with the questions he'd refused to answer. Why was he dressed as a Minorcan? Where was his ship? And why had he come to see her first?

Awareness burst into her mind. Jamie had come to say goodbye to her...*forever.* But why? Until this hour, he'd been unaware that she knew he was the pirate. Perhaps he'd found out someone else in St. Augustine had uncovered his identity. That meant he and Marianne and—*Lord, have mercy*—the children, were all in danger. Surely they would have to flee East Florida. And yet he had come to see her, to bid her goodbye. He was leaving her, as he always had done, but this time there was no hope of his returning.

She flung herself into his arms. "Oh, Jamie, I do love you so."

He held her for a moment, kissing the top of her head. "May God watch over you, my sister."

Sniffing, she struggled to regain her composure and at last gave him a trembling smile. "A word of advice, dear brother. Before you see your sweet wife, do take a bath. You have almost knocked me over."

He snorted out a laugh and chucked her chin. "I will do that."

With obvious reluctance, he released her and turned to take his leave of Anne. Then he slipped out the front door. Through the window Dinah could see him hurrying toward the back yard. A few moments later, a noise sounded at the front gate, and Cook struggled through carrying two burlap bags bulging with supplies. At the same moment, the familiar smell of Artemis's apple-scented hair dressing reached Dinah's nose, and her heart almost stopped. He emerged from his nearby bedroom and gave her a sly grin, then turned to Anne.

"What are we having for our midday meal, my dear?" He stroked his long, narrow chin. "Freshly caught fowl?"

Chapter Twenty-Seven

"I must say, Moberly, this is most displeasing to me." Admiral George Rodney eyed Thomas through his quizzing glass. "To have a captain with a list of laurels like yours resigning in the midst of a war? And just when we have those blackguards and their French allies with their backs to the wall? Just when you came so close to catching one of their most bothersome pirates?"

Thomas stood before his irascible superior officer trying not to shuffle like a new midshipman. "I understand your thinking, sir, but—"

"Why, Captain Brett here has nothing but praise for you." The admiral waved his bony, blue-veined hand toward the transport captain, who stood by the bulkhead in borrowed clothes. "Without your quick actions, his crew would have been lost…drowned, every last one of them. Not to mention the cargo you were able to retrieve." He stood and paced behind his dark oak desk, a massive, ornate piece of furniture appropriate for the admiral's large cabin aboard his flagship. "How can you leave His Majesty's service when you are certain to bag the pirate on your next try?" A cough that seemed to come from the bottom of his lungs punctuated his words. "Sit down, Moberly." He indicated a chair facing the desk and resumed his own seat behind it.

Thomas shifted his sword to the side and eased himself into the oak chair. He had not slept well for the past four days since encountering Templeton's ship, and his body ached with a fatigue equal to the exhaustion of his mind. Countless doubts and suspicions had filled his thoughts, and he still could not sort out truth from speculation.

Discovering that his brother-in-law was the notorious pirate had shattered his trust in everything and everyone. Even Dinah had not escaped his suspicions, but he could not resolve that until he saw her. She had never seemed anything but thoroughly transparent in her devotion to the Crown. Further, unlike other women he had known, including his late wife, Dinah was utterly lacking in artifice, and her concern for her brother's safety had appeared genuine. But then, Templeton had always seemed a staunch Loyalist, too. Perhaps she had learned her acting skills from him.

"Tell me, sir." Admiral Rodney stared down his long, slender nose at Thomas. "Did you get a good look at the fellow?"

Thomas swallowed. This was the moment he'd dreaded, but he still did not know how he would answer. He raised an agonizing silent prayer for God's wisdom as promised in scripture. "At that distance, not a *good* look, sir." Not a lie.

"But enough to recognize the blackguard if you saw him again?"

"Yes, I would." Still not a lie. But then, silence about the truth was a lie in itself. And in this case, a hanging offense. "Sir, may I have a word with you in private?"

The admiral's naturally high-arched eyebrows rose

another half inch. "Of course." He nodded to the transport captain and his own ship's commander. "Gentlemen."

The two men left, followed by the admiral's green-liveried steward.

"Now." Admiral Rodney leaned across his desk, and a conspiratorial smile curved his lips upward. "What's this all about?"

Too late, Thomas recalled the man's reputation for greed. He must think the *Dauntless* carried goods recovered from smugglers and perhaps he coveted a share. But it was too late to stop.

He cleared his throat. "Sir, I find myself in an awkward situation." He chewed his lip, praying for the right words.

"Go on, lad." The admiral's smile broadened.

Time to roll out the big guns. "My father, the late Lord Bennington—"

"Ah, yes." The smile disappeared, replaced by a grimace and a frown. "I should have said something when you first came aboard. How thoughtless of me. Please accept my condolences."

"Thank you, sir." Thomas coughed into his fist, stalling, praying. "He placed a great deal of trust in an American loyalist merchant captain who became his partner in imports and exports."

"Yes, yes." Rodney's frown bent into an impatient scowl. "What of it?"

"That captain—"

At a sharp rap on the door, the admiral raised a frail hand. "One moment, Moberly." He stared toward the door. "Come."

A slender, youthful lieutenant entered and saluted. "Admiral Rodney, sir, Commodore Hunt wanted me to inform you that his purser has disbursed uniforms to the rescued merchant sailors who've signed on with us. And Dr. Savage has reported that another of the merchant sailors has died from his wounds and another lingers near death."

The admiral uttered an oath and slammed a fist down on his desk, causing his inkwell to tip. He caught it before damage was done. "Moberly, I have told you I am unhappy with your decision, but you know my own history is fraught with such choices. Remember, like me, you can come back at any time." He stood and straightened his coat and reached for his bicorne hat.

Thomas jumped to his feet. *Lord, just how far should I push this?*

Rodney settled the hat on his head. "As you requested, you may sail the *Dauntless* back to St. Augustine, where you will be relieved of your command. There you are to turn the vessel over to Brandon. That worthy man is overdue for his own ship, wouldn't you say? As for that protégé of your father's, I understand the new Lord Bennington will choose his own favorites, and this fellow might be left out in the cold. Write me a letter about him, and I'll see what I can do."

Thomas clenched his teeth to keep his jaw from dropping. "Yes, sir." Should he try again? "But—"

"You must excuse me. Write that letter. When I receive it, I'll use my influence as best I can." He walked toward the door, his frailty obvious in his cautious gait. "However, right now I have something more important to do. As you may know, I have always made it a practice to be solicitous toward the concerns of the lower deck, much to the disapproval of my brother officers." He waved a hand carelessly in the air. "Matters not to me. I have never failed to grip the hand of a man, whether soldier, sailor or merchantman who lay dying upon my ship. Now, if you will excuse me." He exited the cabin, leaving Thomas to his thoughts…and fears.

Had he done all to report Templeton's treachery? Must he still attempt to give an account of what he knew? Honesty had required him to try, but what did this insane conversation mean? That the Almighty…no, his *Father* in heaven countenanced the pirate's actions? Or at least his escape from retribution?

Praying had been difficult these last four days since the *Dauntless* had sailed from the scene of the disaster off the coast of East Florida down to the West Indies. The transport ship had been part of a flotilla delivering supplies, arms and ammunition to Martinique, where Admiral Rodney and the British fleet awaited orders regarding the war. Separated in a storm from the British frigates that protected the supply vessels, the transport became easy prey for Nighthawk. Now those stolen arms would fuel the rebellion. Would fuel the hopes of the rebels. Would validate Templeton's piracy. And where was God in all of this?

Could Templeton be a Christian *and* a pirate? If so, did that mean God countenanced the rebellion? Were there not godly Englishmen praying for victory on the battlefields of South Carolina, Virginia and Massachusetts? And yet every day men like Charles Fox argued in Parliament for the release of the colonies from British rule. If Christians on both sides prayed, whose voices were heard in heaven?

His mind still reeling over the conversation with the admiral, Thomas returned to the *Dauntless*. Surely God had answered his prayers, diverting the admiral's line of thinking as Thomas tried to divulge Templeton's treachery. What else could he have done without becoming insubordinate? But the Articles of War demanded that he report what he knew about Templeton, or he could be tried before the Admiralty and hanged for treason. Very well. For his own survival, Thomas would write to Admiral Rodney with all the necessary information. And in the interval, Templeton would have more than sufficient time to avoid capture. Madly, that thought gave Thomas a sense of relief.

Mr. Brandon received the news of his imminent promotion to captain with his usual self-control, an attribute that had always served him well as an officer. By the next morning, they had their orders in hand, and Thomas stepped aside while his first officer gave the orders to return to St. Augustine.

Hinton received the news of Thomas's coming retirement with little emotion, although a glimmer of approval flitted across his eyes upon hearing it. He proclaimed himself willing to remain in Thomas's service and hovered about the cabin as if trying to prove himself indispensable. The steward already knew every breath Thomas took and had been surprisingly undisturbed by the appearance of the document proclaiming the colonists' independence. A man would be unwise to let such a discreet servant go, for it gave Thomas the freedom to examine the declaration at will.

Despite Hinton's ability to anticipate Thomas's every need, he had yet to become a mind reader, which proved helpful as Thomas agonized over Freddy's possible involvement with the rebellion. As close as Templeton and Freddy had been these past four years, with Templeton working as a liaison of sorts between the plantation and Bennington, the two men undoubtedly shared the same ideology. Within a few days, Thomas would no longer have the duty to find out if his brother was a traitor, and he welcomed that freedom. But he also knew he would not feel at peace until his questions about his brother's loyalty had been answered.

As the *Dauntless* skimmed over the waves of the Florida Current, he wondered at his own feelings—or lack of feeling—regarding this voyage. After eighteen years—four as captain of this vessel—this last turn at command surely should have more effect on him. But other than enjoying the brisk ocean breezes and the privileged fare at his table, he came to realize he cared not a whit if he ever sailed again, much less as captain.

However, when St. Augustine's wooden watchtower came into view, his heart grew heavy with dread, for now he must face Dinah. And he found the prospect far more daunting than his interview with Admiral George Rodney.

Chapter Twenty-Eight

"I am afraid you do not understand, Mr. Richland."
Dinah leaned away from the middle-aged plantation
owner, whose odors of tobacco smoke and rum nearly
overpowered her. "I am betrothed, as Mr. Hussey
should have told you. Therefore, I cannot marry you."
She scooted off of the settee and moved to a chair several feet away. Only one lamp lit the darkened parlor,
and she shivered in spite of the warm room's stifling
atmosphere.

Mr. Richland chortled, an unpleasant sound that
grated on Dinah's nerves. "And I am afraid *you* do not
understand, Miss Templeton. Mr. Hussey has told me
about your, eh, *betrothal,* but where is the proof of it?
My spies, if you will permit that term, have informed me
of no gentleman callers here at the Hussey residence."
He inspected his fingernails and brushed them across
his sleeve.

Spies? Dinah pulled in a deep breath to stave off
her threatening dizziness. Had Artemis told this man
about Jamie? She swallowed hard before trying to speak
again.

"You are correct, sir." Having failed to repair the fan
Thomas had given her, she waved her old one before

her heated face. This hot August weather had caused many St. Augustine citizens to become ill and she did not wish to join their ranks. "I do not understand. But my confusion comes from wondering why you would wish to marry someone who so clearly does not wish to marry you." *Who clearly has come to despise you.* How could she explain herself more plainly?

Mr. Richland's eyes narrowed and his leering grin sent a sick feeling into her stomach. "Oh, you will soon warm to me, my dear. And you will find that being the lady of a fine plantation will be more than ample reward for your, eh, pleasant company *at my side*." He chuckled, as if he'd told a joke.

A violent shudder swept through her. This man reminded her of the snake that had almost bitten her before Thomas killed it. How could this vile man have such a pleasant son?

"You may find that my fiancé, Captain Moberly, objects to your assumptions and insinuations—"

"Ha!" His grin grew into a sneer. "Captain Moberly, indeed. Do you think I am a fool, madam? The good captain has been in St. Augustine for close to a week and has not once set foot on your street, much less into your house. Is he then your adoring suitor? Your fiancé? I think not. As I said, I have spies. Why else do you think I came here today? I was waiting to see if your assertion was true. Clearly, it is not."

Dinah grew cold inside and out. Her throat constricted and her mind went blank. Thomas here? For a week? What madness was this? Why had he not come? *Please, Lord, help me.* Again, she pulled in a long, calming breath. "Your persistence amazes me, as do your wild reports. I will not discuss my fiancé with you further." She rose and swept from the room.

At the back hallway, Artemis met her and seized her wrist. "Very good, Miss Templeton. Your arrogance befits the aristocratic lady you soon will be. But you have aimed your haughtiness in the wrong direction."

"You were listening." Dinah tried to pull away, but his bony fingers held her in a death grip. "Of course. You've as much as sold me to him like a slave. But why?"

Artemis shrugged. "Political advantage. And as my friend Mr. Richland so gallantly stated, you will find being the wife of a wealthy plantation owner has inherent rewards. That is, as long as you please him."

She had been wrong. Mr. Richland might be a boor, but Artemis was the snake. "What could you possibly gain from this, Artemis? My paltry inheritance?"

"As I said, political advantage." He pulled her toward her bedchamber. "I will deliver to him a wife of superior beauty, grace and *innocence,* a combination of qualities absent in most marriageable young women in this area. He, in turn, will grant me the five hundred acres required of an assemblyman."

He kicked the smooth wooden door open and shoved her inside. She would have fallen if she had not caught herself on the bedpost.

"You will stay here until you decide to cooperate." Artemis turned to leave.

Dinah regained her footing and chased after him into the hall. "You cannot force me to marry that man."

He whirled around and gripped her shoulders. "You will do as I say." His words blasted over her face like a dragon's fiery breath. "If you do not, I will have you declared a madwoman and I will confiscate your inheritance. And lest you think Governor Tonyn will rescue you—" his self-satisfied sneer matched Mr. Richland's "—he will have nothing to do with a woman whose brother is the infamous pirate Nighthawk." He smirked. "And do you really think anyone will believe Captain Moberly does not know of Templeton's activities? Why else has this brilliant, *heroic* captain failed to catch the pirate? Shall I point that out to our esteemed governor?"

Dinah gasped. She had never considered the possibility that Thomas might have been letting Jamie escape.

"Then again," Artemis said, "perhaps the governor will decide to imprison you. That would be another option for getting you off my hands." He pushed her back toward her shadowed room and once again shoved her inside, then pulled the door closed.

She heard the click of iron on iron as the lock latched into place. Only then did she notice that her interior bolt had been ripped from the wood.

For a moment, tears welled up within her, and she longed to throw herself on her bed and weep, just as she had when Jamie came to bid her goodbye two weeks ago. But something inside her held on, like a ship's anchor in a storm. She would not submit to this blackmail. God would help her.

Indeed, He would help her climb through the window. She rushed to the narrow glass opening, pinned aside the mosquito netting, and studied the ten wood-framed panes, built securely to withstand hurricane winds. Only the bottom two rows could be opened, and the gap would be hard for her to climb through. But she must try.

Yet, if she left, where would she go? To find Thomas? Or perhaps she should again call him "Captain Moberly." Her heart ached to think of losing him through no fault of her own. But then, if he had been using her to learn about Jamie and perhaps even Frederick, he'd never loved her in the first place.

After these many weeks of not seeing him, she found it distressingly easy to believe the worst. All her life, she had been alone. Her dear foster mothers and Anne had loved her in their own ways, but she had never felt the deep bond of sisterhood they all enjoyed. Perhaps it was due to her restless spirit. They had been content with their lives, while she had always wanted to be someplace else doing something different. Well, this situation certainly was different, but hardly what she'd longed for.

She slumped into her chair by the window. Night was falling over St. Augustine. After twilight, no decent woman walked the city's streets for fear of the drunken soldiers who found their amusements where they could. The very men to whom she ministered when they were ill could not be trusted to recognize her, much less to guard her virtue, if she should be so foolish as to venture out.

Hearing sounds within the house, she went to the door to listen. Identifying the voices, she realized Anne had come in from the kitchen house after her nightly meeting with Cook to decide on the next day's meals. Perhaps Anne could make Artemis see reason. Dinah pounded on the door.

"Anne, help me," she cried. "Help me." Pain shot up her arm from hammering on the hard wood.

"What has thou done, husband?" Anne's voice sounded from the back of the house. Hope stirred within Dinah. Never before had she heard her foster sister speak in anger.

Footsteps padded across the tabby floor. "Why has thou imprisoned my sister? Dinah, are thee well? Ouch! Artemis, let go of me."

"Dinah is well, my dear."

His growling voice made Dinah shudder. She had never known him to be cruel to Anne. How could anyone be unkind to such a dear Christian lady? Had his ambition driven him so far that he would harm his own wife? Fear for her foster sister coursed through Dinah.

"I am not hurt, Anne," she called through the door. "Never mind. We can sort this out in the morning."

"There, you see." Artemis's tone had softened. "Now turn in, wife. I have a guest in the parlor who requires my courtesy. And do not think to open this door. I have the only key to the lock."

"Yes, Artemis," Anne murmured. Then their footsteps scuffed away, and silence reigned in the hallway.

Dinah glanced again at the window. At first light she would find a way to crawl through it and seek help. But from whom? If Thomas no longer cared for her, she had no one to turn to.

After an agonizing night of little sleep, she decided to go to Mr. Leslie and ask for some of her money. Although she had seldom ridden, she would hire a horse and go to Bennington Plantation. Even if Frederick was a traitor to the Crown, he and Rachel would not deny her a place of refuge from a forced marriage. She prayed she would be able to make her way to King's Road before Artemis realized she'd escaped.

Before dawn, she dressed in her oldest gown, then bundled up a second dress in a small satchel and glanced around the dark bedchamber to be sure she had everything she would need. Her drawing supplies would have to stay. Her extra pair of shoes. Her straw hat. No, she would need the hat once the sun rose. And of course she packed her broken fan. Perhaps that would be all she had left to remind her of Thomas's love.

Her room was on the shadowed west side of the house so little morning light reached the grassy yard between her window and the lavender field. She wiggled the lower panels of the narrow window and found the hinges rusty. Answered prayer! She kept at the task as quietly as possible and finally bent the section far enough inward to give her space to climb through.

Hope blossomed like the purple blooms still dotting the field. She shoved her leather satchel out and dropped it to the ground, then tossed out the hat. She glanced back at her dark room one last time, took a deep breath, and lifted one foot to begin her escape. Before it reached the window's casement, her satchel flew back inside, nearly knocking her down.

Dinah's heart jumped to her throat, and a sick feeling filled her stomach.

A dark form stood just beyond the glass. "Sorry, miss, so sorry." The soft, deep voice of the male slave was filled with sympathy. "Mr. Richland says you must not go out." In the shadows, she could see him turn to the right and then to the left, as if checking for something… or someone. "I won't tell him you tried." He shoved her hat back inside. "So sorry." He dropped down, disappearing from view.

Dinah forced the bent window panels back into place and latched them. Again the urge to weep roared up within her, but she stamped it down, replacing despair with anger. Unlike Anne, she would not submit to Artemis and his ambitions. She would resist at every turn, no matter what they did to her. Even if they dragged her before a minister, she would refuse to speak the words that would bind her forever to that uncouth slave owner.

Chapter Twenty-Nine

"Mrs. Hussey, how may I serve you?" Thomas buttoned his coat as he entered the common room of the barracks. Hinton had wakened him only moments before and had hastily helped him dress. But Thomas's apprehensions over the lady's astonishing visit left no time for the finer points of grooming, nor even opening courtesies. Ladies did not come to the officers' quarters, even women of ill repute. And no one came here before sunrise unless the matter was most serious.

Dark half circles underscored the weariness in her eyes, and her rich auburn hair was as tousled as his. The mere fact that this Quaker lady had emerged from her house without wearing her customary bonnet struck alarm into Thomas's chest.

"Captain Moberly." Her voice caught, and she bit her lip and stared down, apparently trying to regain her composure. "I fear m-my husband has let his ambitions overthrow his good judgment."

Thomas swallowed his rising anger. This good woman was not at fault for her wretched husband's misdeeds, whatever they might be. "Please sit down." He touched her arm to escort her to an overstuffed chair and sat across from her. "What has happened?"

For the first time in their brief acquaintance, Mrs. Hussey glared at him. At least it seemed like a glare in the dim morning light. "Where has thee been, sir? My Dinah has almost wasted away in grief over thy cruel abandonment." Tears appeared in her dark eyes, but her lips formed a rigid line.

Thomas opened his mouth to speak, but in truth, he had no answer. The instant Mrs. Hussey said "*my* Dinah," he knew all his suppositions about his betrothed had been wrong. "Please tell me what has happened to bring you here, madam." And what did "wasted away" mean? His alarm increased.

She withdrew a handkerchief from her pocket and dabbed her cheeks. "Thee met Mr. Richland at the governor's ball. He has long pursued Dinah, but she will not have him."

Thomas shifted uncomfortably as guilt slammed into his conscience. "The boy is hardly a danger—"

"I refer to the senior Mr. Richland, and he is indeed a danger. He and Artemis have awaited thy return and watched to see if thee visited Dinah. When thou did not come, my husband made a pact with the man to trade her for a plot of land…as if she were his property, his *slave*." She spat out the word. "Artemis has imprisoned her in her bedchamber and will not release her until she agrees to marry that man." Mrs. Hussey shook her head and shuddered, as if her own words made her ill.

His beloved Dinah held captive by that jackanapes? Rage roared up within Thomas. To keep from saying something he would regret, he jumped to his feet, paced the wooden floor and ran a hand through his hair. But then guilt cut into his anger. He could have prevented this.

"If thou will not honor thy betrothal vows, at least take my dear friend to her cousin's plantation. If thou dost not wish to be in her company, then assign the duty to some other—"

"Please, madam, I beg you to stop." Condemnation heaped itself upon Thomas at her every word. "I am devoted to Dinah." *At least I was until—*

"Then go to her and keep her from being forced into marrying that man." Mrs. Hussey stood and walked toward the door.

Thomas followed close behind. "Madam, you must permit me to finish dressing so that I may see you safely home."

The face she turned toward him was a study in serenity. "I thank thee, Captain, but my God will take me home in safety as surely as He brought me here."

The instant she stepped out through the double front doors, Thomas located a sober soldier on duty. "You there, would you be so good as to follow Mrs. Hussey at a discreet distance and make certain she arrives home unharmed?" With no authority over anyone in the army garrison, Thomas could only hope the man would not refuse his request.

"Aye, sir." The slender, middle-aged man lifted his musket with scarred hands. "For that good lady, I'd fight a pack of wolves. Now, that husband o' hers—"

"I implore you, my good man, do not waste words. Make haste."

To his relief, the affable soldier saluted and hurried off to do the task.

Thomas released a deep, weary sigh, then inhaled

another galling dose of guilt. He had never hesitated before going into battle, and yet he had postponed confronting Dinah about her brother. There was no reasoning in it. He had returned to St. Augustine fully intending to deal with the matter immediately.

But resigning his commission had taken time. First there was the required paperwork, and then the letter Admiral Rodney had requested. But Thomas had agonized over divulging the truth about Nighthawk and in the end had been unable to expose his brother-in-law. Instead of an accusation, he wrote a vague letter requesting support for another of his father's favorites, making no mention of Templeton. Not one person in the world knew what Thomas knew, and if someone discovered it, he would simply have to pay the price.

But even with that decision made, Thomas could not go to Dinah. Instead, he spent hours writing letters of explanation to his friends in the admiralty. After that, his lengthy visit with the governor. Then the tailor measured Thomas for his new civilian wardrobe and came back later for fittings. Poor excuses, all of them, and he'd known it at the time. But the days slipped by, and it grew easier not to see Dinah at all, although his heart still ached with the pain of her perceived betrayal…and his lost love.

Now this. Mrs. Hussey clearly had no idea how her words had affected him, yet the good woman's affirmation of Dinah's innocence made his indecision nothing short of evil. He should have trusted his first instincts. Should have trusted Dinah.

He hurried up the staircase three steps at a time and returned to his quarters. With Hinton's help, he finished dressing and made his plans for setting things to right. At least he had no concerns about anyone in the city being suspicious of Templeton. During his visit with Governor Tonyn, he had reported his encounter with the pirate. From Tonyn's reactions and responses, Thomas concluded without doubt that no one suspected a thing. He could walk away, or rather, *sail* away from St. Augustine with a clear conscience and let history sort out the details regarding whose side God fought on in this war.

And whether or not Dinah would forgive him for his negligence and sail away with him was a question he hoped to answer before the end of the day.

Overnight, Dinah's bedchamber had become stifling without the benefit of the cool night air breezing in. She was confident the kindly slave who guarded the window would not try to enter and harm her, but nonetheless, she felt safer with the panes locked in place. Somehow it gave her a sense of controlling a small part of her life.

Sunlight began to brighten the lavender field, and sounds drifted through her door, murmured words she could not make out. Metal struck metal, and a grating squeak sent a shiver down her spine. The door swung in, and Artemis stood there with the lock in his hands. Cook scurried into the room, her eyes wide with questions and fear. She set a tray of eggs, bread and coffee on Dinah's small table, left the room, then returned with a pitcher of hot water.

"Are you all right, Miss Templeton?" The gray-haired woman's weathered face was pale, and her thin lips quivered as she spoke.

"I said keep quiet," Artemis growled. He lifted his hand as if he would strike the woman.

She backed away down the hall, apologizing to Dinah with a shrug of her thin shoulders.

"And you." Artemis leaned against the doorjamb. "Put on your best day dress, the purple one, and be ready in half an hour. You're going with Mr. Richland."

"What?" Dinah recoiled as if he'd actually struck her. "Why, that would be indecent for me to go alone with him to his house. How can you do this to me, Artemis? We grew up together. Went to Meeting together."

He snorted. "And your brother's fellow rebels tried to tar and feather me for my loyalty to the Crown. Well, East Florida is a new world for me. When the war ends, I shall not go back to whaling. Such a filthy business. Instead, I'll be walking the clean, polished halls of government as this colony prospers."

"But you don't believe in slavery." Dinah choked back tears. She would not let this man see her weep. "How can you sell me like a slave?"

He released another dismissive snort. "Hardly a slave, although you will be mistress over many of them. And don't worry about being alone with Mr. Richland. You know full well that his mother lives there, and she will see to the propriety of things." He reached in to pull the door shut. "After a few days of enjoying their hospitality, you will gladly marry the gentleman."

"But—"

He slammed the door and the sounds of the lock being secured echoed through her room.

Dinah eyed the tray of food. She'd eaten little these past days and reason demanded she keep up her strength. Once Artemis freed her from the room, she would get away from him. All that chasing around with the children had reminded her of how fast she could run. She downed the food and coffee, then washed herself and put on the lavender dress, as he'd ordered. Let him think she would yield to his plan. Once they reached the gate, she would break away and dash to Dr. Wellsey's house two streets over. Joanna would help her. She should have thought of them before. How alarmed they would be over her situation, but she had no means to deliver the news to them.

She knelt beside her bed and prayed for the Lord's blessing on her escape. Prayed that Anne and Cook would not be hurt. Prayed that Thomas—what? She had no words to say to God on his behalf, only a heart that ached bitterly over the way he had abandoned her. Just as everyone else in her life had done. Misery and despair ground into her, dissolving her optimism, and she bowed her forehead against the quilted counterpane.

"Please, God." It was all she could think to pray.

A voice within reminded her of the Scriptures she had read these past few days: *He hath made us accepted in the Beloved.* And another: *I will receive you and will be a Father unto you, and ye shall be my sons and daughters, saith the Lord Almighty.* Finally: *For he hath said, I will never leave thee, nor forsake thee. So that we may boldly say, The Lord is my helper, and I will not fear what man shall do unto me.*

As surely as if God had reached down and pulled her into a warm, paternal embrace, peace swept over her and into her soul. God would be her Father. What a precious promise. It drove away the despair and filled her with joy. He would be her helper, would guide her and protect her, no matter what happened. No matter what Artemis and Mr. Richland did to her.

Once again, the grating sound of the key in the lock came through the door. It opened, and Artemis scowled at her. "Come with me."

Dinah stood and gave him a smile. "Yes, Artemis."

She scooped up her broad-brimmed straw hat and walked toward him.

He blinked, and his jaw dropped. Doubt furrowed his forehead, but then his eyes narrowed. "What's this all about, this smiling compliance?"

She stared back at him. "God is my helper, Artemis. You can do me no harm."

Again, his face crinkled with doubt, and perhaps a small hint of shame. But too soon, his scowl returned. "You have it all wrong, girl. I mean you no harm. I simply want to be rid of you."

"No!" Anne burst from her bedchamber, rushed to Dinah's side and clamped her arms around her waist.

"Woman, I've told you—"

Artemis gripped Anne's wrist and tried to separate them, but Dinah clasped her dear friend's waist in return, and they clung to each other in desperation. Unable to separate them, he raised his hand to strike.

Anne jutted out her chin. "If thou dare, then do it. But I will never let her go."

His hand hovered, then slammed against the wall, and both she and Dinah flinched. Anne's labored breathing cut into Dinah's soul, but they did not disconnect, nor did either one weep.

"Very well." Artemis gripped Dinah's upper arm and dragged the two of them down the hall and out the front door. Cursing, he stopped and released them, where they fell back against the wall of the house.

Outside the open front gate, Mr. Richland stood beside his small carriage. Beside him stood Thomas, his hand resting on the hilt of his sword.

"Thomas!" Dinah released Anne and ran to him, stopping short of throwing herself into his arms. "You came at last." Uncertainty rained down upon her. His presence did not ensure her present or future safety.

The love radiating from his sky-blue eyes erased her doubts. "Forgive me, my love." His formal tone did not dismay her, for he took her hand and kissed it with great tenderness. "God willing, we shall not be separated again." He gazed beyond her to Anne, who sank to the ground in silent sobs. "Mrs. Hussey, are you unwell?"

"Never mind my wife, Captain Moberly." Artemis moved in front of Anne. "And you can unhand Miss Templeton. She is promised to Mr. Richland here, and there is nothing you can do about it."

His expression filled with hauteur, Thomas stepped between Dinah and the plantation owner. "I believe you are mistaken, sir. Miss Templeton and I are to be wed."

Dinah's heart swelled with happiness. *Thank You, Lord.*

"Indeed?" Mr. Richland traded a smirk with Artemis. "And what have you to say about that, Mr. Hussey?"

"Ahem." Artemis's artificial cough stilled Dinah's joy. She had no doubt about what his next words would be. "Now, tell me, Captain, would you not like to know the identity of the pirate you have been seeking? This Nighthawk fellow? For a small sum—or the rights to this chit's hand, I will gladly divulge his name to you, along with the names of all of his, um, cronies and family members."

Dinah's heart seemed to stop. Now all would be lost. *Peace,* her inner voice murmured. She steadied herself with a bracing breath and moved close to Thomas. To her surprise, his face bore a frown of confusion.

"I cannot imagine the importance of the pirate in regard to my betrothed, sir." He gave his head a little shake. "However, since you bring him into the conversation, I will tell you that I've encountered the fellow myself. Caught sight of him through my spyglass."

Dinah thought she might swoon. He'd seen Jamie, knew the truth. What would he do? But if she fainted, she would miss it. Another bracing breath steadied her.

Artemis's scowl deepened. "If you speak the truth, Moberly, then you know who he is. You can be hanged as a traitor if you try to hide his identity. I will see to it myself."

"On the contrary, I do not know the man I saw that night." Thomas's lips curled upward into a sly smile. "Will you contradict me? Will you threaten one of His Majesty's officers?" Again his hand went to the hilt of his sword.

Dinah looked away, trying to sort out what Thomas had said. Mr. Richland caught her eye and his sneer proclaimed his disgust.

"Enough, Hussey." He stepped up into his small, open carriage. "The man wouldn't lie about this, not after the way he vowed to catch the pirate." He spat on the ground before turning his attention back to Dinah. "You will regret your choice, madam. As my wife in East Florida, you could hold a status equal to that of an English countess. If you marry this man and live in England, you will be a shame to your husband's family, a common, uncouth American." He lifted his buggy whip and snapped it against the horse's rump. The animal lurched forward and pulled the conveyance down the lane.

Dinah slumped against Thomas and he wrapped one arm around her.

"Dear one, we have much to discuss." He eyed Anne. "Mrs. Hussey, I would not leave you here with this—"

"My husband, Captain Moberly." Anne approached Artemis, who stared after Mr. Richland without expression. "Come, husband." She gripped his arm. "We also have much to discuss."

Artemis yanked his arm away from her and glared at Thomas. Gradually, rage faded into a bitter snarl. He spun on his heel and strode into the house, slamming the door behind him.

"Anne, what will you do?" Dinah rushed to her friend and embraced her.

Anne sighed and kissed Dinah's cheek. "No matter what hardships beset our paths, God's ways are best. He will be my strength and my guide. Perhaps one day my husband will come to himself and return to the Lord. Until then, my place is with him." She gazed toward the door, then back at Dinah. "Go now. If thee but ask, the Wellseys will surely give thee refuge until thy wedding day. I will send thy belongings to Joanna." She gave Dinah another kiss, then disappeared inside the house.

Dinah moved into Thomas's open arms and felt the comfort of his embrace. But one thing stood in the way of her complete happiness. She gazed up at him through her tears.

"Thomas, did you truly see Nighthawk? See him clearly?"

He brushed a hand over her damp cheek. "I did."

"And…but…" How could she ask the question? How could she not?

"As I said, I do not know the man I saw that night." His intense look explained it all. Truly, she did not know the man Jamie had become either. "We have much to discuss, but—" he kissed her forehead "—there's no hurry."

"All right, then." She buried her face in his chest. "May we go now?"

"Not until you forgive me."

Dinah looked up to see genuine concern in his eyes. "For what?"

He exhaled a long sigh. "I promised to return, but did not."

She gazed up into his handsome, winsome face, so filled with devotion and worry, and her heart overflowed with love. "But you did, for here you are."

His smile burst through the gloom like a sunrise. "And I shall never leave you again, Lord willing."

He had said that a while ago, but she'd thought it was for Artemis's sake. "I understand when you must leave to do your duty. I promise not to complain." She grimaced just a little. "Well, I promise to *try* not to complain."

He chuckled. "My only duty from this day forward is to take care of you, my beloved."

She gasped. "What have you done?"

He leaned his forehead against hers, that most endearing gesture that signified their deepest affection and communion. "I have resigned my commission. I fear, my darling, that you must set aside your ambitions to be a British captain's wife. Will it suit you just as well to be the wife of a country gentleman?"

"Oh, yes, Thomas. But I didn't dare to dream of such a thing. Are you sure you wish to do this?"

"Yes, my dear Dinah, I am very sure."

He bent to kiss her, pulling her up in his arms and deepening the kiss as if he would never let her go.

And she had no desire that he should do so.

Epilogue

September 1780
St. Johns Towne, East Florida Colony

"Ladies and gentlemen—" Reverend Johnson closed his prayer book and looked out upon the congregation of St. Andrew's Church in St. Johns Towne "—may I present to you Captain and Mrs. Thomas Moberly."

Thomas gazed down into the most beautiful face he had ever seen. His beloved bride's cheeks glowed, and her brown eyes sparkled with invitation. He lowered his head and placed a chaste, teasing kiss on Dinah's lips. She rose up on her toes and claimed another and this time, he wrapped his arms around her and showed her what a real kiss was all about.

Had they chosen to marry in St. Augustine, Thomas would not have ventured to be so bold, but the people of this smaller community appeared to have fewer qualms about a husband kissing his new wife. To his relief, the congregants chuckled and murmured their approval.

Freddy and Rachel hurried forward to offer congratulations. Behind them came Hinton and his Nancy, who had married in St. Augustine before accompanying

Thomas and Dinah on the trip to St. Johns Towne. Thomas and his steward would have much to teach their brides about life in England, but for now, he wanted his lady to enjoy the wedding celebration without any anxieties about the future.

After the others had given their congratulations and filed out of the small church, Reverend Johnson's wife bustled toward them and embraced Dinah. "My dear, you are a beautiful bride." She wiped away a tear. "How I envy you going home to England." She hesitated for an instant. "Of course, it is not home to you yet, but it will be." She shook her head. "But never mind. We have a feast awaiting you outside, so come along." She began to walk away, then turned back. "Oh, Captain, I haven't enjoyed a wedding this much since your dear sister married Captain Templeton four years ago. By the by, what a shame he and Lady Marianne had to rush away last month and miss your happy day. I never did discover the why and wherefore of that unexpected journey." She raised her eyebrows, clearly seeking a response.

Thomas glanced at Dinah, whose serene smile conveyed her confidence in him. Her peace had not come easily. When they had spoken all the truth to each other about their loved ones' deceptions, she had wept bitterly, and his own mind had been deeply troubled. But they agreed to hide what they knew during this final visit.

For Thomas's part, he would never reveal their loyalties because Freddy clearly was not active in fighting against His Majesty's troops. Further, the recent victories of Tarleton's combined British forces in Georgia assured that the rebellion would soon be put down. Here in East Florida, Freddy and his family would be able to continue their happy, prosperous lives, unaffected by the madness happening in the northern colonies.

"Mrs. Johnson." Thomas inclined his head toward the minister's wife. "We deeply appreciate your kindness in preparing our wedding supper. I am famished." He placed a quick kiss on Dinah's cheek. "And you, my dear?"

"Oh, yes. Famished."

They followed Mrs. Johnson to the back of St. Andrew's, and once they emerged into the fading sunlight, Thomas felt as if they had passed through the door to their future. Only a few more obstacles lay before them, all of which he and Dinah agreed they could surmount as long as they were together.

November 1780
Hampshire, England

"Are you certain you wish to do this?" Thomas hugged Dinah close as their covered carriage moved over the dusty road to Bennington Manor.

"Of course I do." Her heart filled with gratitude over his protectiveness, which had not abated since he'd rescued her from Artemis nearly three months before. "And best to get it over and done with. Even if Lord and Lady Bennington despise me, I shall not be dismayed, for I have your love."

"And you always will." Thomas bent down to give her a kiss and she received it eagerly. Then, with a sigh of contentment, she laid her head against his shoulder and toyed with her fan. The fragile silk had not torn when she struck Jamie, only the ivory had cracked. Thomas had miraculously repaired the damage with the same degree of skill he'd applied to repairing her heart.

England was a beautiful country, even with winter coming on and the days growing shorter. Traces of green remained on the hillsides and trees, and the local farmers had almost completed their harvest. The air was filled with the fragrance of herbs and mown hay.

Her arrival last week at Thomas's—and now *her*—country house would always remain one of the happiest days of her life, next to the day they first met, the day when he proposed and their wedding day. She would somehow manage to forget their storm-tossed voyage from East Florida to Portsmouth aboard a British merchant ship, a harrowing six weeks that had tested her almost beyond bearing. Love triumphed, of course, but she would never cease to marvel that Thomas had managed to live at sea for eighteen years.

She prayed daily for Anne and, reluctantly, for Artemis. She prayed for Frederick and Rachel to be safe and to stay out of the rebellion. Most often, she prayed for the safety of Jamie, Marianne and their children, wherever they might be.

The carriage turned a corner, and through the curtained window Dinah could see the massive manor house, with its three stories of gray stone walls and tree-lined drive. At the front door, they were greeted by an austere, gray-haired butler, whom Thomas addressed as Blevins. The man escorted them to an exquisite drawing room.

Dinah had never seen such opulence as the furnishings of this room: brocade settees and tapestry chairs, velvet draperies, exquisite vases filled with hothouse roses, a massive marble hearth with statues of Zeus and Hera on either side. The giant painting of a battle scene above the mantelpiece impressed her with its artistry. Thomas told her the man on horseback in the center was the late George II. Behind the king rode a black-haired young man who looked very much like Thomas, and indeed, he was the late Lord Bennington, Thomas's father. At this pronouncement, Dinah's eyes welled up with tears for the old man who had given his all for his king, but could never show love to his own four sons.

"Lord and Lady Bennington." Blevins's monotone announcement could not have come at a worse time.

Dinah breathed rapidly to regain her composure and grew lightheaded as a result. What an awful time to feel faint. They would surely misunderstand the cause.

The couple looked like bookends. The earl was not much taller than Dinah, and the countess a little shorter. Both wore high, white-powdered wigs and lavish silk clothing, she in rose, and he in green. Their round faces and corpulent bodies proclaimed their enjoyment of many hearty meals.

Thomas squeezed her hand, left her in front of the hearth, and strode to his brother and sister-in-law. "Lady Bennington, you are the very picture of elegance." His bow to the woman was lower than any Dinah had ever seen him execute.

"Thenk yew, Captain Moberly." She held out a gloved hand, and Thomas kissed it.

The lady held her nose in the air, as if something smelled bad, but Dinah knew Thomas smelled very fine wearing his new citrus cologne. At this bit of snobbery, the last of her tears disappeared.

Thomas turned to his brother. "Bennington, how well you wear your elevation."

"Quite." A glimmer of more tender feelings swept over the new earl's chubby countenance, but only briefly. "You look well, Tommy." He studied Thomas up and down through a quizzing glass. "Very well indeed."

The quizzing glass turned in Dinah's direction at

the same moment Lady Bennington stared at her and sniffed.

Thomas stiffened. He reached out to Dinah, and she walked to his side, her head held high. He put his hand around her waist and pulled her into the shelter of his arm.

"Lord and Lady Bennington, may I present my wife, Mrs. Moberly."

Dinah dutifully curtseyed, as custom required, but she also smiled at her new sister-in-law. "I am honored, my lord, my lady." The titles did not roll easily off of her tongue, but she would not shame Thomas. Some small hint of her Quaker beginnings nagged her that all men were equal before God. Clearly these two would not agree with that Scriptural teaching.

Both of them stared at her boldly, as if she were a horse they would not consider purchasing.

"Well," Lord Bennington said.

"Indeed." Lady Bennington sniffed yet again.

An awkward silence ensued, during which Thomas's grip on Dinah's waist tightened. But he had no cause to worry. This couple's obvious disapproval of her bordered on being comical, but she would behave herself. Foolish or not, the earl and countess held great power in this country, and Dinah would do nothing to cause them to turn their wrath upon Thomas.

Blevins once again stepped into the room. "Mr. and Mrs. Robert Moberly," he said in a droning monotone.

"Tommy!" Another Moberly gentleman—this one tall and dark-haired like Thomas—strode in with a lovely, brown-haired woman on his arm. "God's mercy has brought you back to us." Well-fed, but not as plump as the earl, this gentleman bore none of the hauteur of his eldest brother. He pulled Thomas into his arms, and Thomas responded with equally enthusiastic back-slapping.

"Robby, you old dog. Look at you. The picture of health." Thomas pulled back and turned to the lady. "Grace, you are lovelier than ever." He held out a hand to Dinah and drew her into the small circle that excluded the lord and lady of the manor. "Robby, Grace, may I present my wife, my own dear Dinah."

"Oh, my dear sister." Grace Moberly embraced Dinah with all the enthusiasm her husband had bestowed upon Thomas. Then she took Dinah's face in her hands, kissed one cheek and wiped away her own tears. "Now that we are both Mrs. Moberly, I shall call you Dinah, and you must call me Grace to avoid confusion."

"I am so pleased to meet you…Grace." Dinah's vision blurred, and she blinked several times. This was the sweet lady Marianne had described so glowingly, and the warmth in her gaze bespoke all to be true.

Thomas belatedly kissed Grace's hand, then her cheek. "Are you…*well,* madam?"

The concern in his eyes alerted Dinah to the deeper question he was asking, and she held her breath awaiting her new sister's response.

Grace smiled warmly, as if she comprehended their anxiety on her behalf. "Indeed, I am well, as is our daughter Anne Marie, born just over seven weeks ago."

Thomas released a long sigh, his relief obvious, and voiced his congratulations. Dinah sent up a silent prayer of thanks and would not fear when her own time came.

A glance revealed that the earl and countess had moved to a settee and now watched the proceedings as if observing a play—through their quizzing glasses, of course. They did not appear displeased with the actors, merely bored.

"Now, we must all get acquainted." Grace put one arm around Dinah's waist and the other around Thomas's arm, then drew them toward the chairs across from their host and hostess. Grace sat upon the arm of Dinah's chair and rested a hand on her shoulder. "I am so thankful the Lord has brought you to us. We shall be such friends, my dear Dinah. I promise you."

Dinah glanced at Thomas and saw his slight nod and the grin that played at the corner of his lips. She gazed up into Grace's lively face, knowing instinctively that she had found a sister and confidante. But most of all, she had her own true love, who had surrendered his own ambitions for her happiness. And she planned to spend the rest of her life, Lord willing, making Thomas very happy he had done so.

* * * * *

Dear Reader,

I hope you've enjoyed this journey back in time to 1780 St. Augustine, East Florida Colony. I've been fascinated by this obscure chapter in American history ever since I first discovered my home state belonged to England from 1763 to 1783, which included our American Revolutionary War.

When I began this series, my aim was to extol the zeal of the Patriots who fought for independence from England. But after writing about two couples divided by the struggle, I wanted to present a couple who shared the belief that England would and should be victorious over the rebelling colonists. Many American-born Loyalists who suffered great persecution from the Patriots fled to St. Augustine, where they found a peaceful, bustling town with a full social life. While I may not agree with their opinions, I do believe that when trials come, every person can look to God for help in time of need.

Thank you for choosing *At the Captain's Command*, my third Revolutionary War book. In these stories, I hope to inspire my readers always to seek God's guidance, no matter what trials may come their way.

I love to hear from my readers, so if you have a comment or question, please contact me through my website, *www.louisemgouge.com*.

Blessings,

Louise M. Gouge

QUESTIONS FOR DISCUSSION

1. At the beginning of the story, we learn that Thomas's brother and sister have married Dinah's cousin and brother. How does this help them become friends right away? What prejudices does each have to overcome before he or she can truly consider romance?

2. Thomas's mother died at his birth, and his father was a distant, angry parent. What influences help him to realize that God is a far different Father from his earthly father?

3. What is your view of God? Do you see Him as a loving, gentle Father or a demanding parent whom you can never please?

4. When Thomas discovers that his good friend is also his nemesis, he feels betrayed. Do you think he did the right thing not to report Nighthawk to the authorities after his first attempts failed? Do you think your response is influenced by your feelings regarding the outcome of Revolutionary War?

5. Have you, like Thomas, ever been deeply betrayed by someone you trusted? How did you respond?

6. As an orphan, Dinah has been lonely all her life. Even her relatives seem to reject her. How does her spiritual journey help her to see God as her loving Father? Have you ever felt utterly alone and friendless? How did you deal with it?

7. Dinah's cousin and sister-in-law appear to be kind, generous ladies, yet they seem to turn a cold shoulder to Dinah. Was their behavior justified in those turbulent times? Have you ever been snubbed by friends or relatives? Were you able to forgive them? Despite their treatment, were you still able to feel good about yourself?

8. Dinah's feelings of being alone extended even to God. Although she believed in Him, she felt He was distant and she wasn't important enough for Him to notice. Do you think she felt that way because she had been orphaned? How did she resolve her doubts?

9. Have you ever felt that God is far away and not listening to you? Did you resolve your doubts? If not, what would change your opinion?

10. Which character changes the most in the story, Dinah or Thomas? In what ways did each one mature and become stronger? In what ways did they stay the same?

11. At the end of the story, both Dinah and Thomas assume that the British will be victorious over the American colonists. How do you suppose each of them will react when the colonists win the victory and establish a new nation "conceived in liberty"?

INSPIRATIONAL

Inspirational romances to warm your heart & soul.

Love Inspired.
HISTORICAL

TITLES AVAILABLE NEXT MONTH

Available May 10, 2011

KLONDIKE MEDICINE WOMAN
Alaskan Brides
Linda Ford

HANNAH'S JOURNEY
Amish Brides of Celery Fields
Anna Schmidt

ROCKY MOUNTAIN PROPOSAL
Pamela Nissen

THE UNEXPECTED BRIDE
Debra Ullrick

IHCNM0411

REQUEST YOUR FREE BOOKS!

2 FREE INSPIRATIONAL NOVELS
PLUS 2
FREE
MYSTERY GIFTS

Love Inspired

HISTORICA

INSPIRATIONAL HISTORICAL ROMANCE

YES! Please send me 2 FREE Love Inspired® Historical novels and my 2 FREE mystery gifts (gifts are worth about $10). After receiving them, if I don't wish to receive any more books, I can return the shipping statement marked "cancel". If I don't cancel, I will receive 4 brand-new novels every month and be billed just $4.24 per book in the U.S. or $4.74 per book in Canada. That's a saving of at least 23% off the cover price. It's quite a bargain! Shipping and handling is just 50¢ per book in the U.S. and 75¢ per book in Canada.* I understand that accepting the 2 free books and gifts places me under no obligation to buy anything. I can always return a shipment and cancel at any time. Even if I never buy another book, the two free books and gifts are mine to keep forever.

102/302 IDN FDCH

Name	(PLEASE PRINT)	
Address		Apt. #
City	State/Prov.	Zip/Postal Code

Signature (if under 18, a parent or guardian must sign)

Mail to the **Reader Service:**
IN U.S.A.: P.O. Box 1867, Buffalo, NY 14240-1867
IN CANADA: P.O. Box 609, Fort Erie, Ontario L2A 5X3

Not valid for current subscribers to Love Inspired Historical books.

Want to try two free books from another series?
Call 1-800-873-8635 or visit www.ReaderService.com.

* Terms and prices subject to change without notice. Prices do not include applicable taxes. Sales tax applicable in N.Y. Canadian residents will be charged applicable taxes. Offer not valid in Quebec. This offer is limited to one order per household. All orders subject to credit approval. Credit or debit balances in a customer's account(s) may be offset by any other outstanding balance owed by or to the customer. Please allow 4 to 6 weeks for delivery. Offer available while quantities last.

Your Privacy—The Reader Service is committed to protecting your privacy. Our Privacy Policy is available online at www.ReaderService.com or upon request from the Reader Service.

We make a portion of our mailing list available to reputable third parties that offer products we believe may interest you. If you prefer that we not exchange your name with third parties, or if you wish to clarify or modify your communication preferences, please visit us at www.ReaderService.com/consumerchoice or write to us at Reader Service Preference Service, P.O. Box 9062, Buffalo, NY 14269. Include your complete name and address.

LIHI

*Amish widow Hannah Goodloe's son has run away,
and to find him, she needs help—which circus owner
Levi Harmon can provide. If Hannah can convince him.
Read on for a sneak preview of HANNAH'S JOURNEY
by Anna Schmidt, the first book in the*
AMISH BRIDES OF CELERY FIELDS *series.*

HAVE REASON TO BELIEVE that my son is on your train,"
annah said. "I have come here to ask that you stop that
ain until Caleb can be found."

"Mrs. Goodloe, I am sympathetic to your situation, but
irely you can understand that I cannot disrupt an entire
hedule because you think your son…"

"He is on that train, sir," she repeated. She produced
lined piece of paper from the pocket of her apron and
inded it to him. In a large childish script, the note read:

*Ma, Don't worry. I'm fine and I know this is all a part
" God's plan the way you always said. I'll write once I
et settled and I'll send you half my wages by way of gen-
al delivery. Please don't cry, okay? It's all going to be all
ght. Love, Caleb*

"There's not one word here that indicates…"

"He plans to send me part of his wages, Mr. Harmon.
hat means he plans to get a job. When we were on the
rcus grounds yesterday, I took note of a posted advertise-
ent for a stable worker. My son has been around horses
s entire life."

"And on that slimmest of evidence, you have assumed that
ur son is on the circus train that left town last night?"

She nodded. She waited.

"Mrs. Goodloe, please be reasonable. I have a business
run, several hundred employees who depend upon me,

not to mention the hundreds of customers waiting along th
way because they have purchased tickets for a performan
tonight or tomorrow or the following day."

She said nothing but kept her eyes focused squarely
him.

"I am leaving at seven this evening for my home a
summer headquarters in Wisconsin. Tomorrow, I will me
up with the circus train and make the remainder of the jou
ney with them. If your boy is on that train, I will find hin

"Thank you," she said. "You are a good man, Mr. Ha
mon."

"There's one thing more, Mrs. Goodloe."

Anything, her eyes exclaimed.

"I expect you to come with me."

*Don't miss HANNAH'S JOURNEY by Anna Schmidt,
available May 2011 from Love Inspired Historical.*

Love Inspired **HISTORICAL**

Save $1.00 when you purchase
2 or more Love Inspired® Historical books.

SAVE
$1.00

when you purchase 2 or more
Love Inspired® Historical books.

Coupon expires September 30, 2011. Redeemable at participating retail outlets in the
U.S. and Canada only. Limit one coupon per customer.

52609783

65373 00076 2 (8100)0 11736

d TM are trademarks owned and used by the trademark owner and/or its licensee.
10 Harlequin Enterprises Limited

Love Inspired

Miriam Yoder always thought she'd marry her neighbor, a good dependable man. But then local veterinarian John Hartman catches her eye, a handsome, charming man who is not Plain. Miriam is confused, but must listen to her heart to truly know which man will claim her love and her future.

Miriam's Heart
by Emma Miller

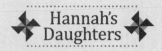

Available May
wherever books are sold.

LI87